Full Figured 12:

Carl Weber Presents

Full Figured 12:

Carl Weber Presents

La Jill Hunt
and C. N. Phillips

www.urbanbooks.net

Urban Books, LLC
300 Farmingdale Road, NY-Route 109
Farmingdale, NY 11735

The Biggest Loser Copyright © 2018 Urban Books, LLC
Lusting for a Big Girl Copyright © 2018
Urban Books, LLC

ISBN 13: 978-1-945855-21-4
ISBN 10: 1-945855-21-5

First Trade Paperback Printing May 2018
Printed in the United States of America

10 9 8 7 6 5 4 3 2 1

*This is a work of fiction. Any references or similarities
to actual events, real people, living or dead, or to real
locales are intended to give the novel a sense of reality.
Any similarity in other names, characters, places, and
incidents is entirely coincidental.*

Distributed by Kensington Publishing Corp.
Submit Orders to:
Customer Service
400 Hahn Road
Westminster, MD 21157-4627
Phone: 1-800-733-3000
Fax: 1-800-659-2436

Full Figured 12:

Carl Weber Presents

La Jill Hunt

and C. N. Phillips

The Biggest Loser

La Jill Hunt

Chapter One

The ringing of the phone caused me to turn over. I wasn't asleep, but the sound still disturbed me. I reached over onto the nightstand and looked at the name on the screen: the office. I thought about ignoring the call but decided to go ahead and get the conversation over and done with.

"Hello," I answered.

"Good morning, Zen. I hope I didn't wake you."

I looked at the time. It was only eight fifteen, and Graves Realty, where I worked as an account manager, didn't even open until nine. The woman on the other end, who had been my boss for the past four years, knew me well enough to know that I was an early riser and didn't sleep past five thirty, not even on weekends.

"No, Gayle, you didn't," I told her.

"Well, I was just checking to see how you were feeling."

"I'm doing a little better."

"That's good. Do you need anything?"

I closed my eyes and thought about all the things I needed; then I simply responded, "No."

"Well, okay. I hope you're getting plenty of rest."

"I am."

"We miss you around here. Mr. Graves even asked about you."

I found that hard to believe, because even though he still came to the office once a month to attend our staff meeting, Jerry Graves, the owner of the company, was damn near seventy and could barely remember his own name. I had a lot of respect for the man, though. He had taken a small, family-owned business and turned it into a multimillion-dollar real estate firm that handled the biggest commercial properties in the city. All things considered, I doubted that Mr. Graves even knew I was out sick.

"Oh." It was the only response I could think of. There was an awkward silence.

"Well, Zen, I hope you get well soon. Did you get the flowers we sent?"

"I did. They were really nice. Please tell everyone I said thank you."

"I will. Well, please let us know . . . uh, if you need anything."

"I will. Thanks for calling," I said then ended the call. I put my phone back on the nightstand and looked around my bedroom. I didn't want to get out of bed, but the overwhelming urge to pee that I had been ignoring since waking up was now too much to bear. I sat up, unable to avoid noticing that the other side of the bed was still made. I slowly stood and went into the bathroom, purposely not turning on the light. I emptied my bladder then washed my hands, making sure to avoid looking in the mirror.

A few moments later, my stomach growled, reminding me that I hadn't eaten since leaving the hospital. On the way to the kitchen, I passed through the living room and saw the pillow and blanket laying on the sofa. He was gone. Probably where he always was: work. Even after what had just happened, I knew he was not going to miss work. I told myself not to complain, because one of the reasons I fell in love with him was the fact that he was a hard-working man.

I started to feel faint and continued into the kitchen. Dishes filled the sink, and crumbs from what looked like Chinese food were on the counter. I reached to open the refrigerator, and I froze. My heart began pounding, and I almost stumbled backward. I told myself to look away, but I couldn't. I could hear Dr. Anderson's voice in the distance. . . .

"No heartbeat . . . I'm sorry . . . happens to women your age . . . high risk . . . emergency surgery."

"Surgery? What? When?" I asked between sobs. My life was in turmoil.

"Right now," she said.

I gasped. "Will I be able to . . . Can I still . . .?"

"Zen, it's going to be okay. The doctor knows what's best," Var whispered, reaching over and taking my hand into his. I stared at the IV sticking out of my arm. I didn't even remember when he had come to the hospital.

"But . . ." I whispered.

"It's fine. I promise you we're gonna get through this together. I promise."

I looked up, and we stared at one another. I wanted to believe him. He'd been so nice since we found out, but now that this had happened, I wasn't sure.

"We are?"

"Yes, we are. We're gonna get through it together. I'm right here."

"We've gotta get you prepped, Zen. I'm gonna need your signature." She handed me a clipboard and a pen.

"I don't know," I said, still trying to wrap my head around everything that was happening. I started crying all over again, this time even harder. I pushed the clipboard away and shook my head. I needed time to think.

"Zen, listen. I know this is a lot to take in, but your life is at stake here," Dr. Anderson told me.

"Can't we do something else?" I pleaded. "Anything but this."

"If I could, you know I would." Dr. Anderson looked as if she wanted to cry right along with me.

"I'm not going to let you die, Zen. Sign the damn paper." I could see the tears in his eyes as he leaned over and kissed my forehead. It was easy for him to tell me to sign the paper. He already had a daughter when we met. We had been trying for two years to get pregnant when it finally happened. These past four months had been the happiest of my life. I was finally going to be a mom. Now, I was living a nightmare.

I scribbled my name on the paper, and he kissed me once again right before they whisked me off to surgery.

The last two days since I'd been released from the hospital had been a blur. This was the first time I'd even left my bedroom. Now, I was standing here, staring at the small piece of paper hanging on the refrigerator door. The ultrasound. The photo of my unborn child. Our unborn child. Our baby. His baby. Our baby, which would never be born.

I closed my eyes and opened the freezer door, taking out a gallon of butter pecan ice cream, then grabbed a spoon and walked out of the kitchen to return to my bed. I was glad he wasn't there to see me; to tell me that I shouldn't be sitting in the middle of the bed eating ice cream. As much as I wanted him to be there, I was glad that I could find comfort in the sweetness all alone, one spoonful after another.

Chapter Two

It took what seemed like a lifetime for me to make it from the sofa, where I had been lying, to the front door. When I opened it, my best friend Bailey was standing on the other side, holding a beautiful potted calla lily, which she knew was my favorite.

"What, no chocolate?" I gave her a half-grin.

"No, absolutely not," she said, hugging me as she walked in and followed me into the kitchen, where I placed the flower on the table. I hadn't seen her since she came to visit me in the hospital. That was almost a month ago.

"How are you feeling?"

"I'm feeling better. I'm healing up nicely." I shrugged.

"And mentally? How are you feeling?"

I didn't know how to answer her question, so I didn't. Instead, I asked, "I'm thirsty. You want something to drink?" I went to stand up, and a sharp pain went through my abdomen, causing me to wobble just a bit.

"Oh, my goodness. Zen, are you okay?" Bailey jumped up to help me.

"I'm fine, girl. I just moved a little too fast, that's all."

"Are you sure you should be moving around at all?" She gave me a concerned look. "Where is Var? Why isn't he here with you?"

"He's at work. And I told you, I'm fine."

"You're not fine. You're acting like you're about to pass out."

"Well, that's because I'm fat." I laughed.

"Shut up, Zen." Bailey sat back down and shook her head.

"Well, one thing the doctor mentioned was that my weight may have contributed to what happened." I swallowed hard, repeating the words Dr. Anderson had said while she was looking over my chart.

"You're not even that big, Zen."

"You know that's a lie. I've always been big. I've gained a lot of weight, as if you didn't notice."

Bailey and I had been friends since high school. At five feet eight inches, we were both taller than average, but our bodies were very different. My shoulders were wider, and I had always been what most people would call "big-boned." Now, at almost thirty years old, I was what the medical field considered morbidly obese.

"Yeah, but you also had a reason to gain weight," she said, ever the supportive friend.

"I'm three hundred and four pounds, Bailey."

Bailey's eyes widened. "There's no fucking way, Z."

"Yes, I got on the scale today. And my blood pressure has been up for the past couple of years."

"Well, we know why that is." She rolled her eyes at the photo of Var and me on our last vacation, which hung on the fridge near the ultrasound photo.

"Don't be like that," I said with a sigh.

"Be like what? You know I haven't been feeling Var for a while now. First of all, he needs to put his baby mama in check. And then, I ain't like it when he—"

"She hasn't caused us any drama in a while now, Bailey, and you know things have gotten a lot better. We've both been working hard and getting our shit together," I said, not wanting to even get into the ups and downs of my roller-coaster relationship.

Even though Var and I had been together for almost five years, we'd had more than our fair share of hiccups along the way. There were even a few breakups and makeups when Var chose to "take some time" away from me. But he always found his way back. We'd been going strong for the past year, and although my pregnancy wasn't planned, Var said he was excited about becoming a father again.

Bailey wasn't convinced. "Working hard was never the issue for neither one of you," she said. "You're both workaholics. But where's the ring he promised you last year when you took him back?"

"It made more sense for us to get the house, especially with the—" I couldn't finish the sentence.

Talk of a ring and a wedding had been put on hold once I found out I was pregnant, and we began the search for our new home. Var insisted that purchasing a house was the best move for us to make. Finding the right house had taken us a few months, but we did: a four-bedroom, three-bath, ranch-style home with a two-car garage and a large backyard. When I first saw the price, I felt that it was a bit out of our budget, but Var convinced me that if I put in a few more hours at work and made a little more money, we could afford it. Our offer had been accepted just days before the miscarriage. Although I had lost the baby and didn't want to move, Var was still pressed about us buying it.

"Oh, Zen, I'm sorry. I shouldn't even be talking about this right now." Bailey reached over and grabbed my arm.

"It's okay, B," I told her, wiping the corners of my eyes. "Damn, I've cried so much the past week that I thought I was out of tears. I guess I was wrong."

"Please don't cry, Zen. Oh, Lord, now I'm crying." Bailey started sniffling and got up to grab the roll of paper towels, taking one for herself then passing me one.

"We're a hot mess." I shook my head and wiped my tears. "For real, B, I'm good, and I'm getting better. But I do need to drop some weight," I said.

"I can help you with that. I can stand to lose a few pounds myself. We can meal prep, hit the gym, go walking. However you wanna do it. I got you, Z. Whatever it takes." Bailey gave me a reassuring smile.

I loved my best friend, and I knew she was going to be a great support system. She always had my back.

I looked at the package of Oreos and the bag of Doritos laying in the middle of the table. "I guess I need to get rid of these."

Bailey grabbed the bag of chips and opened it, popping one into her mouth. "Hell, Z, we ain't starting today," she said with a laugh.

"Girl, Var constantly brings snacks and food home. I mean, that's one of the reasons I gained so much weight. We eat out all the time, and when we ain't eating out, we're eating takeout." I sighed. "That's gotta change."

The sound of the front door opening caused us to turn around. Var walked through the front door and into the kitchen, carrying two large boxes of pizza.

"What's up?" He placed the pizza on the stove.

"Hey," Bailey and I said simultaneously.

"I didn't know you were bringing pizza. I thought you were going to the grocery store," I told him.

"Well, we know you ain't gonna cook, I ain't feel like cooking, and we both hungry, so I picked this up," he replied, taking a paper plate and putting three slices of pizza on it. He then grabbed the ranch dressing from the refrigerator, poured some on the pizza, and put the plate in front of me. "Here you go, baby. You want pizza, Bailey?"

"Nah, I'm good," she replied.

"More for us," he said with a shrug. "Z, you want orange soda or Coke?"

"Bottled water," I told him.

He shot me a strange look. "You try'na be cute because Bailey here?" he teased.

"Not at all," I said, looking at the delicious pizza before picking up a slice and biting into it. "I guess I'll go ahead and enjoy it now, because this diet is about to be cruel."

Bailey shook her head. "It won't be that bad. I promise."

"What diet?" Var asked, scrunching up his face.

"Bailey is gonna help me lose a few pounds," I told him.

He frowned. "Why? You don't need to lose anything. You look fine the way you are."

"It's not about how she looks. It's about her being healthy," Bailey replied.

"Exactly. And you heard what the doctor said," I reminded him. "I just need to make some lifestyle changes. Nothing major."

"Okay, whatever you wanna do, Zen. You wanna go on a diet, then do it. Don't be try'na take no leftover pizza to work with you on Monday, neither." He laughed.

"You're not funny, Var." I rolled my eyes at him.

"Wait. Monday? What are you talking about? She just had surgery," Bailey snapped.

"She had surgery a month ago. I know that. And she's been moving around a lot more. She's going back to work."

Bailey looked at me. "I thought the doctor told you not to go back for six weeks."

"Well, she said I could—"

"The doc said *up to* six weeks, and if she feels better, which she does, she can go back. It's not like she works construction." Var laughed. "Ain't that right, Z?"

"Yeah, that's true," I said quietly, avoiding eye contact with Bailey.

"Besides, her boss calls her every other day asking when she's coming back. They been ready for her to come back," Var said.

"And you're fine with her going back to work after what she's just been through?" Bailey's voice was so cold that I felt goosebumps on my arm.

"Hey, it was her decision, not mine. But if she says she's ready, I ain't gonna tell her she can't. You know how Zen can be. She loves to work. That's one of the things I love about her. We have goals we're trying to reach: we buying this house, and then we're trying to get a new car. I can't do all that by myself. She knows she gotta do her part. That's what makes us a team. Besides, no point in her laying around here moping about what happened. It's time to move on and make some major moves." Var walked over to the sink and washed his hands before opening the box and taking out a slice of pizza. "Hand me one of those paper plates, Z."

I passed him a plate, and he left the kitchen without saying another word.

"What the—"

I held up my hand. "Don't, please."

"Zenobia Chanel Ferguson Brooks, have you lost your mind?" Bailey hissed.

"No, Bailey. It's okay. I've been out of work long enough, and the truth is, I miss it."

"Fine, then work from home. I'm sure you have plenty of stuff you can be making or sewing right here. You don't have to go into the office."

"You know Var doesn't consider that *real work*." I laughed, making air quotes around the last words.

Bailey was right about the sewing. I did have several people who were eager for me to get back to my first love, sewing and interior design, but since landing the account management position at the real estate firm, I hadn't had the time to sew as much as I used to.

"I don't give a shit what Var thinks," Bailey scoffed. "I get it, Zen. You love LaVar, always have, but you also have to love yourself too."

I shook my head. "I know you mean well, but I'm good. You know if I wasn't, I would tell you."

"Zen, you're not ready to go back. Just take a little while longer," she pleaded. "At least just go back part-time for a couple of weeks."

"I'll think about it," I said weakly. I hated lying to my best friend, especially when I knew she had my best interests at heart, but there was no way I could stay out of work for another two and a half weeks. It had already been decided that it was time for me to return, even when my mind and body didn't agree.

Chapter Three

"You're back?" Gayle, my manager, looked up from her desk after I tapped on her door. Lloyd Dickerson, another manager, who also happened to be the son of the firm's owner, was sitting in one of the leather chairs in front of her.

"Zenobia, glad to see you're doing better." Lloyd smiled at me. Unlike everyone else in the office, he always called me by my real name. Lloyd was good looking, which made constantly the subject of conversation among females in the office, who talked about everything from the designer suits he wore to the scent of his cologne. Even I had to admit that I had noticed him a time or two when he walked by.

"Uh, thanks," I said. "Gayle, can I talk to you for a second?"

"Sure, come on in." She waved her hand and beckoned for me to come inside.

Lloyd remained seated, and I hesitated. After a few seconds, he got the hint and said, "Oh, I'm sorry. Let me get on out here and make this quota so I can keep my job. Welcome back, Zenobia."

I stepped aside so he could walk out before I entered the small room.

Gayle sat up in her chair. "You look amazing. But how are you feeling? I didn't expect you back for another couple of weeks."

"Well, I'm not a hundred percent yet, but I think I should be ready by Monday." I sighed, looking around and noticing a large white board with the names of all the account managers, including mine, along with the number of dollars collected for the month so far. Those on target to meet their monthly goal were in green; those who were below par were in red. I located my name, which was in black, along with the word *sick*. When I made the decision to go back to work early, all the long days, late nights, worrisome account holders, and harrowing goals and quotas had somehow slipped my mind. As I sat across from my supervisor, it all came back to me. A slight tinge of anxiety caused my blood pressure to rise, and that was the last thing I needed to happen.

"I'm so happy to hear that you'll be back. I know you see our numbers are down tremendously." Gayle hopped up and walked over to the board to erase *sick* from beside my name.

"Well," I said, remembering my conversation with Bailey, "I'm thinking it will probably be better if I came back part-time instead, if that's okay."

The smile on Gayle's face slipped slightly.

"Just until I'm one hundred percent, which will be sooner rather than later," I told her.

"Well, I'm sure that won't be a problem. I will have to let Lloyd and his father know so they can approve."

"I'd appreciate that." I stood up.

"So, we'll see you on Monday?" she asked as if to make sure I was still coming in.

"Yes, Monday morning, nine a.m.," I said before I walked out of her office and went down the hallway to my cubicle. Several of my coworkers greeted me, and I couldn't help but notice the hint of sadness in their eyes as they spoke to me. Word of my pregnancy had just gotten around when the mishap occurred. I could tell that they were trying to be as polite as possible.

"You're back so soon?" Lila, whose cubicle was right beside mine, jumped up and hugged me. She was a younger girl who was hired right after I was. I liked her a lot, and her lighthearted spirit was one of the things that made my job a little easier.

She pointed to the dress and black heels I wore. "You stay fly, Zen. I swear."

"Thanks, and well, I'm back, but it's only going to be part-time for a couple of weeks," I told her.

"Well, even if it's only a couple of minutes, we're glad to have you back here." She smiled. "How are you feeling?"

"A little stronger each day," I said with a sigh.

Lila nodded. "I understand. My sister went through the same thing. She says she's available to talk if you need to."

"Thanks, but I'm fine," I said.

Lila's phone began ringing, so she stepped back into her workspace. I sat at my desk and looked at the pile of papers that lay on top.

If anyone had told me that I would be sitting behind a computer day after day, talking to tenants about their delinquent accounts, I would have said they were crazy. I had always dreamed of working for a real estate firm, but not as an account manager. I wanted to stage homes and possibly work at a design firm. But, after I finished college with a degree in visual arts and was unable to find a job in my field, Var suggested that I accept the fact that maybe it wasn't going to happen and I just needed to do something that paid decent money.

At the time, I was working at a fabric store, and although I wasn't making a lot of money, I enjoyed my job. Then, the mother of Var's daughter took him back to court for an increase, and things got tight for us. The stress and strain took a toll on our relationship, and we decided to take a break. Another friend of ours mentioned to him that she was moving and suggested I apply for her position with the firm. I did, and landed the job, which paid more than I expected. But I earned each and every dime. Soon after, Var and I started dating again, and he asked me to move in. I was ecstatic.

Now, as I listened to Lila becoming increasingly irritated at whomever was on the other end of the phone, and I stared at the pile of paperwork in front of me, I was beginning to feel overwhelmed. I stood up, gave Lila a quick wave, and headed down the hallway.

"So, Gayle says you're back on Monday, huh?"

Lloyd's voice startled me as I waited for the elevator to arrive.

"Yeah." I nodded.

"Well, it'll be nice to see your smiling face around here, even if it's only for a few hours a day." He grinned at me.

The elevator doors opened, and we both stepped on. I pushed the button for the lobby, and the doors closed.

"You going all the way down?" I asked.

He took a step toward me, looked me up and down in a way that took me by surprise, then said, "If you want me to."

I blinked for a second, trying to gather my thoughts, but before I could respond, the elevator stopped. A couple of other people got on, both of whom spoke to Lloyd, and he moved away from me. I glanced over at him to try to read his expression, but he looked away. When the elevator reached the next floor, he got off without a good-bye and disappeared down the hallway.

What the heck was that all about?

Chapter Four

I walked into the house, and for the first time since coming home from the hospital, I walked into the bedroom that held all of my sewing and craft materials. I called it my salon. A large shelf held bins of fabric, appliques, books, and magazines. There were also jars of thread, buttons, and other materials that I tried, unsuccessfully most of the time, to keep organized. This room used to be my safe haven, where I could escape from the chaos of the outside world and design and create whatever my heart desired.

I sat in the chair in front of my machine and picked up the soft cotton material covered with ducks. I had planned to make pillows and wall coverings from the fabric. Now, it seemed pointless. A lump swelled in my chest, and I tried to force it down, but I couldn't. I put the fabric down, hurried back out of the room, and ran into the kitchen. The bag of Doritos that Bailey had snacked on a few days before was still in the middle of the table. I opened the bag and began eating the chips by the handful as I sat and cried. Then, when I realized the bag was empty, I cried even more. My life was spiraling out of control, and my emotions were all over the place. I put the empty bag in the trash, went into the living room, and lay on the sofa, where I fell asleep.

When I woke up, it was dark, and Var still wasn't home. I sat up and rubbed my eyes, then checked the time. It was almost ten o'clock. I took my cell phone from my purse and sent him a text. It wasn't like him to stay out late, especially during the week, but I knew wherever he was, most likely it was work related. There was a time when Var would come home late and I would assume he had been out with some other woman—and I would be right. But, when I moved in with him and he gave me the car he no longer drove, I knew he was finally ready to settle down and be faithful. He had come a long way and earned the trust that I now had in him.

I heard someone fumbling at the front door and got up. Before I could get to it, I heard the lock turn, and Var backed inside carrying something.

"Hey, baby." He smiled when he saw me standing near the doorway. "Can you grab my keys out the door for me?"

He was dragging something, so I moved so he could get past me.

"What in the world?" I asked, walking back inside after getting his keys.

"Boxes," he said, pointing to the folded pieces of cardboard. He walked over and gave me a kiss.

"Boxes?" I asked, looking up at him. "That's where you've been?"

"Well, me and a couple of the other loan officers went and had a couple of drinks at Coppola's, then I stopped at Walmart and grabbed some boxes. Did you eat?" he asked.

I thought about the entire bag of Doritos I'd devoured before taking a nap and shook my head in an effort to clear the memory, but Var took it as me saying no.

"Let's go to Hooters and grab wings and nachos," he suggested.

"It's late," I said. One of the small diet changes Dr. Anderson had suggested was that I not eat so late. Even though I hadn't changed my eating habits completely, I had been trying to not eat after seven p.m.

"Okay, but I'm still hungry, and I know you are too. You're already dressed. Where are your shoes?"

I smoothed the soft fabric of the black-and-white printed dress I was still wearing and tried to recall where my shoes were. "In the salon. But—"

"Perfect. That's exactly where these boxes are going anyway," he said, picking them up.

"What? Why?"

"That's the first room we're packing up."

"But Var—"

He disappeared down the hallway, the boxes in his arms, returning a few moments later, carrying my pumps.

"Var, I really don't feel like going anywhere," I told him.

"Come on, Zen." He put the shoes on the floor and pulled me to him. "We haven't had a late-night dinner date in forever."

"I know, but I had a long day, and I'm really tired."

"Tired from what? Playing on your sewing machine?" He said it teasingly, but I wasn't amused. When he made jokes about my sewing, I knew he didn't mean any harm; which was why I tried not to let it hurt my feelings too much. But sometimes, like tonight, it did.

"I went into the office to talk to Gayle," I replied. I was about to tell him what had happened with Lloyd on the elevator, but then thought it best I didn't mention it. I also didn't say anything about my working part-time for a couple of weeks. It didn't really matter, though, because he was already rambling on about something else. I hadn't even realized I zoned out until I heard the word *move*. I turned my attention to what he was saying.

"I'm trying to make this move smooth and organized. We can get as much packed up as possible the rest of the week and this weekend before you go back to work," Var said.

"Wait. What are you talking about? What's the rush?" I frowned. "I mean, I know I'm going back to work, but I'm still not a hundred percent. I still have to take it easy."

"Baby, this isn't a game. Our offer for the house was accepted. We gotta pack up and get into our new place. I turned our thirty-day notice in today."

I felt like I still needed time to process everything, but Var wanted me to jump right back into life as if nothing had happened. Tonight, I was too tired to protest, though, so I swallowed any reservations I was feeling and put on my shoes so we could go out to eat.

Returning to work part-time was easier said than done. My plan was to work until about noon or one o'clock each day, but somehow, I ended up working my normal schedule and leaving with everyone else at five. By the time I made it home each evening, I was exhausted, but Var wasn't trying to hear it. He insisted that we go through each room, purging and packing in preparation for our move. It was as if he couldn't wait to leave. I had started to feel excited about the move, but nowhere near as much as he was. A few times, I had come home to find him already there, packing things and moving boxes around. He wouldn't even let me sit down for a rest before he was recruiting me to work with him. Between work at the firm and the late nights packing with Var, I was exhausted. It would catch up with me midmornings at work.

"Girl, I feel the same way," Lila whispered when she caught me yawning during our monthly staff meeting. The owner, Mr. Graves, was going on and on about something he had been reading from a slip of paper for the past ten minutes, but he was stumbling and mumbling to the point that no one was listening.

"We all do," said another coworker who was sitting behind me.

The door to the large meeting room we were assembled in opened, and Lloyd walked in, causing everyone to turn and look. You could hear the whispers of almost every female as he took a seat at the front of the room with the other management staff.

"So, he's going to be working out of this office now?" I leaned over and asked Lila.

"Yeah, he's been moved to this location permanently," she said.

"I thought he was the property manager over at Westwood."

"Not anymore. We get to enjoy all of that eye candy now." The girl sitting behind me giggled.

Mr. Graves continued mumbling into the microphone. The sound of his voice was making me sleepier than I already was.

"Well, now that he's over here, they need to let him handle the meetings. We would def be way more attentive, that's for sure," I suggested.

"Now, that's a good idea." Lila laughed.

"Yes. You're right about that, girl." A few other female employees near us laughed and agreed.

"And I bet the number of top performers each month would increase too." I sighed.

"Oh, I would definitely be in that number," another girl stated, causing Lila to laugh even louder. I elbowed her as I looked up and saw Lloyd staring at us.

When the meeting was finally over, I went into the break room to get a cup of coffee. I had just hit the brew button on the Keurig when Lloyd walked in.

"Hello, Zenobia."

"Hello, Lloyd."

"I see we both need a little afternoon pick-me-up, huh?" He stared at me.

"Yeah, a little," I said politely, turning around and staring at the brown liquid pouring into my favorite coffee mug.

"Nothing like something rich, sweet, and hot to brighten up the day. It's my personal favorite." He licked his lips and leaned on the counter beside where I stood.

The machine stopped, and I quickly grabbed my mug and headed toward my desk. When I sat down, my hand was shaking so much that I nearly spilled coffee on my desk. There was no doubt about what Lloyd meant by his statement, and he had made me feel very uncomfortable.

"You forgot this."

I jumped when I heard the voice behind me. I turned around in my chair to see Lloyd standing in the middle of my cube, smiling, with my cell phone in his hand. The lock screen displayed a picture of Var and me hugging.

"Thanks." My voice was shaky as I stood and held my hand out for him to give me the phone.

He took a step toward me, so close that I could smell his cologne and see the faint five o'clock shadow on his face. He pressed the phone against me, and I grabbed it. His fingers lingered along my breast, and he leaned in close and whispered, "Nice picture. That's one lucky man."

"Hey, Zen." Lila's voice came over the cubicle wall.

Lloyd winked and eased out of my workspace as silently as he had entered a few moments earlier, leaving me speechless and afraid.

Chapter Five

"He did what?" Bailey yelled through the phone.

I explained for the third time what had happened in the break room and at my desk an hour earlier. The incident had left me so shaken that I left work early without saying anything to anyone, not even Lila.

"What did you say? Did you go the fuck off?" she asked.

"I ain't say or do anything." I sighed, now feeling like I should have had a bigger reaction when the incident happened. My mind became filled with what I could have done differently; then I wondered if maybe, because I hadn't reacted differently, I was blowing things out of proportion.

"You should've slapped the shit out of him," Bailey snapped.

"But maybe he was just joking and didn't mean to do anything wrong." I thought out loud. "He didn't really say anything wrong."

"You left work because you were so upset. And it's not what he said; it was the way he said it. He violated your personal space. You've gotta go to HR."

"What?" I said, slamming on the brakes because I had almost run a red light. I was driving Var's Acura that had basically become mine when he bought his new car a few months ago. I still had my old Honda, but I loved this car as if it were my own.

"That's sexual harassment, Zen," she said.

"No, it's not. He didn't grab me or anything," I protested.

"He touched you, and he made comments of a sexual nature."

The light turned green, and I proceeded. "I'm just gonna avoid him from now on."

"Trust me, you have to report him. Lemme ask you this: are you gonna tell Var what happened?"

"Hell no. Are you crazy?" I shook my head as if Bailey could see me through the phone.

"Because you know he would go up to that office and tear that office up, then kill that dude. That's how you know it's sexual harassment."

"I don't know, Bailey." I pulled into the driveway. Eager to change the subject, I asked her about work. Bailey was a programming director for the radio station, and she not only kept me up to date on the latest celebrity gossip, but we always got great seats at concerts and other freebies.

"Today was nothing special. Oh, we do have one of the Housewives of Atlanta coming through next week, though," she said.

"Really? Which one?" I became excited about possibly meeting a cast member from one of my favorite TV shows.

"Child, I don't even remember," Bailey replied.

It amazed me how nonchalant she was when it came to the people she came across all the time. The only person I'd ever heard her become star-struck about was Prince, her all-time favorite artist, whom she got to meet right before he passed away. Everyone else was just ordinary to her.

I opened the mailbox before unlocking the front door. Once I was inside, I began sifting through the pile of mostly bills and sales ads. But one envelope, in particular, stood out to me.

"Here we go with this bullshit again."

"What? What's wrong?"

"Var got another letter from Child Support Enforcement. His baby mama probably found out we got the house, and now she's probably trying to take him back to court for an increase." I sighed as I opened the envelope. Scanning the letter, I expected to see the name if his son's mother, along with a court date. Instead, the name listed was not one I was familiar with.

"Lemme call you back, Bailey."

"What's wrong?"

I hung up the phone without saying another word. Sitting at the kitchen table, I reread the letter, slower this time. As I realized what the letter stated, my heart felt as if it was exploding into a million pieces. I didn't wipe the tears that streamed down my face. I let them fall one by one, wetting the papers that I held in my hand.

When Var finally walked through the front door an hour later, I was still sitting at the table. I hadn't moved from the spot I'd sat in when I got home; not even to turn on the light when the sun began to set.

"Shit, you scared me," Var said when he passed the entrance to the kitchen and saw me sitting at the table. "Why the hell are you sitting in here in the dark?"

I didn't answer him. I just sat and stared.

"What's wrong?" he asked, turning on the light. I still didn't move nor answer. "Zen, you're scaring me. Baby, please tell me what's going on. Are you okay?"

"Who is April Hughes?"

Var cocked his head slightly to the side and frowned. "Who?"

"April Hughes." I repeated the name.

"Oh, uh, she—"

"When the fuck were you going to tell me?" I asked before he could finagle a lie.

"Tell you what?" He shrugged, confused by my question.

"How long was it going to take? What was your fucking plan?" I blinked and waited for his answer.

"Zenobia, I don't know what the hell you're talking about."

"Don't, Var," I warned.

"Don't what?"

"Please don't stand there and act like you don't know what I'm talking about."

"Zen, damn it. I ain't acting. I don't know what you're talking about."

"I'm asking you one more time. When the fuck were you gonna tell me you and April Hughes had a fucking newborn, LeVar?" I threw the papers across the table at him.

"Zen," he said softly, reaching for me.

"Don't fucking touch me, Var." I jumped up from the table. A familiar sharp pain shot through my abdomen as if to remind me once again that the baby I once carried in my womb was no longer there.

"Zenobia."

"Congratulations, Var. At least now I know what the fuck you did with all the baby stuff I bought. Yeah, took it to the Goodwill, huh? You lied about that too." I laughed sarcastically. "I can't believe this shit. Well, at least I know now why you've been in such a rush to move too. You ain't want that damn letter to come to this house."

"I know this looks bad, Zen. Please just let me explain."

"This explains a whole hell of a lot. That break you needed, the one where you said you needed space because you didn't feel that I was pulling my share of the weight and I wasn't working up to my full potential? It was all because you wanted to be fucking some other bitch. If that's what you wanted, Var, that's all you had to tell me," I snapped at him.

"Zen, real talk, I just found out about this myself. I wanted to tell you."

"But you didn't!" I screamed.

"Because I found out about her saying the baby was mine the night you were rushed to the hospital. How the fuck was I gonna tell you about this when that just happened?" He had the nerve to raise his voice at me, and I looked at him like he was crazy.

"Are you yelling at me?" I asked.

"No." Var lowered his voice. "But, Zen, that ain't my baby. She's lying."

"Y'all make the perfect couple then. You're both great liars." I walked out of the kitchen and headed down the hallway toward our bedroom, "A match made in fucking Heaven."

Our bedroom was a cluttered mess from all the packing we were in the middle of doing. I spotted the travel bag that I had taken to the hospital in the corner, and I put it on the bed, tossing some clothes for the rest of the week into it.

"Zenobia, stop it, please." Var went to touch me again, but I snatched away from him.

"Move out of my way, Var."

"I'm not letting you leave," he said, standing in front of the bedroom doorway with his arms folded across his chest like some fake superhero. "Not until we talk about this."

"*Now* you wanna talk about this? What the fuck is there to talk about?" I frowned, grabbing my pajamas and underclothes out of the drawer. "We should've talked about this a year ago when you convinced me to get back together with you. Oh, that was after I got the new job and you said I was ready for what you were trying to build in your life. You know what, Var? You had me thinking that I was slacking, which was why you wanted space, when the entire time, it was you wanting to be a whore. And you have the nerve to talk about your daddy."

I knew that what I said would hit a nerve. Var's dad had constantly cheated on his mother, so much so that he had several other children outside of his marriage. Var's motivation in life was to achieve everything his father hadn't: great career, big house, nice cars, and the ability to provide for his mother.

"I'm nothing like him." Var looked like he wanted to hit me, but he knew better.

"I asked you, Var. I asked you were there other women when we were apart, and you swore there weren't."

"Zen, she's lying. You don't need to leave. It's an order for a blood test. That baby ain't mine."

"It doesn't even matter at this point, Var." I zipped the bag and put it on my shoulder.

"So, this is what you really wanna do, Zen? You just wanna leave before we know if this is even my baby? You just wanna walk away from everything we're trying to build here?"

I held my tongue, refusing to answer him. Looking at Var, I saw that it wasn't hurt in his eyes, but anger, and that disappointed me.

"Fine then, Zenobia. Carry your ass. Go ahead and leave." He stepped out of the doorway, and I walked out.

Chapter Six

After leaving the apartment, I went to Bailey's condo. I called out sick for the remainder of the week, and in addition to avoiding work, I also avoided Var's calls and texts. Bailey was the amazing, supportive friend she had always been since eighth grade, but she would only allow me to have a pity party for so long.

"So, what's your game plan?" she asked me on Sunday night while I was camped out on her sofa, eating nachos and watching reality television.

"I don't know," I said.

"Have you talked to Var?" she asked, sitting on the other end of the sofa and putting her feet under the blanket that was covering me.

"Nope. What's there to talk about? How he's been lying for the past year? Surely you can't expect me to talk about that. Talk about how not only does he have one baby mama to deal with, but now two? How he has a newborn by some random chick; a new baby that he can hold and kiss, and I have nothing? Is that what we're supposed to talk about?" I asked, my voice filled with sarcasm.

"Well, those aren't the exact topics I was thinking about, but now that you mention it, I do wanna know why the fuck he's been lying to you for a whole damn year, personally." She shrugged.

"Fine, then you ask him. I know he's been blowing your phone up as much as he's been blowing up mine."

Bailey nodded. "Yep."

"Well, next time he calls or texts you, ask. I don't give a shit."

"Zen, it's okay to give a shit. There's nothing wrong with that."

"Funny thing is, I really don't. I'm done, Bailey."

"If you say so." The way Bailey said it let me know she didn't believe me. Truth was, I didn't know if I believed it myself. I was beyond hurt; I was devastated. But being with Var was something I had always wanted. From the moment we met nearly five years ago, I had been smitten with him.

When he had first approached me, I thought it was a joke. He was fine as hell, and so were the other two guys sitting with him at a nearby table, while I sat at the bar. I had just finished my last final exam and was waiting for Bailey so we could celebrate the moment with plenty of drinks and happy hour appetizers.

"Hello." He smiled at me when he walked over.

"Hi," I said, trying not to stare at his dimpled smile, which showed off his perfect white teeth.

"It's me, Var."

"Okay, Var. What's up?" I prepared myself for what I knew was gonna be some BS. I had been plus-size my entire life and had learned that most guys thought that all "big girls" had low self-esteem and could be approached any kind of way. That was not the case with me. I knew that I was beautiful, fashionable, and had a lot to offer. Any man that I chose to date would be the lucky one, not me. Knowing this allowed me to discern between the guys who were decent and the ones who were trying to play games. As I sat there looking at Var, with a body like a fitness model even in simple jeans and a T-shirt, I wondered what kind of game he was about to try.

"I have a confession," he started.

"Then you also have a problem," I told him.

He gave me a confused look. "Why is that?"

"Because I'm not a priest, and we're definitely not in a church." I looked up, then around.

"You're funny. I like that. But I do have something to tell you."

"What's that?" I turned slightly to get an even better view of him.

He took a deep breath then, to my surprise, he said sheepishly, "I've had a crush on you for a while. Since the sixth grade."

"What are you talking about? I didn't even know you in sixth grade." I looked at him like he was crazy.

"We were in Miss Turk's class. Shell Elementary?" he said adamantly.

I shook my head. "I have no idea who Miss Turk is, and I don't even know where Shell Elementary is."

"Olivia, stop playing."

"See, that's where you're wrong. My name isn't Olivia," I told him.

"Damn, I'm so sorry. I thought you were this girl I had a crush on for years. Her name was Olivia Pritchett. Man, my boy Rich even told me it was you. You look just like her." He sighed. "I apologize."

"It's cool. No apology needed," I told him.

"Well, at least let me buy you a drink. That's the least I can do. What are you drinking?"

He bought me a glass of wine then went back over to his table. A few minutes later, Bailey finally arrived, and we started our celebration. We were on our third round when Var came back over to me.

"Damn, he's fine," Bailey whispered a little too loudly in my ear.

"Hello again," he said.

"Hello." I laughed, now feeling quite giddy from my alcohol consumption.

"I know you're not Olivia, but you didn't tell me your name."

"You didn't ask me." I shrugged.

"You're right. Can I get your name?"

"Zenobia, but you can call me Zen," I replied.

"That's beautiful. Well, I came back over here because I have something to tell you."

"You and these confessions. What are you, an Usher album?" I shook my head.

"Again with the humor. That's a good one."

"Welp, spill it." I clapped my hands and rubbed them together as if I were preparing to hear some juicy gossip.

Var leaned over and whispered, "I've got a crush on you."

I tossed my head back and laughed heartily. "Dude, I'm not the girl from sixth grade. You do not have a crush on me."

"I know. I've had a crush on you for a while now." He looked down at his watch. "For about thirty minutes."

"You are hilarious, you know that?" I searched his face, waiting for the punchline of what I suspected was going to be a joke, but there was none.

Var asked me for my number, and I gave it to him. He called the following day and the day after, and every day after that. We started dating, and he quickly captured my heart. I wasn't naive to the fact that when most people saw Var and me, or when they found out we were dating, they were a bit surprised. Granted, I was cute, but in the words of my best friend, Var was built like an action hero and as gorgeous as a soap opera star. I could see them wondering how I ended up on his arm. Not only was he good looking, but he was passionate about everything he did, including making me into the woman he thought I could be.

Var loved the way I looked; he never complained about my size and actually let it be known that he enjoyed my being thick and curvy in all the right places. There was no lack of physical affection from him, whether we were in public or home alone. He enjoyed hugging, touching, rubbing, and loving on me. But what he didn't like was that I was what he considered a dreamer. "I get it, Zen, you like making stuff and decorating, but you shoulda known finding a job in that field that pays decent money was gonna be hard," he told me when I still hadn't found a job almost a year after graduating. He was ready to do more things in life, such as travel, buy a home, and start investing. I really didn't have a decent job, and most of my money was going to pay my student loans.

I knew I was becoming somewhat of a burden, and it caused a lot of tension between us. Whenever he would come home and find me sewing or looking at design magazines as I helped our family and friends with design ideas for their homes, his demeanor would change. Eventually, I stopped, hoping it would help our relationship, but he still decided we needed a break. I moved out; however, even when we were apart, we remained close. He suggested that getting my MBA would enhance my design degree and maybe open more doors for me. So, I went back to school. Then, I landed the job with the property management company.

Now, here we were. His advice had paid off. I had a decent job, made lots of money, my bills were paid, we were finally making moves—and he had a new baby.

"I'm going to start looking for a place this week," I said. I knew Bailey enjoyed living alone, and I wasn't trying to invade her personal space. "I won't be crashing here too long. Don't worry."

"Shut the hell up, Zen. Don't act like you didn't have shit upstairs in the guest bedroom before all of this happened.

You know you're welcome to stay here however long you need to. When you're ready to talk to Var, you will. And that doesn't mean you have to decide to stay with him or leave him. You're dealing with a lot, including that bullshit on your job with that Lloyd dude."

At the mention of Lloyd's name, I shook my head. "I don't even wanna think about that."

"You have to think about it. Eventually, you've gotta go back to work, and when you do, you need to report his disgusting ass." Bailey took the plate of nachos that I hadn't touched since our conversation began, and put it on the coffee table. "Zen, not only did he say some out of line shit, but he touched you inappropriately. That's a straight workplace violation. He needs to be fired."

"But—"

"But nothing. You've put too much time and energy into that place to have an asshole like him run you away. Don't let him get away with this shit, Zen."

I looked at Bailey. She was right. My relationship with Var was important, and something that was going to take time for me to figure out. My job was just as important to me, and something that needed to be handled immediately.

Chapter Seven

"I hope you know we take these allegations very seriously, and we will investigate and let you know our findings."

"Thank you." I nodded at Priscilla Osborne, the tall, blond woman who worked in Human Resources.

My original plan was to confront Lloyd about what had happened and tell him that if it happened again, I was going to HR. I had an entire speech planned in my head and had even practiced in the mirror while putting on my makeup. Bailey gave me a strong pep talk before we both left for work, and I blasted Kirk Franklin in the car during my morning commute. I was ready to face the day, until I heard my name being called across the parking lot as I walked toward the building.

"Welcome back." Lloyd smiled. "We missed you."

I tried to walk as fast as I could to avoid him, but he somehow caught up with me.

"Thanks," I said, making sure I didn't make eye contact as I scanned the parking lot in hopes that someone else would be nearby that I could approach in an effort to avoid him. I could feel my anxiety growing. When I didn't see anyone, I stopped abruptly and said, "I . . . uh, I left something in my car."

I turned around and rushed back to my car, where I sat and cried from sheer frustration. I was about to leave when Lila tapped on my passenger's side window.

"Good morning!" She grinned.

"Morning." I smiled weakly.

"Are you okay?" Her smile faded, and a look of concern came across her face.

"I'm fine," I said, using the back of my hand to wipe my tears. I opened the door and headed toward the building, this time with Lila by my side, cheerfully babbling about her weekend and the office happenings while I was out.

By the time I made it to my desk, I felt a little better. There was plenty of work for me to catch up on, and I focused on responding to emails and important voice-mails. Once my clients realized I was back in the office, my phone began ringing nonstop.

"Zenobia Brooks," I answered.

"Hey, Zen."

I sat up and stared at my computer screen.

"What do you want, Var? I'm working."

"I wanna talk to you."

I lowered my voice and spoke directly into the micro-phone of my headpiece. "I don't give a damn about what you want, Var. I'm hanging this phone up, and don't—"

"Zen, I get it; you're mad. You have every right to be upset with me. I was dead-ass wrong. But we need to talk."

"Well, right now is not the time or place to have this discussion."

"Can you come by the house later so we can talk?" he pleaded.

"I don't know. I'll call you when I get off. I have to go," I told him.

"Zen, I love you. You know that, right?"

"Bye, Var." I ended the call. Leaning back in my chair, I stared at the computer. Before his call, I was so engrossed in work that for the first time in days, I hadn't thought about him or his paternity situation. Now I stared at my computer screen and couldn't even recall what I had been doing. It was time for a break. I pushed back from my desk and turned around in my chair to see Lloyd standing in the doorway of my cubicle.

"You know, Zenobia, I'm sure you already know this, but there is something about you that just mesmerizes me. I finally realized what it is when I watched you step out of your car this morning."

I didn't say anything as I stared at him, smiling at me.

"You are like the Michael Jordan of the office. It's your shoes. They're so damn sexy." His eyes went to my feet. I wore a pair of grey Ferragamo pumps that also happened to be one of Var's favorites too.

"Lloyd . . ."

"Oh, hey, Lloyd, I was just looking for you in your office." Gayle, who happened to be walking by, stopped when she saw him. "We have that call in ten minutes."

"I'm headed to the conference room right now. You can lead the way," he said, walking behind her.

I sat for a few more minutes before I was able to stand and compose myself. Then I went straight to Human Resources. Priscilla, who had been checking up on me just as much as Gayle while I was out sick, welcomed me into her office and listened carefully as I explained what had just happened in my cube, and the other incidents as well.

"So, what happens now?" I asked. I thought that reporting what Lloyd had done would bring me relief. Now I wasn't so sure. For some reason, I felt like a kindergarten student who had gone to the teacher and tattled on someone for teasing me. Priscilla didn't seem to have a reaction one way or the other to what I had told her. Then again, I didn't know what I was expecting her to do.

"Well, we're going to need you to give a written account of what you just told me. And like I said, we will do a full investigation. One thing this company does not tolerate is violation of any kind against employees." Priscilla gave me a nod. "We will bring Lloyd in and discuss what happened with him."

I gasped. "What? Right now?"

"No. Like I said, we need a formal written statement. I will speak with management, and we'll conduct the investigation. Right now, focus on the statement, and if he approaches you again, let me know immediately. Do you feel comfortable going back to your desk, or do I need to move you temporarily?" she asked.

"I think I'll be okay. I'll just try and avoid him as much as possible." I stood up. "But I'm gonna get that statement over to you as soon as possible."

"I'm sorry this is happening to you, Zen, especially in light of everything else you've had going on." She gave me a sympathetic look. "Please let me know if you need anything."

I walked out of her office and turned the corner to the elevator. I saw Gayle and Lloyd talking outside the conference room and immediately turned around. I walked back into Priscilla's office and said, "I'm gonna go ahead and leave for today. Can you let Gayle know?"

"No problem," she said.

At the rate things were going, I was spending more time away from my office than I spent actually working. When would things get easier for me?

Chapter Eight

"I'm proud of you." Bailey smiled.

"Why? I didn't do anything." I shrugged. I had called her when I left work, and we met at Olive Garden for lunch. I was sitting across from her, staring at the menu, trying to decide if I was going to be sensible and order soup and salad, or order the Tour of Italy, which was what I really wanted.

"Wrong. You stood up for yourself. You took a stand and let the powers that be know what that asshole did. You did a lot."

"If you say so. We'll see what happens. I just really want them to tell him to leave me the hell alone, and I'll be fine. I was gonna just tell him myself, but Gayle walked up, and I thought about what you said, so I went to Priscilla," I explained.

"And that was the right way to handle it," Bailey assured me.

"Oh, and get this: Var called my desk phone right before it happened."

"Shit, you had a rough morning from the jump, girl. And here I thought my motivational speech and healthy breakfast was gonna be the start of a great day."

"Tomorrow we're listening to trap music and eating waffles," I said with a laugh.

"So, what did Var say?"

"He wanted to meet and talk. Says he wants to come by. I told him now isn't the time. I need time to think this thing through, and I don't need him in my ear while I'm figuring out what I want to do," I said.

"I get that."

"He keeps saying that this chick is lying."

"She might be. You know how chicks are. To be honest, I wouldn't be surprised if she was. And for real, I don't wanna see you walk away from Var over a lie that some chick told."

"It's not even about her, though. Var never mentioned this chick to me."

"And he probably never would have if this hadn't happened, either. But then again, y'all were on a break. I told you you shoulda been out getting yours because he was out getting his." Bailey gave me an I-told-you-so look, and I rolled my eyes.

"Well, I was getting mine. The difference is I was still getting it from him when I got it."

"I knew you were still screwing him."

"Not as much as you think, but Var was acting like he wasn't even entertaining anybody else. And then, even after he found out that she said he was the father, he still didn't mention it. How long was he going to keep this from me? Was he ever going to tell me? And what if it does turn out to be his baby? Then what? I already deal with enough baby mama drama with Karli. Now I gotta deal with another chick?"

"Oh God, I don't think anyone could be as psycho as that bitch. She is the absolute worst."

Karli, the mother of Var's seven-year-old daughter Venus, was crazy, and she had a low-key personal vendetta against me. When we first started dating, she was nice, but when Var and I moved in together, the pleasant demeanor suddenly changed. She became distant and cold. Then, although he had always been supportive financially, physically, emotionally, and had a great relationship with Venus, Karli took him to child support court once she found out I was pregnant. Ironically, the eight hundred dollars that Var had been paying monthly was lowered to five hundred. Karli was livid. She packed Venus up and moved six hours away. She said it was to be closer to her sister, but I knew better. Karli was like a lot of other people who thought that Var would never settle down with a big girl, especially when all of his exes, including his baby mama, were built like video vixens who captured the attention of every man in every room they entered. His decision to be with me was insulting to her, and she wasn't pleased. As bad as I felt about Var not being able to spend every other weekend with his daughter as he always had done, I was glad that I no longer had to deal with the games Karli would play to disrupt our lives.

The waitress came over, and before I could say anything, Bailey quickly told her, "Two waters, please. And we'll both have the *zuppa* Toscano and the salad, please."

"I'll be right out with your drinks and bread," the young girl said as she took our menus.

"Nope, we're good on bread," Bailey answered. Both the waitress and I gave her a confused look.

"Heffa, it's Olive Garden," I said.

"Fine, two breadsticks," she relented. "That's it."

"Sure thing."

"Lifestyle changes, remember?" Bailey said.

"Small steps, remember?" I reminded her. "Who comes to Olive Garden and doesn't get breadsticks? That's not a lifestyle change; that's just disrespectful."

Bailey laughed. "You're so dramatic."

I pulled out my phone and checked my Facebook account, scrolling to a photo Var had been tagged in.

There was Karli, smiling alongside Venus, and another woman holding a baby with the caption "Big Sis and Lil Sis finally meet. #siblings #twins." I was shocked. It was obvious Karli had posted it to be hurtful, and it worked. My heart broke into a million pieces for what felt like the hundredth time as I zoomed in on the picture and stared at the baby that looked just like Var. No blood test was needed. I knew he was the father, and our relationship was over.

Chapter Nine

I sat at my desk and stared at my computer. I had been attempting to complete the formal statement Priscilla told me to submit, but I was too distracted. I wasn't the only one who had seen the picture posted on Facebook, and I had gotten so many calls and messages that I turned my phone off. Any glimmer of hope that I had for Var and me to somehow move past this was gone. Not only had he betrayed my trust by keeping his paternity situation from me, but he had placed me in an embarrassing situation in front of everyone.

Bailey and I had gone straight into SCI mode (Sistas Collecting Info) on both of our phones and began finding out everything we could about April Hughes. We discovered that she was the daughter of Var's former boss. I wondered if his being with her had anything to do with him getting promoted twice within a year.

There was a light tapping on my cubicle wall, and Molly, one of the security guards, stuck her head in. "Hey, Zen."

"What's up?" I looked up from the computer.

"You have a visitor downstairs."

"Huh?"

"That handsome fiancé of yours is in the lobby. I tried calling your desk, but it kept going straight to voicemail," she said.

I looked at my work phone and saw that I hadn't logged back in after my lunch break, which I spent at my desk because I didn't want to chance running into Lloyd. There was no telling how many calls I'd missed.

Var was the last person in the world I wanted to see. I thought about having Molly tell him I wasn't in, but I was sure he had seen the car in the parking lot. The one good thing about staying with Bailey was that she lived in a gated community, and he since he didn't know the code to enter, he couldn't get to me. Here, I didn't have that luxury, especially since he was familiar to some people.

"Thanks," I told her. "Tell him I'll be down in a few minutes."

"I gotcha." Molly turned and left.

I turned back to the computer and inhaled as I stared at the half-written statement. Priscilla had asked me to have it to her before two o'clock, and it was already after one. I had to get it done. I locked my computer screen then headed downstairs to face Var for the first time since I'd left the house.

When I got to the lobby, Var was standing near the front door. He smiled when he saw me walking toward him; I didn't smile back. Normally, I would have been filled with anticipation of the strong embrace he always greeted me with, along with a kiss on my neck. Instead, I was emotionless and didn't even get close enough for him to touch me.

"Hey, baby." His voice was low.

I glanced around the lobby, checking to see who was watching us. Molly was showing the receptionist something on her cell phone. Two other co-workers were engaged in a conversation near the elevator.

"What do you want?" I folded my arms across my body.

"Zenobia, we gotta talk about this."

"I told you I would talk to you when I'm ready, Var. I'm not ready yet." I tried to remain calm so I wouldn't make a scene.

"Well, when will you be ready? It's almost been a week."

My neck snapped, but I caught myself before raising my voice an octave and giving Var the cussing out he truly deserved. Instead, I quickly walked out the front door and headed over to the wooden gazebo on the side of the building. It had originally been placed there as a nice place for people who wanted to have lunch outside, but it had somehow become the unofficial smokers' lounge. I could smell the lingering scent of cigarette smoke as I stepped inside.

I quickly turned around and faced Var, who was right behind me. Until then, I hadn't even noticed his fresh haircut, which made the waves of his hair even more visible. The navy blue suit he wore was custom made and one of my favorites, and the tie was one I had given him on Valentine's Day. Based on his attire and the smell of his Tom Ford cologne that I loved, it was clear that he had planned to see me at some point today.

"Let me explain something to you, LaVar Thompson. You don't have to tell me how long it's been, because believe me, I know. I know that damn letter arrived in my mailbox seven fucking days ago. I know you've been lying to me this entire time. I also know who April Hughes' daddy is, and I know that you already know I saw that fucking picture that Karli's bitch ass tagged you in. Everyone knows, Var." I spat the words at him. "You're an opportunistic bastard, Var. And one of the reasons I didn't wanna have this conversation with you is because I am so disappointed in you."

"Zenobia, that's not my—"

"If she ain't your baby, then neither is Venus, because they look just alike, like their daddy. So, please spare me, and don't disrespect me with some explanation that I really don't even need."

"You're not even gonna let me—"

"There's no explanation needed, Var. You slept with her, got her pregnant, and now you have two baby daughters to raise. At least your two baby mamas seem to get along." I gave him a fake smile.

"I know I fucked up, Zen, and I'm sorry about all of this. I swear I just found out when I did, though. I couldn't tell you. There was no way I was gonna hurt you like that—"

"Couldn't have hurt any worse than how I feel right now."

"Zen, you know we've always said we could get through anything together and we'll always have each other's back. We can get through this." He stepped closer to me. "You know neither one of those chicks mean anything to me. We've gotten through other shit, Zen. We can make it through this. Come home."

I shook my head. "First of all, they're the mothers of your children, so they should mean something to you. Second, why are you acting like I'm overreacting, like this is no big deal?"

"Because in the grand scheme of things, it isn't. It's not as if I cheated on you. We weren't together when it went down between me and that chick. Second, I've stuck by you when you had shit going on yourself, don't forget."

I could feel beads of sweat forming on my forehead and between my breasts. "What the fuck is that supposed to mean?"

"Zenobia, I took care of you financially for a whole year after you graduated. I stood by you when you didn't have a job," he stated. "I made sure you were good because I believed in you and believed in us."

"Are you really standing there saying this?" I said, shocked by what he was saying.

"What?"

"Var, I had a job. I was in the process of starting my own business when *you* decided *you* needed a break from us because *you* were stressed . . ."

"And I pushed you to go back to school and get your MBA and become the success that you are. Hell, look at where you're working now."

"Is everything okay?" Molly asked, standing in the middle of the walkway.

I was embarrassed because I had no idea how much she'd heard. "We're fine."

"Okay." Fortunately, she took my word for it and turned to walk back inside.

"Shit." I looked down at my watch and realized we had been standing outside talking longer than I anticipated, and I had less than twenty minutes to send Priscilla the formal complaint. The conversation with Var had gone on long enough, and there was nothing more I had to say. "I have to get back inside."

"I'm not done," he said.

"I am." I left him standing in the gazebo. Walking back to the building, I noticed the same coworkers that had been gawking over Lloyd in the staff meeting were staring at Var as they passed him.

I went back to my desk and unlocked my computer. I was exhausted physically, mentally, and emotionally. He was the one who had been deceitful, and yet, he tried to make me feel as if he was supposed to get a pass of some sort and I was to just accept what he had done. The situation at home with Var and the situation at work with Lloyd seemed to mirror one another, and I was not going to be the victim to either one. Suddenly, my fingers began to fly across the keyboard, and I detailed what Lloyd had done and how it made me feel. When I was done, I secured the email and sent it to Priscilla, making sure to send a copy to myself. For the first time in a week, I felt like I wasn't going to cry at any moment.

Chapter Ten

The remainder of the week went by quickly, and by the time Friday arrived, I was beyond ready for the weekend. Even though it was casual Friday, I still wore a dress and heels, because when I ran by the house to grab a few more of my things, I was so afraid that Var was going to come home while I was there that I forgot to grab a pair of jeans and sneakers. I walked into the building still wearing my Chanel shades that I had put on because the sun was so bright on the ride to work.

I spoke to the receptionist as I passed her desk. Normally, she was bright and perky, but something about the way she said good morning seemed a bit off. As I waited for the elevator, a few other coworkers walked up. When the doors opened, I stepped on and pushed the button to hold the door open for them, but they told me to go ahead. When I got to my floor, I could feel the stares and heard the whispers as I walked down the corridor.

"Okay, what the hell is going on?" I asked Lila, who was already sitting at her desk eating oatmeal and listening to the morning radio show that Bailey produced. I knew if something was going on, she would be the one to know.

"Good morning to you too." She turned around and smiled. I was relieved when her reaction was normal, and I wondered if I was being paranoid. "Aren't you dressed kind of fancy for it to be a Friday? That dress is everything, and so are the shoes."

I relaxed, figuring that was the reason people were looking at me strangely, because the black-and-white wrap dress, along with my favorite red heels, was a bit dressy. I had also gotten my hair done the night before.

"Thank you."

"And the hair is fabulous too. You and Var got a hot date after work?" She laughed.

"No, definitely not. People were looking at me like I was a foreigner, so I thought something was wrong." I sighed.

"Nope." She scraped the bottom of her bowl and stood up. "I gotta go rinse this out. You need anything from the break room?"

I went into my cubicle and grabbed my coffee mug and handed it to her. "Breakfast blend, please. Sugar and cream. You're the best."

"That's what I've heard."

I laughed, and as Lila walked off, I looked up and saw Gayle and another coworker looking in my direction. When they saw me looking, they both turned and went the other way. In the pit of my stomach, I knew there was something going on, and this was about more than just my dress.

"Well, you were right," Lila said when she came back and handed me my coffee.

"I told you," I said, taking it from her and setting it on my desk. "Are they gonna announce another manager that they hired instead of me?"

I was expecting Lila to laugh, but she didn't. The look on her face let me know that whatever it was, it was serious.

"Did someone die? Is someone sick?" I frowned.

"No, but people are talking about you," she whispered. "Did you report that Lloyd touched you?"

My heart began pounding. Priscilla had assured me that although an investigation would take place, what I reported would be in strict confidence. If people were talking, then clearly they knew, but I hadn't told anyone, not even Gayle or Lila.

I nodded. "Yes, he did."

"What? When? Why didn't you say something to me? Oh my God, Zen," she hissed.

"It happened right here in my cube. He also made some inappropriate comments to me, so I reported it."

"Good morning, Zen. Lila, can I see you in my office?" Gayle's voice interrupted our conversation.

"Huh? Oh, sure." Lila nodded and followed her out, throwing a quick glance back at me.

I tried to concentrate but couldn't. I wondered if Gayle needing to speak to Lila had anything to do with what people were saying. I tried to reach Bailey on her cell phone, but she didn't answer, so I sent her a text. She didn't respond, so I sat and waited nervously for Lila to come back.

It seemed as if it took forever for Lila to return to her desk. When she did, I didn't waste any time going to speak to her.

"What the hell did she wanna talk to you about?" I whispered.

Lila shook her head and whispered, "Not here. We can't talk in here."

"What? Fuck that. I need to know what the hell is going on, Lila. Tell me."

She gave me a helpless look, then peeked out of her cubicle to make sure the coast was clear before she said, "They asked me questions about you and Lloyd: if I'd seen him in your cube or heard him speaking to you."

"What did you say?" I frowned.

"I told them that I'd seen him in there a couple of times, but I couldn't hear you guys talking." She said, "Then they asked if you'd ever complained or said anything to me about anything he'd said or done. I told them no, because you hadn't."

"I told you this morning what he did." I leaned against her desk.

"I know, and I started to say something, but I knew their next question would probably be what did you say, and I didn't wanna make things worse than they already are," Lila explained.

"What do you mean?" I was taken aback by her statement.

"Zen, I know this is gonna sound bad, but I don't think they believe you. People are saying that you're lying."

Instead of taking the elevator up two floors to Priscilla's office, I rushed into the stairwell and climbed the stairs. I could barely catch my breath and had to pause for several minutes before I opened the door and entered the corridor that led to her end of the building. I knocked on her door, but no one answered. I had just turned around to leave when I heard her call my name.

"Zenobia, here I am."

"I need to talk to you," I told her.

"Well, I was actually going to have you come in later this afternoon."

"This can't wait until then. I need to talk now."

She unlocked her door, and we went inside. I sat in the same chair that I had been in earlier in the week. After she placed the manila folder she was carrying on her desk, she settled into her chair.

"How are you doing?" she asked.

"You told me that what I told you would remain confidential, and now there's this chit-chat all over the office that I lied about what Lloyd did. How do you think I'm doing?" I asked.

"I know you're upset, and I can understand your frustration. Your complaint was kept confidential; however, we are in the middle of investigating the allegations, and I explained that to you. We brought Lloyd in to address what you said happened—"

"We? Who is we?" I asked.

"Well, myself, of course, and another member of management," Priscilla replied.

"Please don't tell me the other member of management is Gayle," I begged.

"Actually, it is."

"No wonder everyone knows and they think I'm lying. She has the biggest mouth in this building, and she runs behind Lloyd like she has a schoolgirl crush on him," I said, my voice full of frustration.

Priscilla remained emotionless and said, "Well, we did speak to Lloyd, and he denied that he did anything inappropriate, verbally or physically. He said he did pick up your cell phone from the break room where you had a brief conversation about the kind of coffee you like. Then he brought the phone back to you. He denies having any physical contact with you."

"That doesn't surprise me. And what about what he said to me in the parking lot?"

"He said he simply complimented you on your shoes, that's all." Priscilla shrugged.

"This is some bull. So, basically, it's my word against his?" I shook my head and looked past Priscilla to the plaques and framed photos on her shelf.

"Unfortunately, that's how these things turn out sometimes. But it's not over yet, and we haven't come to any conclusion at this time, which is why I was waiting until this afternoon to talk to you."

"Don't even worry about it. There's no point in even investigating him at this point."

"Zenobia, he's not the only one we're investigating now."

Her words took me by surprise. In all the time I'd worked at the property management company, I had never seen or heard anything out of the ordinary until my own experience with Lloyd.

"There are other men in the office doing this?" I asked.

"No."

"I don't understand," I said, confused.

"Zenobia, Lloyd has made allegations against you. He was told that you made comments of a sexual nature to others during a staff meeting last week."

At that moment, I wished the floor would open up and swallow me. Was he really trying to flip this back on me? I was starting to wish I had never gone to report him in the first place.

Chapter Eleven

"Are you sure this is everything?" Bailey asked.

"Yeah, this is it." I looked around the bedroom to make sure I had gotten all my belongings. It had only taken a couple of hours for us to pack everything up, mainly because Var had most of it boxed up before we got there. We hadn't seen one another since the day he showed up at my office, and the only conversation we had was via text messaging, when he let me know that we had until the last day of the month to be out of the townhouse. When we arrived to get my things, he was polite and cordial, and then instead of staying at the house while we picked up my things, he said he had a couple of errands to run and left.

"I hope all of this fits into the back of the truck." Bailey picked up one of the boxes marked "shoes" and grunted, "Damn Zen, you and your damn shoe addiction."

"Mine isn't nearly as bad as yours. Hell, you have an entire bedroom dedicated as a shoe closet." I picked up another box, and we headed out the door and loaded them onto the U-Haul that I had rented. It was the first load, and I was already tired and sweating. I leaned against the truck and said, "I know I said I was glad Var left, but now I'm wishing he was here to help us carry these boxes."

Bailey laughed. "I was just thinking the same thing. But come on, we gotta keep the momentum going. Besides, this is great exercise."

"I never thought I would say this, but I'd rather be at the gym," I joked.

Since I moved in with her, Bailey had insisted that I tag along with her to the gym three times a week. She said it was to keep her company. I usually ended up walking alongside her on the treadmill while she ran and chatted about her day at the station, and surprisingly, it didn't even feel like exercise, just girl talk, which we did daily.

"Hey, Zen!"

Bailey and I were bringing out another load of boxes when Jose Caldwell, the handyman our landlord used, rushed over and took the box from me. He was a nice-looking Hispanic guy who was always available when we needed something done.

"Thanks, Caldwell. I appreciate it."

Once he loaded it onto the truck, he took the box that Bailey was carrying as well, then asked, "I know you pretty ladies ain't moving by yourselves. That's too much stuff. Where's Var?"

"He's not here. And we're just moving my things," I told him.

He blinked for a second, then said, "Well, I can't let you do this by yourself. I'll be more than happy to help."

"You don't have to do that, Caldwell. I'm sure you have work you need to do," I told him.

"I am working. The property owner sent me over to do a quick inspection to see if any repairs need to be made—which I already know there aren't. Heck, you actually made improvements to the place that he should've deducted from the rent." He laughed. "You know I always said that whenever I was here."

"You got that right," Bailey agreed. "This place is way nicer now than when they moved in. Did you see what she did with that fireplace?"

"Man, I walked in to fix the dishwasher and saw that fireplace and thought I was in the wrong place. Not just that, but the way she has, well, *had* it decorated was straight out of a magazine. I told my boss about your talent and told her she needs to hire you," he said.

"Zen is one of the most gifted and talented designers I know. I can't wait to see what she does with my place now that she's my new roomie." Bailey gave me a quick hug.

I appreciated their votes of confidence, especially since I wasn't feeling gifted or talented these days. I really hadn't felt anything. In a matter of a few weeks, I had lost a baby, my relationship, my job, and my home.

"Well, I have plenty of time to spruce it up for you, that's for sure," I told her, thinking about my current unemployment status.

It hadn't taken long for Priscilla to investigate the sexual harassment claims that Lloyd had made against me. Both women who had been sitting behind me during the last staff meeting confirmed that they'd overheard my statement about numbers increasing if he would be conducting the monthly sales meetings. The tables had somehow turned, and I now looked like I was pursuing him instead. Priscilla and Gayle both suggested that I resign before the findings were submitted to the board of directors. I sat across from them at the table in the conference room, too shocked to say anything. I could hear Lila's words echoing in my head: *They don't believe you.*

"So, he gets away with this and I have to quit? Is that what you're telling me?" I had said, finally breaking the silence that filled the room.

"Like I explained, Zenobia, it was pretty much your word versus his," Priscilla answered.

"But that's not the case, because clearly, you're taking his word over mine." I frowned.

"There were witnesses to what you said," Gayle explained.

"That's crazy, because what I said wasn't even of a sexual nature, and what the two so-called witnesses said about him was way worse than my simple-ass comment. Not to mention that one of them—" I was about to spill the beans about how one of the chicks was plotting to seduce Lloyd, but I stopped. It was pointless.

I glared at the two women, who stared back at me like I was some kind of alien who had just arrived and asked them the formula for rocket fuel so I could return home. To them, not only did I look strange, but this entire situation was unbelievable. Here I was a damn near three-hundred-pound black woman accusing the most attractive man in the office of being sexually inappropriate toward me when there were plenty of other skinnier, prettier women who were ready, willing, and able to do whatever, whenever he wanted. To them, it made no sense at all.

Since being hired, I'd been dedicated, hard-working, and an all-around team player who came to work early and stayed late. I was the model employee. Lloyd had only been in our office for a month, yet I was being asked to leave. I couldn't believe it. I was just as disappointed in the company I worked for as I was in my ex-fiancé.

"I was out of work for a month because I lost my baby. I came back before I was even released by my doctor because you told me you needed me back here. Gayle, you've been my supervisor from the day I started, and I've never given you any trouble. You've told me time and time again that I've been considered for management positions, none of which I've ever gotten, by the way, because they've gone to less qualified people with less seniority and less education, including that perverted asshole Lloyd, and I've never complained. But this is just . . . sad." I shook my head.

"Zen, you are a great employee—" Gayle started, but I didn't let her finish.

I stood up and announced, "I quit."

"You don't have to leave today. We were thinking you would stay for the rest of the month." Priscilla placed her hand on the table.

"You're crazy," I said, frowning at her.

Gayle tried speaking again. "I'm so sorry, Zenobia. I truly am. You know if you need letters of recommend—"

"Fuck you and your fake sympathy—and you can keep your recommendation," I told her.

"Zenobia, that's really uncalled for." Priscilla gave me a disappointed look. "I know you're upset, but there's no need—"

"Oh, I'm sorry if you expected my reaction to this bullshit to be a little more professional, but it's not. I'm over all of this, and I'm over all of you." I opened the door to walk out.

"Wait. I have to call and have security escort you to your desk to get your personal belongings," Priscilla said.

"You want to embarrass me even more?" I asked.

"No, that's not what we want to do. You know that's our policy, Zenobia." Gayle was now turning red in the face.

"That's the policy when people are fired. I quit, remember." I turned around, and this time I was out the door before they could stop me.

I ignored the looks and whispers as I walked back to my cube. I snatched the pictures and motivational sayings off my walls and put them on my desk, then realized I didn't have a box to carry anything in. I reached in my desk drawer and took out my purse and keys.

Lila walked in. "What happened?"

"I told them to fuck this place."

"What?" Lila's eyes widened with surprised.

"They told me I could either resign or be fired, so I quit. You were right; they didn't believe me."

"Noooooo!" Lila gave me a hug. When she released me, I could see the tears in her eyes.

"It's cool. Can you do me a favor?"

"Sure, anything. What do you need?"

"Priscilla is probably calling Molly and the cavalry to come up here and haul my big ass out of here."

Lila gasped. "She wouldn't dare."

"She says it's company policy." I repeated the reason I was given.

"That's if you were fired."

"I know that. Anyway, can you pack my desk up for me and I will pick my stuff up from you later? I don't trust anyone else here except you."

"You know that's not a problem." The tears Lila had been holding back began to fall. We had become close, and I was going to miss her.

"Stop it." I grabbed a Kleenex from my desk and handed it to her. "You know we'll still talk all the time."

"I know." She sniffed.

I gave her one final hug good-bye and left.

"What's next?" Caldwell asked, bringing me back to the reality of packing up and moving instead of remembering my last day in the office.

I sighed. "We got all of my stuff from the bedroom and master bath. I guess next is the salon."

"Lord, that's the one room I've been dreading," Bailey teased.

"What's the salon?" Caldwell asked as he followed us down the hallway and into the room.

Var had told me that even though he boxed up my clothes and shoes, he hadn't touched anything in the salon because it was too much to deal with. As I looked around the space, I was glad that he felt that way. I would rather do it myself than running the risk of him doing it and throwing stuff away that he thought was unnecessary, which he had the tendency to do.

"This is where the magic happens—well, it used to happen, before she lost her mojo," Bailey teased, bumping my arm. "But we're gonna get that back soon enough."

"Wow, this is a lot of stuff." Caldwell laughed. "Where do we start?"

I looked at him and said, "Are you sure you don't have anything else you're supposed to be doing? This is gonna take a minute."

"I told you it's cool," he said.

Handing him one of the empty boxes that were leaning against the wall, I told him, "I guess you can box up those books and magazines. I'm not gonna empty the caddies; we can just tape them shut, and I could put them in storage along with the sewing machine and the serger."

"What? Why would you do that?" Bailey looked confused.

"Because it's easier than trying to box them all up. We can just—"

"No, Zen. I'm talking about why you would put your sewing stuff in storage."

"Where else am I gonna put it?" I asked.

"Um, my house where you're living," she said.

I laughed. "I know my room is pretty spacious, but there's no way that's gonna fit in there."

"But it'll fit in the shoe room. Especially if I move some of the shoe boxes out." She shrugged then added, "Hand me the tape."

I looked at my best friend and fought the tears that I felt forming. "Bailey, you don't have to do that."

"You said you wanted the drawers taped up. Make up your mind, woman." She exhaled dramatically.

"Wow, you're a good friend," Caldwell commented as he grabbed the roll of packing tape on the floor near the boxes.

"I have ulterior motives. I told you she's about to hook my place up, so I don't need her giving me any excuses about not being able to do it because her stuff is in storage," Bailey told him.

"I knew you were being too nice. I don't know any woman who would willingly give up her shoe room," Caldwell said.

With the three of us working, it didn't take long to get everything in the room packed up, boxed, and loaded. Caldwell did all the heavy lifting and made sure my machines were secure. He even offered to meet us at the storage facility and then Bailey's house to unload the truck.

I was doing a final walk-through of our place when Var returned.

"Damn, y'all finished already?" He looked surprised.

"Yeah, we're done. I'm making sure I got everything," I told him

"Caldwell helped," Bailey volunteered.

"Caldwell? Why the hell did you call him?" Var snapped at me.

"I didn't call him, Var. The property manager sent him over to check the place out," I explained.

"I don't know what for. The keys don't even get turned in until day after tomorrow. He probably brought his Spanish ass over here to be nosy and see if we left anything he could take."

"Var, you're tripping. Caldwell ain't even like that, and you know it." I shook my head.

"What I do know is that he was always commenting on

how nice our shit was like he was casing the joint. And you used to encourage him, always pointing out how you did this or made that. I told you how I ain't like the way he used to look at you when y'all would be chatting it up."

Caldwell had never done anything suspect, and he'd always been nice and respectful each and every time he'd come over to the house. Var had never liked him, especially the fact that, unlike him, Caldwell always noticed if I did something to our house. Whether it was major like the redesign of the fireplace, or minor, like changing the furniture around, Caldwell noticed and gave me compliments. Var was never the jealous type, but me receiving compliments on my design skills always bothered him. I believed it was because he thought it might inspire me to go back to pursuing it full time.

"Again, you're tripping. He was never like that. You just didn't like him for some strange reason." I took my key off the ring and handed it to him. "Here."

Var just stared at the shiny copper in the palm of my hand with a look of sadness. "Zen, we gotta get through this."

"You get the paternity test results back, Var?" I asked.

He looked up at me, took the key, then looked away. "Yeah, I got them."

"That's what I thought." I sighed. I knew that the test had to have come back listing him as the father. Had it not, he would've told me.

"I know this is a lot to ask, considering what we've just gone through, but I love you, Zen, and I want us to be together. Moving into this house doesn't even feel right without you. How am I even gonna do all of this by myself? We've both worked so hard for this."

"You were the one who wanted to go through with that house, not me. And honestly, with your new baby and all,

I don't know how you're gonna handle it. But I'm sure you will. I can't help you," I told him.

"Yes, you can. We're a team. I've apologized, and this baby is not something I planned or even knew about, but she's here," he said.

"Are you crazy? Clearly, you've lost your mind." My voice rose, and I took a step toward him. I had taken about as much as I could tolerate from him.

"Come on, Zen. Let's go." Bailey, who'd been quietly waiting near the door, walked over and put her hand on my shoulder.

"No, I haven't lost my mind. I'm the one that's fighting for us, and you say I'm crazy?" Var asked.

"What do you expect her to do, Var? She just lost her baby, and now you want her to step up and be stepmom of the year? That ain't fair. Your baby mama been out of pocket for years, and you've never checked her on her bullshit. Zen has always been the one to turn the other cheek. And she's a good one, because the only cheek I would've given her was the one I sit on to kiss. You are crazy." Bailey tugged on my arm.

"Fine, Zen, go ahead. Let your single, miserable friend convince you to leave your relationship so she can have someone to be miserable right along with her!" Var yelled.

"Fuck you, Var. You're right; I am telling her to leave your opportunistic, arrogant, selfish ass. Go be with your baby mama. Move her into your house, and then maybe her daddy will promote you again to help you pay for it, you asshole!" Bailey yelled back at him. "I'd rather her be miserable by herself than with your whack ass!"

"Screw you, Bailey. You never wanted to see her happy anyway. You were always jealous because Zen could keep a man and you couldn't," Var responded.

"Var, you need to stop it. Don't stand there and act like some kind of fucking victim like this ain't your fault. I swear, you are a self-centered, narcissistic hypocrite, and you need to seek counseling," I said.

"And you're whack as hell!" Bailey repeated.

It was me who then pulled Bailey out the front door. We climbed into the U-Haul and looked at one another in silence for a few moments, then we burst out in laughter.

"You just had to have the last word, huh?" I gasped, trying to catch my breath. "What was that? You're whack as hell?"

"Well, he is," she said matter-of-factly, and we pulled out of the driveway, away from my former home with whack-ass Var.

Chapter Twelve

Six Months Later

"Is that all you need today, Mrs. Powe?" I asked the customer as I put the items she had purchased into a plastic bag.

"Yes, Zen. Thank you so much for all your help. I don't know what I'd do without you." The tiny, gray-haired woman smiled. "The ladies in my book club are gonna be jealous when they come to my house and see these pillows I'm making."

"Well, you have to let me know what they say."

"I will. See you next time."

I walked Mrs. Powe out the front door of Loehman's Fabrics, where I was finally working after being unemployed for almost five months. It wasn't where one would expect to find a talented, educated black woman with two degrees, but here I was. My Loehman's paycheck didn't cover all my bills, but thankfully, the seamstress work I did for clients put a little more money in my fairly empty pockets.

Bailey didn't charge me anything for rent, and when I tried to give her cash, she refused. So, I made sure to bring groceries and household supplies in weekly, and whenever we went out for drinks, I paid for at least one round. I also did a phenomenal job redecorating her house, especially because of my store discount. I really enjoyed working at the store, but I knew I needed to find a better job soon.

"Can I help you find something?" I asked a lady who had been lingering among the bolts of sheer polyester for a little while.

"I don't know. I'm so confused," she said, running her fingers along the material.

"What are you looking for?"

"My husband and I just got new living room furniture, which I love, but now our drapes don't match. I want to change them, but he's saying they look fine. I just came in here to look, really," she said.

"New living room furniture. Nice. What color is it?" I asked.

"I love it. They call it Fresco, I believe. It's brown leather, but is has tapestry cushions and pillows." She was beaming as she described her décor.

"It sounds gorgeous. Do you have a picture?"

"Well, darn it, I don't. That would probably be helpful if I did, huh?" She laughed.

"A little. But, no worries," I told her just as the store phone began to ring, "Excuse me for one second."

"Oh, you're fine, dear," she said.

I walked behind the counter and answered, "Loehman's Fine Fabrics, this is Zen."

"Hey, Zen, I got a client for you."

"Caldwell?"

"Yeah, I tried calling your cell but got no answer, so I called the store. What time do you get off? I told him you would meet him." Caldwell was talking so fast that I couldn't grasp what he was saying.

"Wait, slow down. What are you talking about? *Who* are you talking about?" I asked.

Since helping me move, Caldwell had checked on Bailey and me pretty frequently, and we had even hung out at happy hour a couple of times. We learned that not only was he a talented contractor, but he was also smart and funny. Caldwell also had no problem letting anyone who needed any type of seamstress know that I was available. He had even told one woman I could design and sew her wedding gown, which I certainly couldn't do. I had to stress to him that my specialty was interior design, not fashion. So, when he called talking about a potential client, I had to clarify before agreeing to meet with them.

"My mother's best friend's son just moved back, and he needs some work done to his townhouse. I went over to do an estimate for him. His mother wants him to hire a designer, and I told them about you," Caldwell explained. "I told them you charge two-fifty an hour."

"What?" My voice was so loud that the customer I'd been helping raised her head and looked over at me.

"That's how much you told me designers make, right?" he asked.

"Well, yeah, ones who work for design firms, Caldwell, which I don't." I couldn't believe this dude.

"Well, I guess they're cool with the price, because they asked when you could come by, and I told them probably today. So, what time do you get off?"

"Uh, I, um, seven," I said.

"Cool. I'll let them know and text you the address," Caldwell said. "See you when you get there."

Before I could protest any further, Caldwell hung up. I put the receiver back on the cradle and walked back over to my customer.

"I am so sorry about that," I apologized. "Did you find anything you think may match?"

"Not really. I think I'm gonna take a picture and bring it back, if that's okay." She waited for my response. When I nodded, she seemed relieved.

"That's fine. I'll be here and ready to help you find the perfect fabric," I promised, and she left.

It was two minutes after seven when I hung up my uniform apron and clocked out. I grabbed my purse out of my locker in the storage room, said good-bye to Maggie, my boss, and walked out the door. Once I got in the car, I took my cell phone out of my purse and saw I had two missed calls from earlier. There was also a text from Caldwell, with an address where we were supposed to meet.

The phone began vibrating, and Bailey's name and picture flashed on the screen.

"What's up, girl. How was work?" she asked after I said hello.

"It was cool. What about you?"

"Same ol' same. Nothing spectacular," she said. "I'm grabbing my bag and changing at the gym. You on your way?"

"Uh, well . . ." I started.

Bailey interrupted me. "No excuses. I don't wanna hear it."

We had continued our weekly "girl talk" workout regimen on the treadmill three to four times a week. Bailey also kept her promise about adopting and keeping healthier eating habits. With my best friend's support, I had lost well over fifty pounds and felt better, and Bailey was now training to run her first 5K race. She had invited me to participate, which I respectfully declined.

"I'm not making an excuse, I swear. Caldwell called—"

"Ohhhhh, nooooo. Now I know this is about to be some BS. What did Juan Valdez want?" Bailey laughed.

"Bailey, that's not nice. Don't do that," I scolded her.

"Do what? As much as he teases me about my forehead and my fingers? You're kidding, right?"

I laughed, because Caldwell and Bailey constantly teased one another, sometimes to the point that I could hardly breathe from laughing so hard. They had both grown up with older siblings, which had seemed to help them learn to joke others.

"He set up a meeting for me with a potential client."

"Oh God, he doesn't have you making someone else's wedding dress, does he?"

"No, it's someone remodeling a home."

"What? That's great," Bailey said with excitement. "Wait, what's wrong? Why do you sound like you don't wanna go?"

"Because he told them I was a designer and I charge two-fifty an hour," I explained.

"Yes, Caldwell! You better do the damn thing and make it happen for my girl."

"Uhhh, I'm gonna tell you like I told him. That's what design firms charge. I don't work for a firm."

"Zenobia, shut up. You hold an art design degree that you earned from a highly esteemed university, and you graduated with honors, which demonstrates that you know what the hell you're doing. You also hold an MBA, which you also earned with honors, which demonstrates that you not only know what the hell you're doing, but you've mastered it. Clearly, whoever it is doesn't have a problem with what Caldwell said, because they wanna meet. You know white folks don't mind spending money with people they like and trust. They ain't thinking about a firm. They need to know if you're good at what you do."

"I don't have my portfolio together. I don't have swatches . . ."

"Stop it. I told you no excuses."

"I thought that only applied for the gym."

"No, that applies to this too. You go to that meeting and tell them what you can do. I'm sure Caldwell has sung your praises, which is what sparked their interest in the first place. If they need more references, tell them to call me. Better yet, bring them by the house so they can see for themselves. Zen, you got this."

I took a deep breath and said, "Okay, okay, I'm going."

"You walk in that meeting with your head held high and all the fabulousness that's in you, so they can see just by looking at you that you're the best person for whatever they need you for."

"Except a wedding gown," I joked.

"Definitely not."

"Thanks, Bails."

"You're welcome. Call me when you're done so we can go celebrate." She said, "I love you."

"Love you too," I told her.

It took me fifteen minutes to get to the address that Caldwell had sent. It was a townhouse settled in the center of a cul de sac. Caldwell's pickup was parked out front, along with a gray Infinity SUV. I parked on the street and said a quick prayer before getting out. I looked at the black slacks and multi-colored blouse that I had worn to work, wishing I had on a pair of heels instead of the sensible flats on my feet.

"You must be Miss Brooks." To my surprise, it wasn't a white woman who opened the door, but a nice-looking, older black woman. Her eyes were warm and inviting, and her voice was soothing. She reminded me of Geraldine, my aunt that raised me. She had passed away the summer before my freshman year of college.

"Zenobia," I said softly.

"That's such a pretty name. I'm Georgette Miller. Come on in," she said. "Jose and Josh are upstairs."

"Thank you." I stepped inside and looked around. The house definitely needed some work. The tile floor was cracked; you could see where the carpet had been pulled up, and all the walls needed painting. As we continued farther inside, I glanced into the kitchen and saw that there weren't any appliances, and the countertops had been ripped out.

"We appreciate you coming to meet us. Caldwell said you were coming straight from work."

"Yes, ma'am. I work at Loehman's Fabrics. It's not that far from here."

"I know exactly where that is. It's such a nice store. It's so organized and not cluttered like so many other fabric places. Plus, you all have unique material in there." She smiled warmly.

"I enjoy it."

Loud footsteps came down the stairs, and Caldwell walked in and greeted me. "Zen, you made it."

"I did." I laughed.

"Well, Mama G, Josh, this is the young lady I was telling you about. Zen, this is Mama G." He pointed at Georgette, then said, "And this is Josh."

Caldwell moved slightly, and the guy behind him stepped forward. He stood about half a foot taller than Caldwell, who was six feet, and he didn't seem very friendly. He actually looked irritated, and I was almost afraid to extend my hand to him.

"Nice to meet you," I said.

"You too." He gave my fingers a light squeeze, and I felt a little better, even though he was barely smiling as he did so.

"Why don't we give you a tour?" Georgette suggested.

I followed them through the entire house, most of which was just as damaged as what I'd already seen. The previous occupants had really destroyed the place. There were three bedrooms, including a large master suite upstairs. The backyard had what looked like it used to be a nice patio, and the fence needed to be replaced. In spite of the damage, all in all, the house had a lot of potential, and I already had ideas forming in my head.

"Your place is really nice," I said.

He shook his head. "I ain't saying all that. It used to be at one point."

"No, really, it is," I said. "It just needs a little TLC."

Caldwell agreed. "That's what I told him, Zen. This place has so much potential."

"Well, that's the plan, to give it a little TLC and restore it to its full potential. Caldwell says you can help us get it done." Georgette seemed a lot more excited about the remodel than her son did.

"Definitely," I told her. "I don't know who was living here before that trashed it like this, but I've seen Caldwell's work, and I know he can have this place ready for new tenants before you know it. It's going to make a great rental property. I would love to help bring it back to life."

There was a shift in the room, and I could tell that I had said something wrong. Just then, Josh's phone rang, and he said, "I have to take this." He stepped away from us quickly.

"Did I say something wrong?" I asked, confused.

"Not really," Georgette said. "It's just that Josh gave this place to my younger son a couple of years ago when he moved. He was the one living here, until he died a few months ago."

Chapter Thirteen

"Well, how did it go?" Bailey asked as soon as I walked into the house. I could hear Sean T's voice yelling from the TV in the den, which let me know she had opted to stay home and work out instead of going to the gym.

I walked in and plopped down on the sofa. Bailey, dressed in leggings, a sports bra, and sneakers, was sweating as she mimicked the moves demonstrated on the screen in hopes of achieving her hip-hop abs.

"Not good. Not good at all," I told her.

"Why? What happened?" she asked, still moving to the beat of the music.

"I don't think the owner was feeling me. I don't think he was feeling anything, to tell the truth," I said.

"Are you sure you're not being dramatic?"

"No, I'm not. I think I gave him the wrong impression. I commented that whoever was staying there pretty much ruined the place, and it turns out it was his brother, who's now dead."

Bailey stopped and turned around. "Oh, that's not good."

"Nope, not at all. It was a very awkward moment, to say the least. But even more so because I offered to help bring the place back to life," I added.

"Damn, Zen, you're right; that definitely did not go well at all. But I'm glad you went and got the experience of meeting with potential clients. Next time, you will be ready. This is God giving you a hint to get your portfolio and stitch-witch . . ."

"Swatches?"

"Swatches, stitches—whatever it is you said you didn't have, now is the time for you to get it ready."

"I gotta admit, when I was walking through that house, my mind was full of ideas, Bails. Oh my God, the kitchen is completely empty. I mean gutted. There's not even a sink in there." I closed my eyes and leaned my head back. "Do you know the kind of magical transformation I could do in there?"

"What happened to the sink?" Bailey asked.

I sat up and looked at her, shaking my head. "Does that even matter?"

"I'm just wondering, that's all." She laughed. "But do you see how you're talking right now? The excitement in your voice? This is why I say you're meant to do this."

"But I didn't get the job. They didn't hire me." I exhaled. "Bailey, I appreciate you being my personal cheerleader and all, but I gotta find another job that—"

My phone began vibrating in my purse. I fumbled but didn't make it in time and missed the call. As soon as I took it out, it began vibrating again, and I answered immediately.

"Hello."

"Hello, Zenobia, it's Georgette Miller. Is this a bad time?" Her voice over the phone was just as warm as it had been in person, and it made me smile.

"Hi, Mrs. Miller. No, it's not a bad time at all." I motioned for Bailey to turn down the volume on the television where Sean T was still yelling at her to squat lower. She grabbed the remote and hit the mute button so she could eavesdrop.

"Please, call me Georgette. Well, I was wondering if Josh and I could meet with you tomorrow and go over a few things, if your schedule permits."

"Sure, that's not a problem. I don't have to work until tomorrow afternoon, so anytime tomorrow morning would be best." I gave Bailey an excited look.

"How about ten o'clock?

"Ten o'clock is perfect," I told her.

We agreed to meet at the Starbucks not far from the fabric store. I thanked her, and as soon as I ended the call, Bailey began dancing around the room.

"I told you. I told you." She was grinning like a fool.

I laughed. "Calm down. She just wants to talk to me about some stuff. She didn't say I was hired."

"She's gonna hire you. Trust me. If she wasn't, she wouldn't have called so soon."

"Well, I guess you were right; I need to start getting my shit together," I told her.

"You're damn right. Let's go get these switches you were talking about."

We went upstairs to what was now my mini salon, which still held plenty of Bailey's shoes. I located the portfolio I had created in college, and we were able to update it by using pictures from my cell phone of work I'd done here and there, in addition to the redecorating I'd done in Bailey's house. It wasn't exactly the professional design portfolio I'd hoped to have when meeting with a potential client, but it was better than nothing, and it did show my work.

I arrived at the Starbucks fifteen minutes early. Even though I had already met Georgette and Josh, I was still nervous. I was surprised when I walked in and saw her already sitting at a table in the corner, working on a laptop. She smiled when she looked up and saw me.

"Good morning, Zenobia. You're early."

"Good morning. You're earlier than I am," I told her.

"That scarf is gorgeous. I love it," she said as I sat across from her.

"Thank you."

"Where on earth did you get it?"

"Actually, I made it," I said, looking down at my scarf as I placed my bag on the chair beside me.

"It's beautiful. You want some coffee or a latte or anything?"

"No, I'm fine. Is Josh here?" I looked around but didn't see him.

"No, he's not coming," she said.

"Oh." I blinked. "Did you want to reschedule for a time when he can meet?"

"No, there's no better time than right now, and the work on that house needs to get done. He's been putting it off long enough."

I decided there was no use in avoiding the obvious blunder I'd made the day before. "I'm sorry about the comment I made. I wasn't trying to be insensitive, I didn't know about your other son," I told her.

"I know you didn't mean anything by it, and no offense was taken. Yesterday was the first time we've gone in the house since Ephriam—that was my son's name—passed away. I think Josh was a bit overwhelmed," she explained.

"Wow, I can understand that. I'm very sorry for your loss," I said.

She nodded, and I understood that she didn't want to dwell on her son's death, so I changed the conversation.

"Well, I did bring my portfolio so you can see a little bit of the work that I've done." I passed her the leather-bound art portfolio with my initials embossed in gold lettering on the front. Ironically, it had been a graduation gift from Var.

Georgette took the book and began flipping through the pages. I sat nervously, wishing I had accepted her

offer and gotten a drink. It would have given me something to focus on instead of fighting the urge to stare at
her to watch her reaction of each picture.

"Caldwell was not lying. You are really talented," she
said. "Did you find this sofa in a local store, or was it
ordered?"

I looked at the picture she was pointing at. It was a
job I'd done for Bailey's boss recently. "Actually, the sofa
belonged to the woman's mother-in-law. We reuphol-
stered it, and I made the pillows."

"Are you kidding?" She looked surprised. "I thought
this was a designer piece."

"Well, I guess you can say I designed it." I laughed.
"But, no. They were gonna throw it out, but I convinced
them to fix it up instead, and it turned out really nice. We
found the rug at a carpet remnant place downtown, and it
matched up nicely."

"I've seen enough. You're definitely hired."

"But isn't it Josh's place? Shouldn't he see this before
you make a final decision?" I asked. "He didn't seem too
receptive to me, and I don't want to—"

"Zenobia, my son has had a very rough year. He's
not receptive to anyone these days. Please don't take it
personally. Trust me, you'll learn that his bark is much
worse than his bite. He means no harm. But I adore
you, and I'm already a fan of your work. We've already
contracted Caldwell, and he's excited to work with you on
this. I have no doubt that it's going to turn out amazing."
Georgette slid my portfolio back across the table, then
reached into her purse and handed me a folded check.
"Here's your retainer. The house will be ready for Josh
before he's ready for it."

I opened the check and saw the amount: five thousand
dollars! My eyes widened, and my mouth gaped open
before I could stop it.

"Is it enough?" she asked. "Caldwell said two-fifty an hour, so I figured it would be enough for you to get started."

"Uh, yeah, it's fine. Thank you. Can I ask you a question?"

"Sure, go ahead."

I was still a little confused and needed to clarify. "If he's resistant to moving back into the house, why not just have Caldwell do the repairs and sell it or rent it out? Don't get me wrong, I would love the opportunity to redesign it, and I definitely need the work, but wouldn't it be easier? Especially since, like you said, Josh isn't ready for it. After all, it is his house," I finished, then immediately worried that I'd overstepped my bounds. It really wasn't my business how they chose to deal with their loss and move on—or not, in Josh's case.

Fortunately, Georgette didn't seem to take offense to my questions. She smiled and said, "You're right; the house does belong to him, and I'm sure renting or selling is a possibility down the line, but for now, Josh needs this. Call it mother's intuition. I need my son to see that not everything you lose is a loss. There is always beauty in ashes; you just have to find it. As painful as being in that house was for not just him, but me as well, I know that it holds just as many good memories as it does bad. So, I'm going to need for you to kinda work with me and make this happen. That house is important to me, and in spite of how it seems right now, it's important to him. This restoration has to happen."

I didn't know if it was what she said or the way she said it, or even a combination of both, but it resonated in my spirit. Her words drew me in, and I knew that whether she paid me or not, I wanted to do this.

Chapter Fourteen

I promised to check in with Georgette at the end of the week to let her know my progress. She gave me Josh's cell number so I could touch base with him as well and get his input on the remodel and design.

"Are you sure about this?" I asked again.

"I'm positive. I'm excited to see what you do with the house." She gave me quick hug in the parking lot before getting into her shiny Cadillac.

When I got into my car, I took the check out of my purse and stared at it. I couldn't believe I had landed my first real interior design job. This was something I had been waiting for and praying about for so long. It was unbelievable. What made it even more amazing was the fact that it was a total remodel. The house was damn near being gutted and rebuilt from top to bottom. I felt like an artist with a blank canvas.

I had a little more than an hour before I had to be at work, so I decided to ride by the house. I folded the check and put it back into my purse, then dialed Bailey's number as I pulled out of the parking lot.

"Tell me the good news." She answered without even saying hello first.

"Girl!" I said.

"What happened?"

"Bailey."

"Can you please just tell me, Zen? My goodness, you're stressing me out, and I have a meeting in, like, ten minutes," she whispered loudly.

"She gave me the job! Told me she loved my work. Get this, Bails: she gave me a retainer check for five grand and agreed to my rate of two-fifty an hour until the job is finished," I squealed.

"Shut the hell up. Are you serious? I told you. This is just the beginning, Zen. I'm so proud of you."

"Well, I haven't exactly done anything yet, but I am going to make sure this house is absolutely perfect," I told her.

"I know you are. I wouldn't expect anything less of you. Everything you create is perfect, girl. Was her son in a better mood?"

I was so caught up in the excitement of Georgette hiring me that I had almost forgotten she'd done so against her son's will.

"He didn't even show up. It was just her, and she told me that he wasn't too thrilled about this entire thing. I asked her how she expected me to design a house without the owner even wanting me to, and she said, 'make it happen.'" I sighed.

"Hell, she paid you up front, so damn right you're gonna make it happen. But, listen, congrats. I love you, and I'm so proud of you. I've gotta go into this meeting. Tonight, we'll go out and celebrate. My treat."

"Oh, hell no. Tonight, the celebration is on me." I hung up the phone.

When I got to the house, Caldwell's truck was parked out front. I should've known he would already be working. One thing I had learned about him was that his work ethic was out of this world. I understood exactly why he had several contracts with property managers. Not only did he do quality work, but he was dedicated and completed it fast. Bailey had hired him to install shelves in her closet, and you would've thought he was building a shrine of some sort. He was meticulous and made sure it was exactly what Bailey wanted. He also only charged her for the materials he used. Working with him on the house was something I looked forward to.

"Caldwell!" I yelled when I walked inside after realizing the front door was unlocked.

"Who is that?" His voice traveled from the second floor.

"It's me!" I carefully climbed the stairs, choosing not to hold onto the banister, which didn't seem too sturdy. Caldwell was in one of the bedrooms, repairing a cracked wall. His white T-shirt was covered in dust, as were his jeans and work boots. A pair of goggles hung around his neck.

"Hola, mami." He smiled at me. "I take it your being here is a good sign?"

"It's a great sign, Caldwell. I got the job, thanks to you." I walked over and went to give him a hug, but he stopped me.

"No, Zen. I'm dirty," he said.

"I'm not thinking about that dust," I said and hugged him quickly. "Besides, I wear an apron at work. No one will see it."

"I knew she liked you," he said.

"She did. Her son, on the other hand . . ."

"He's just Josh, that's all. He'll come around," Caldwell told me.

"He didn't even show up today. That worries me. After all, this is kinda his house. What's his deal, anyway? And why didn't you give me a heads up about his brother? I was so embarrassed."

"I really didn't think Ephraim—that's his brother—was going to come up." Caldwell shrugged.

"Uh, Caldwell, this was where he lived before he died, wasn't it? How did you think he wasn't gonna come up?" I shook my head.

"Well, that's true. But Mama G knew you didn't mean anything by it."

"I really like her." I nodded.

"Everyone does. And believe it or not, Josh used to be a really cool dude."

"I find that hard to believe." I laughed.

"No, seriously, he was. Our families have always been close, and at one point we were like cousins. Even after he played ball in the league—"

"League? What league?" I frowned.

"He played a couple of years in the NBA. He wasn't a starter or anything like that, but he was a league player. This house was the first thing he bought. He thought it was going to be for his parents, but they wanted to stay in the house where they were living. So, he moved in and lived here for a while. Then, a few years later, after he got married and moved away, he gave the house to Ephraim, who was barely out of high school."

"Wait, Josh is married? Where's his wife? Shouldn't she care what we do to the house?" I was confused.

"She's no longer in the picture." Caldwell shrugged.

"Oh."

"Anyway, he got married and was gone for a while. He rarely came home, and when he did, he didn't stay for long. When his dad died, he came the day before the funeral and left right after the service. He didn't even stay for the repast, and they had some really good cake, too," Caldwell commented.

"Did you really just think about the cake they had at someone's funeral?" I gave him a strange look.

"I did. Come to think of it, they had really good cake at Ephraim's funeral, too. I think the same lady made it."

"Caldwell, please stop talking about cake and go on with the story. I gotta get to work," I said.

"Well, after their dad died, Ephraim kinda started running the streets, and Mama G tried to get Josh to come home and talk to him, but Josh was always too busy. Then, Ephraim died. Josh came back for the funeral, like he did for his daddy's. Didn't stay that long. The house sat here empty. Then, a couple months ago, Josh moved back."

"What made him move home?"

Caldwell shrugged. "No one knows. He just came home."

"So, what does he do now? Where does he work?"

Again, Caldwell shrugged. "I don't know."

I checked my watch and saw that if I didn't hurry, I was going to be late for work. Caldwell walked me to my car. As we stepped out of the house, he paused, looked back, and said, "The thing about this entire situation is that when he first bought this place, it was kinda like the family's man cave. Josh, his dad, Ephraim, me and my brothers, and all the guys from the neighborhood would come over and hang out and talk. Mr. G was a monster on the grill, and he would give us all sorts of advice. Those were the good old days. I guess that's why I was kinda honored when Mama G approached me about doing the work, and that's also why I told her you would be perfect. I didn't want just anyone touching this place."

"I'm off tomorrow, so I guess we can go over some ideas then," I told him.

"I'll be here," he said, then added, "Hey, you better get your new decal before you get a ticket."

"What are you talking about?"

He pointed to the license plate on the front of my car. "Your tag expired last month. A nice-looking black woman driving this nice, fancy car. You know they will pull you over in a heartbeat around here."

I walked over and saw that he was right: the tag had expired a month ago, and I hadn't noticed. My good mood suddenly faded. Although I drove it every day, the fact was that the fancy car, as Caldwell called it, wasn't mine. And I was not looking forward to calling the person it belonged to.

Chapter Fifteen

Although technically I had the day off from Loehman's, I still had a full day planned and left the house early to get a head start. After stopping at the bank to deposit my check from Georgette, I headed to the DMV to see if there was some way I could get the tag renewed without having to involve Var. I had the registration and insurance information, so I figured it would be no problem. I waited in line for almost an hour and a half before my number was called, and when I finally got to the counter, I made certain that I was extremely polite to the customer service worker named Valerie, according to her nameplate, who looked like she would have rather been anywhere else in the world except at work.

"Can I help you?" she asked in a robotic tone without even looking up at me.

"Good morning. I need to renew my license plate, please," I said with a smile that she couldn't see.

"Tag number," she droned.

I slid the registration card across the counter, and she picked it up, still without even glancing up at me. I decided to offer some small talk while I patiently waited.

"How are you doing this morning? Y'all are pretty busy, but these lines are moving."

"Yeah," she mumbled.

"Well, the good thing is the busier you all are, the faster your day will go by and you can get on up outta here, girl."

For the first time since I'd been standing in front of her, she finally looked up and gave me a slight nod. "That's true. Well, it looks like I can't renew this for you."

"Is something wrong?" I began to wonder if Var had done something stupid like reported the tags stolen or something to prevent me from getting the tags without his knowing.

"It's already been renewed and the decals issued," she said.

I should've known that Var had already renewed the tags. He always stayed on top of things like that. Whereas I would wait to pay a bill on the due date, sometimes after, Var would pay it before it was due. He probably had the decals months ago but didn't say anything to me about them.

"Is there anything else I can help you with?" she asked. I could see that she was being sincere.

"No, that was all I needed." I took the registration from her, feeling slightly defeated. "You enjoy the remainder of your day."

"You too," Valerie said. "By the way, your scarf is dope. I really like it."

"Thanks." I smiled as I looked down at my scarf, similar to the one Georgette had complimented me on the day before.

As I walked out of the building, I took out my phone and sent Var a quick text, asking about the decals. I hoped he would send a simple reply, but I knew that was wishful thinking. Just as I suspected, my phone began to ring, and his name appeared on the screen.

"Hello," I answered, trying to be just as polite as I had been to Valerie moments earlier.

"Hey Zen. How are you?"

"I'm well. Thanks for asking."

"I do have the new decals for the car. I tried calling you a couple of weeks ago, but your phone kept going to voicemail," he said.

"Really? You must've been calling when my phone was dead," I told him, knowing that the real reason his call hadn't gone through was because I had placed his number on DO NOT DISTURB when I moved out and forgot to take it off until recently. "Why didn't you leave a message?"

"You're funny, Zen. I know you had me on DND. I sent you plenty of texts that were delivered but not read. I ain't crazy," he replied.

"I know you're not crazy, Var." I sighed as I opened the car door and climbed in.

"When you wanna meet up and get the stickers?"

"I'm actually off today, so whenever," I told him.

"All right, why don't we meet at Doc's at like six?"

"Doc's? Uh, I was thinking more like in the Walmart parking lot."

"Damn, Zen, you can at least let me buy you a drink for old time's sake. Don't be like that." Var sounded like he was pleading. I reminded myself that despite everything that had happened, the car that I drove every day belonged to him. I at least owed him a conversation.

I sighed. "I'll call you at six, Var. We'll decide then."

"Sounds like a plan. Talk to you then."

As soon as the call ended, I dialed Josh's number. When he didn't answer, I sent him a text, asking him to give me a call so we could talk. Next on my agenda was Home Depot, where I was headed when he called me back.

"This is Zen," I answered when I saw his number flashing on my phone.

"Hey, this is Josh Miller. You sent me a text."

"Hello, Josh. I actually met with your mom yesterday, and she gave me the go-ahead on redesigning your place. I was trying to schedule a time when we could sit down and discuss some ideas or any plans you may—"

"Yeah, my mom mentioned that she went ahead and hired you. I don't really have any, so you can just do whatever. Just please make sure everything's up to code," he said.

I was taken aback by his statement. It wasn't exactly my dream job to be designing for a client who couldn't care less what I did with his place. It took a few moments for me to respond. "Well, I'm sure you know Caldwell is going to make sure that everything is up to code, and so will I, but we would both appreciate your input. I'm heading over to Home Depot to look at flooring, and I wasn't sure if you wanted hardwood floors throughout the house, or did you want carpet in some of the rooms?"

Josh exhaled loudly, then said, "Seriously, it doesn't really matter. I don't really care either way. I don't plan on living there. Do whatever you wanna do."

Although I had already accepted the job and been paid, I quickly decided that convincing a stubborn grown-ass man to say what would happen during the reconstruction of his home was way above my current pay grade.

"Okay, well, I guess that's all I need to hear. Sorry to have bothered you," I told him.

"It's cool. I'm sure whatever you do in that house will be fine. Caldwell says you're the best, and I believe him," he said and ended the call.

"Good-bye to you too, asshole," I said aloud. I was tempted not to even go get the samples, but I went ahead anyway. I would remain professional, even if my client was an uncooperative jerk.

My plan was to be in Home Depot for an hour, but when I got inside, as usual, I became caught up in looking at lighting fixtures, toilets, appliances, and everything else instead of what I went in there for. I finally returned to my car two and a half hours later with the samples I needed and dialed Georgette's number.

"Zen, how are you?" Her mellow voice welcomed my call.

"I'm fine, Georgette. I picked up some flooring samples and wanted to bring them by for you to look at, if that's okay. Caldwell says we need to order them as soon as possible."

"Wonderful. Let me text you the address."

"That would be great. See you soon," I said.

"Sending it right over, Zen. Thanks again."

The text came in, and not only did it contain an address, but also a security code and parking instructions. Well, that sure wasn't something you see every day. I couldn't wait to see what kind of house needed such detailed instructions.

I plugged the street address into my GPS. When I arrived, I understood why the instructions were necessary, but I was a little confused. Caldwell had told me the reason Josh's parents didn't want to move was because they wanted to stay in their house, but the address Georgette brought me to was a luxury apartment building.

I parked where she had instructed and grabbed the samples from the back seat, along with my portfolio. I walked to the building, entered the code to the doors which held the elevators, then continued to the designated apartment. When I stepped into the hallway, I admired the thick carpet, immaculate sconces, and artistically painted walls. Based on those features alone, I could assume that the monthly rent was astronomical.

I rang the doorbell and patiently waited. A few seconds later, the door opened, and for a split second, I wondered if I had been given the wrong address.

"Um, hi," I said to Josh, who stood in the doorway.

"What are you doing here?"

"I'm supposed to be meeting your mom. She sent me this address," I replied.

He was dressed in a pair of basketball shorts, a T-shirt, and Nike slides. He obviously had not been expecting me, and based on the way he was looking at me, he was not happy to see me at his front door. I wanted to tell him that had I known he would be there, I would've suggested we meet somewhere else.

Instead, I smiled and said, "Is she here?"

"No, she isn't. And she didn't mention anything to me about coming over and meeting anyone. Come inside, though," he said, opening the door wider. He still couldn't hide the annoyance on his face, but at least he wasn't so rude as to shut the door in my face.

"I can call her or just wait in the car until she gets here," I offered. "It's no big deal."

"No, come on in." He stepped aside and gestured for me to enter.

I hesitated, not really wanting to interact with this cranky man, but then I reminded myself I was hired to a job, and as a professional, I was going to do it well. I walked inside, Josh closed the door, and I followed him into the large living area. It was practically devoid of furniture, containing only a green leather couch, a small coffee table, and one of the biggest televisions I had ever seen, which was mounted on the wall.

"Have a seat," he said, picking up the remote and turning off the blaring TV.

"Thanks." I sat on the sofa and put my belongings close beside me.

"I'll call my mother and see what's going on. In the meantime, you want anything to drink?" he offered.

"No, I'm fine," I told him.

He shrugged and walked out. Not long after, I heard him speaking on his phone.

"Well, you could've called and let me know. What if I wasn't home, or I was busy? . . . I know you asked me earlier if I was gonna be home, but you didn't mention you or anyone else coming through. What if I woulda had company? . . . You ain't funny, Ma. Listen, this girl is here waiting on you, so you might wanna—What? Ma, no. . . . Because I already told you, I don't care. . . . Why? . . . So, you can't just reschedule or come after your meeting? . . . Yes, ma'am. . . . Yes, ma'am. . . . Fine, Ma."

I gathered my things, stood up, and was ready to leave when he came back in the room. "Listen, I'm sorry there was a miscommunication. Like I explained, I called her and told her that I had the samples, and she said bring them over and text me the address and security code. I'll just give her a call and reschedule."

"No, no, you're here, and I told her I would look at what you brought. Just give me a second to get myself together."

"Really, you don't have to."

"I'll be right back," he said.

I remained standing as I tried to decide if I was going to stay and deal with this asshole or leave and enjoy the rest of my day off. I closed my eyes and tried to think of the most professional way to handle this situation. Finally, I decided it wouldn't take that long for him to flip through the samples, especially since he didn't care anyway, so I sat down. When he returned, I had the various hardwood and carpet squares laid out and waiting for him.

"Here you go," he said.

I looked up and was surprised to see him holding a bottle of Pellegrino water toward me.

"Would you like a glass?"

"Thank you. Uh, no, the bottle is fine." I took the water from him, then asked a question that I already knew the answer to. "Would you happen to have a coaster? I don't want to mess up your table."

"No, I don't. You can just set it on the floor." He opened his own bottle of water.

"What? No, that's even worse than putting it on the table. You don't want these beautiful floors to have water stains," I told him. "Do you have a napkin I can set it on?"

"Is it really that serious?" He gave me a strange look.

"Yes, it is." I didn't care if he thought I was crazy. As a designer, how would I look mistreating these expensive floors?

He left and returned a minute later with a handful of napkins.

"Will these work?"

I took the napkins from him, noticing the fast food logo on them, and fought the urge to laugh. "Yes, they're fine."

"I'm sorry if I seemed kinda irritated. I was asleep when you rang the bell, and I didn't know you were coming."

I was surprised by his apology, but happy to hear it. If we had to work together, it would be better if he could chill a little with his attitude. "It's cool, and I promise I won't keep you long. I have the samples right here," I said, pointing to the table.

He reached over and picked through them. "I'm not trying to be mean, but really, I don't know what I'm supposed to be picking or how to pick."

I glanced over at him and saw that he was being sincere. "Well, the first thing we really need to start with, honestly, is a budget. What's your overall budget for the remodel?"

He sat back and stared into space, looking like he was deep in thought. "Honestly, I don't know. The house has been sitting dormant for almost a year. It's been vandalized, and it's in bad shape."

"It's not that bad."

"That house was brand new when I moved in six years ago. Now, it's trash. My bro—" He couldn't even finish the word. He cleared his throat, stood up, and said, "The budget is however much it takes. I know Caldwell ain't gonna hit me over the head. He loved that house as much as we did."

I nodded. "Still does."

"Yeah, he and my mom are on a mission. But, whatever." He picked through the floor samples again. Surprising myself, I felt a twinge of sympathy for him. He was a difficult client, for sure, but he was obviously hurting over the death of his brother.

"We can keep it simple. It boils down to either carpet or not. From what I can see, I'm thinking you don't like carpet." I looked down at the floor.

"Why would you say that? Carpet wasn't an option in here. It's hardwood throughout."

"You don't have any rugs, so that was kind of an indication."

"A rug. I hadn't really thought about that."

I took the time to explain the difference between hardwood, laminate, bamboo, linoleum, tile, vinyl, concrete, and carpet flooring choices. By the time I finished, he was actually able to make an informed decision and chose options for the entire house. He wasn't really excited during the process, but at least he'd shown a little bit of interest, which was more than I'd expected from his previous behavior.

"I'll get with Caldwell and let him know what you picked so we can get them installed," I told him. As I began packing up, I saw that it was almost six o'clock, and I remembered I had to meet Var. This was shaping up to be a day of difficult men for me. "Again, I'm sorry about the mix-up, but I'm glad we were able to get it handled."

"It wasn't a problem." He walked me to the front door and asked, "When you talk to my mom, can you please let her know that I picked the damn floor so she can leave me alone?"

I laughed. "Yes, and I'll tell her that you were nice to the girl who was sitting here waiting on her as well," I said as I headed to the elevator. I could hear him laughing as he closed the door behind him.

Chapter Sixteen

"Damn, Zen, you're skinny as hell. Are you sick? Did you have the surgery?" Var's eyes went from my face to my feet after he hugged me. He looked sexy as hell in his slacks and sports jacket. He wasn't wearing a tie, and the top of his shirt was unbuttoned.

Against my better judgment, I had agreed to meet him at Doc's, a local bar that we frequented when we were together, and one that I had purposely avoided since our breakup because it held so many memories for me.

"You're trying to be funny." I shook my head at him. "No, I'm not sick, and I haven't had no surgery. And you know I ain't skinny neither. But I have lost some weight." I sat on the bar stool beside him.

"Naw, I'm just joking, but you look great. You're still the most beautiful girl in the world to me." He grinned.

I ignored his comment. "How much do I owe you for the decals?"

"Don't be like that, Zen. You know you don't owe me anything for them. What you want to drink?"

"Water is cool," I told him.

It was his turn to ignore my comment, and he asked the bartender to bring me a glass of Chardonnay. The bartender brought my wine, and I sipped it while we made small talk. It felt sort of odd sitting there with Var, chatting like strangers, when just a few months ago we were picking out baby names and preparing to buy a house.

"How's work?" he asked.

"Work is great." I didn't bother to elaborate.

"I can't believe you quit to go back to working at that fabric hut," he said.

"How did you find out I quit?" I asked him, choosing not to respond to the latter part of his statement.

"I tried emailing you at work when you weren't answering my calls or texts. It kicked back a response saying you were no longer with the company, and I know your ass ain't get fired, so I figured you quit. You wasn't really feeling that place anyway, although you were making some kick-ass money," he said.

"Everything ain't about money, Var. Why is it so hard for you to understand that?" I sighed.

"I know that. I said that to point out the fact that you have the education and skills to be making damn near six figures because you've done it before, and right now, you're not working up to your full potential. One thing we've always said was that no matter what, we would always be friends, Zen. What kind of friend would I be if I didn't encourage you to be the absolute best Zen that you can be?" he asked. "You would always talk about how you love and appreciate Bailey because she makes you feel like you can do anything you want: draw, sew, design, lose weight, whatever. But whenever I try, you get all defensive. Why?"

I looked at him, wondering if I should bother to explain the difference to him. After all, we weren't a couple anymore, so why did it matter what I thought of him? Then I decided to tell him about himself. It had always hurt me how little he supported my creative dreams, so I might as well let him know it. "Because, Var, Bailey wants me to follow my heart and go after my dreams. You want me to follow a job and chase after a paycheck. There's a difference."

He answered me with the same argument he'd always used. "I'm all for chasing dreams, Zenobia, but the bills gotta get paid too. That's all I'm saying. Dreams ain't been paying the car insurance every month."

Clearly, nothing had changed, and I was wasting my time sitting here with him. I picked up my glass and drank the rest of my wine, then stood up. "Thanks for the drink. Can I get the decals, please? I need to get home and go to bed so I can go to my dead-end job tomorrow. Oh, and I'll start looking into getting insurance on the car as soon as possible so you don't have to pay it anymore. As a matter of fact, why don't you just tell me how much you want for the car? Draw up a bill of sale, and I'll buy it from you."

He shook his head vigorously. "I'm not selling you the damn car, Zenobia. You want it, you can have it."

"I'll pay you for it. Just let me know how much." I wanted to buy the car so I could cut ties with him for good. I didn't want him to have anything to hold over my head anymore. "For now, I need the decals so I won't get a ticket."

"Zen, can you please—"

"The decals," I repeated.

"They're in my glove compartment," he said.

I beckoned for the bartender, and when he came over, I gave him my debit card. "Can you close out our tab?"

"Sure thing, but it's already on his card." He pointed to Var.

Var rolled his eyes. "Zenobia, you are really tripping."

I ignored Var and said to the bartender, "Please put it on this one. Can you do that?"

"Zen, please stop." Var touched my arm, which was extended toward the bartender.

"This card," I said, this time a little louder so he knew that I meant it.

"No problem." The bartender finally took the card from me and hurried away.

"You really gonna do this?" Var asked.

"Do what? I don't mind paying my bill and yours too. And despite what you may think, I am able to do so. You've always been so damn afraid that you were gonna have to take care of me, and I never asked you to do so. I've always been able to take care of myself."

"I never said you couldn't."

The bartender brought my card and receipt. I quickly scribbled my signature without even looking at the amount and then turned back to Var. "Can we go to your car and get the decals?"

Var got up, and we quickly walked out to his car. He got in, reached into the glove box, and took out an envelope. "Here is the new registration card and the decals. Where's the car? I can put them on for you."

I took the envelope from him. "Thanks. I can do it myself. Maybe you should just let me buy the car from you, Var."

"Zen, I love you so much. I know you said you needed space to think things through, and I've respected that. Can't we please just start over? I don't care where you work. Shit, you don't even have to get a job if you don't want. I just want you back with me." I swear to God his eyes looked a little wet, like he might get emotional or something.

I stared at him, seeing the familiar look of love in his eye. I missed him. That much I knew, but I wasn't sure if I was ready to give him another chance. At the moment, the only thing I was concerned with was getting the decals and leaving.

"Var."

"At least let me take you out. Will you at least think about it?" he asked, his fingers still lingering on my hand.

"I don't know," I said.

"Are you seeing someone else?"

"What?" I was surprised he'd asked that, and I wondered what would make him think I was. Did he think I could move on as easily as he did when he screwed someone else and got her pregnant?

"I'm just saying. You looking good. You seem to be doing well. Shit, why wouldn't you be hanging out with anybody?"

"Now you're the one tripping," I told him. I wished I could believe his compliments, but he was trying so hard to get me back I figured he was just laying it on thick so I'd give him another chance. Still, I couldn't deny that it felt good to hear him saying those things about me.

"You ain't answer the question, Zen."

Something in the back of his car caught my eye. It was a car seat. Suddenly, the emotions came flooding back, and I remembered that my resentment toward him really wasn't about money, it was because he now had a baby, and it wasn't mine.

"Please, Zen."

"I see you've been spending time with your daughter," I said as I pulled away from him.

He realized what I'd seen and quickly spit out, "I love you, Zen."

I didn't say anything else as I walked away and got into what was still his car.

Chapter Seventeen

A week later, we were waiting for the flooring Josh had selected to come in. It was on back order, so it was taking a little longer than I had anticipated. I had chosen a couple of paint samples and was meeting the painter at the house to do an estimate. When we got there, we expected to find Caldwell waiting for us, but he wasn't there.

"Have you talked to him?" I asked the guy.

"I talked to him yesterday. He told me to meet him here at three."

I tried calling Caldwell again, but there was no answer. I sent him a text. We waited another fifteen minutes, but there was still no response.

"Maybe something happened to his phone," I suggested.

"That don't have nothing to do with him not being here," the painter said. "And I have another appointment this afternoon. You don't have a key?"

I wanted to say, "Do you think we'd be standing out here if I had a key?" but instead, I kept my professional face on and just said, "No, I don't."

"Well, I can't get back out here until the end of next week sometime, and if I get another—"

"Wait, give me a sec. Let me make another call right quick," I told him.

I dialed Georgette's number, but her phone went straight to voice mail. Desperate to find a way into the house so the painter wouldn't disappear, I took a chance and called Josh.

"Hello?"

"Hey, Josh. It's Zen," I said. "Have you talked to Caldwell today by chance?"

"No, I haven't. Sorry."

I could tell Mr. Man-of-a-Few-Words was about to hang up, so I quickly asked, "Are you busy right now?"

"Uh, yeah. Kinda."

"Listen, I'm over at the house with the painter. Caldwell told us to meet him here at three, and he isn't here, and we can't reach him on his phone. Is it possible for you to come and let us in so he can get the measurements done?"

"I . . . uh . . ." Josh began mumbling.

"I can come and get the key from you or meet you somewhere to make it easier if you'd like. If we don't get this done today, it may push us behind schedule, and I know how getting this finished as soon as possible is important to you. I called your mom first, and she didn't answer, which is the only reason I reached out to you. We just need to get in the house, that's all," I explained hurriedly, in case he didn't already understand that he was the last person I wanted to call for assistance.

He was so quiet that I thought he had hung up. I was about to do the same when I heard him say, "I'll be there in ten minutes."

I told the painter that Josh was on his way, and I tried reaching Caldwell again, but there was still no answer. My concern grew. I called several more times before Josh's silver Infinity SUV pulled into the driveway. I rushed over before Josh even opened his door to get out.

"Thanks," I said, reaching for the keys. "I can unlock the door and bring them right back, and you can be on your way."

He looked kind of surprised by my anxiousness, but he handed me a keyring. I took it, waved for the painter, and we went inside. I walked around and saw the work that Caldwell had begun doing. The place looked nicer already, and I couldn't wait until the real work began.

The painter took out a notepad and a tape measure. I stood watching him for a few minutes, until I remembered Josh sitting outside, and rushed back to give him his keys.

"Thanks again," I told him.

"Everything okay?" he asked.

"Yep, everything's fine." Rather than stand around and make small talk, I quickly said good-bye and headed to my car.

I took out a box with a can of paint samples and a few brushes and carried it inside. The walls had all been repaired and primed, but we had agreed not to start painting until the new floors had been laid. I popped the cans open and used the brushes to paint a line of each color, then stood back to see which one looked best. I closed my eyes and folded my arms, trying to envision the entire living room with each color on the wall.

"Are you praying?"

I jumped, startled by Josh, who I hadn't heard come inside. " Jesus, you scared the mess outta me."

"My mama said if you jump when someone enters a room, you must be doing something you ain't got no business doing." He smirked. He was dressed a little fancier than the last time we saw one another, wearing a pair of jeans and a nice green, collared shirt. He also had on a pair of the nicest leather shoes I had ever seen, which said a lot, since Var's shoe game had always been on point.

"Well, I'm doing exactly what I'm supposed to be doing. And no, I'm not praying. I'm envisioning."

He walked closer and stood beside me, looking at the wall I was pointing to. "Are you gonna make the walls striped?" he asked, not even joking.

"No, they're not gonna be striped, but these are the colors I think will look best down here. You chose light-colored floors, so I think we should go with warmer-toned walls," I said.

"Oh." He continued staring at the stripes.

"Look at the colors and then close your eyes."

"What?"

"Close your eyes," I said. He shook his head, but I insisted. "Close your eyes. My God, getting you to do something is like pulling teeth, I swear."

He finally closed his eyes. I waited a few moments, then softly said, "Now imagine that you're standing on the floors you picked."

"Okay," he said. His eyes started blinking a bit.

"Don't open your eyes. Keep them closed. Now, think about the three stripes, and then the walls painted one of those colors that make you feel at home." My voice remained calm and soft. "Which one do you feel the most?"

"The one in the middle; the kinda brown one," he said then opened his eyes.

"You sure? What about the burnt orange one?"

"Nah, that's gonna make the room look dim all the time. I like the lighter color better," he said.

"Excellent choice. Actually, that's the one I like too." I smiled. "See, you picked a wall color. And you had an opinion."

"I guess." He shrugged.

"Was there a reason you came inside? Did you need anything?" I asked him.

"Oh, yeah, there was." He held out a slip of paper, which he had been holding, "You dropped this when you went in your trunk. I didn't know if it was important or you needed it."

I took the paper, which turned out to be an old receipt from one of my OB/GYN appointments. Seeing it made me feel like the wind had been knocked out of me, and I swallowed the knot that had formed in my throat.

"Thanks." My voice cracked a little, and I crumpled the paper in my hand.

"Are you okay?" He looked concerned.

"Yes, I'm fine," I assured him. "It wasn't important, but thanks anyway."

The painter came down the stairs and said, "Okay, I'm all done. I tried calling Caldwell, but he ain't answer. If you talk to him, tell him I got the numbers for him."

"Great. I'm thinking something is just going on with his phone because he always either answers or at least responds to my texts," I said.

"A'ight, just let me know." He waved before walking out.

"I hope he's okay, for real," I said, putting the tops back on the paint samples and placing the brushes on a piece of plastic.

"You all done here?"

"Yeah."

When we walked out and made sure the house was locked up, I turned around and stared back at it for a moment.

"Are you envisioning again? This time with your eyes open?" Josh asked sarcastically.

"Actually, I am." I laughed.

"Now what? Picking out a roof color?"

"Nope, shutters and garage door," I told him.

"Huh?"

"Gotta pick a color for the new garage door and the shutters."

"Garage door?"

"Yeah, I know you see that dented door," I joked.

"Damn, I hadn't even really noticed that." He folded his arms. "It does need a new garage door. How the hell did that even happen?"

I walked over and took a closer look at the dent. "It looks like someone might've hit it with a car."

Josh shook his head and said, "I don't understand why my mother can't see that this house is just one headache after another. This is pointless."

"I don't think these are headaches. It's just home repairs. Do you see how amazing this place is? And you must know, because it's the first home you bought. You lived here yourself."

"That was a long time ago." Josh stared at the house for a second, and it was like a dark cloud passed over his face. He said, "I got somewhere to be in a little while. You good?"

"Yeah, I'm good. Thanks again."

We both walked back to our vehicles. I turned around and saw him staring at the house one more time before getting into his SUV and pulling off.

"So, no one has heard from him at all?" Bailey asked later that evening. We were both on treadmills at the gym. She was running, and I was walking.

"Nope, and I've been blowing his phone up like an ex who got a positive test for an STD," I told her.

"Well, damn. That's an analogy I ain't heard before." Bailey laughed. "Are you speaking from experience? Is there something you haven't told me? Is that why you hit Var up the other day?"

"Hell no, and you're trying to be funny. But trust me, I've called him a lot."

"At least your boy didn't act like a complete asshole and came and unlocked the house for you and the painter to get in. That's a good thing."

"Yeah, especially since Jose is insisting that this painter is like the best and acting like he's the only one he wants to work with. I don't understand because it's just paint. But, yeah, Josh actually acted like he had some sense and was even pleasant for a while."

"It's always the good-looking ones who act like total asses."

"How do you know he's good-looking?" I asked. I had never mentioned anything to her about how Josh looked.

"How do you think? I googled him after you told me he used to play in the NBA." Her pace slowed to a brisk walk, which excited me because it meant our time on the machine was almost over.

"Dang, Bailey, I ain't even do that." I shook my head. "Probably because he was such a jerk that I ain't care who he was."

"Well, I did it to make sure he really had money like that, since he said he didn't have a budget. I wanted to make sure he had the loot to pay you," she stated proudly.

"Good looking out, bestie. But it's actually his mother who's paying me, I believe, and her check didn't bounce, so I think I'm good."

"I wonder what his mom does," she said with a questioning look on her face. "What's his mom's name again? Georgia?"

"Georgette." I corrected her. "And don't go googling her, please."

We finished our workout and had just gotten into my car when Georgette called me. I answered on the car's Bluetooth.

"Hello, darling. How are you? I'm so sorry I missed your call earlier. I've been in a seminar all day, and we're just getting out," she gushed. "How are things going?"

"Everything's fine. I was actually calling because I needed to get into the house with the painter, but I was able to reach Josh, and he let us in."

"Oh, really? He did?" She sounded just as surprised as I had been when he agreed to unlock the door for us.

"Yes, ma'am. So, no worries. Thanks for calling me back, though."

"Ask her where she works," Bailey whispered.

"Huh, what's that, dear?" Georgette yelled. "I think your phone cut out."

I shook my head at Bailey to shush her. "I just said thank you, and I'll speak with you later."

"Okay. Speak with you soon," she said.

The call had just ended when my phone rang again, and I was surprised to see Josh's name appear. I didn't answer right away, because I was too busy wondering why he was calling me. It was Bailey who pressed the answer button and said hello, ignoring my threatening look.

"Hey, it's Josh," he said, giving no indication that he realized it wasn't me who answered.

"Hey, Josh. What's up?" I finally said.

"I was just calling to let you know that I found Caldwell."

"Really? You talked to him?" I said. "Something better have happened to his phone, because he hasn't returned any of my calls or texts."

"No, something happened to him."

"Oh my God, is he okay? What happened?" Bailey and I spoke at the same time.

"Huh, who is that?" Josh asked, confused.

"That's my best friend, Bailey. She knows Caldwell too," I explained. "You're on speakerphone in my car."

"Is Caldwell okay?" Bailey asked again.

"Yeah, but he's in the hospital."

"What? Why?" Again, we both spoke.

"Okay, I'm really gonna need for y'all to talk one at a time," Josh told us, then added, "I don't know the details. All I know is that he had emergency surgery, but he's okay."

"Wow. I knew something happened. How did you find out?" I asked.

"I knew you were worried, so I decided to make some calls. I figured I'd update you on what was going on."

"Well, thanks for letting me know. I appreciate it. I am definitely gonna keep him in prayer and hope he gets better." I sighed.

"If I hear anything else, I'll let you know," Josh told me.

"Thanks again, really," I said.

"No problem," he replied and ended the call.

"Well, at least we know where he is, and he's safe," Bailey said.

"Yeah, I guess, but what does that mean about the house we're working on? And my job." Maybe it sounded a little selfish, but it was a genuine concern for me.

"You should've asked Josh. That's really up to him, isn't it?"

I turned and looked at her. "If that's the case, then I'm fired and back to square one."

Chapter Eighteen

I couldn't believe that as quickly as things had started looking up in my life, they fell down, and I was right back where I started. When we got home, I took a shower, changed into a pair of sweats, told Bailey I would be back later, and then I headed to the one place I knew would always make me feel better: Baskin Robbins. I ordered double scoop of mint chocolate chip in a waffle cone with whipped cream and nuts, sat a table in the back, and wiped my falling tears between bites. Maybe Var was right, I thought. Maybe my dreams of becoming an interior designer were stupid and I needed to be realistic. I was thirty years old and living in my best friend's guest bedroom. I couldn't even consider myself a roommate because I damn sure didn't pay half the rent, and without the contract with Georgette, I didn't know when I'd be able to. I finished eating all my ice cream and stared at the waffle cone, feeling as empty as it looked.

"Where the heck did you go?" Bailey asked when I walked in the door an hour later. "I've been calling and texting you, girl."

"My bad. I left my phone in the room. It's on the charger," I told her.

"Are those doughnuts?" she asked, looking at the Krispy Kreme box I was holding.

I nodded guiltily.

"Really, Zen? Why?"

I was too embarrassed to tell her that I had stopped there on the way home after binging on ice cream. I also didn't mention that there were two doughnuts missing from the box because I had already eaten them.

"Because the *hot* sign was on," I answered as if it were no big deal.

"I can't believe you. You know we're in training," she said. "I'm throwing these out."

"Don't play, Bailey," I said in a threatening tone.

"I ain't playing. I don't need this temptation, and neither do you."

"Don't tell me what I need," I snapped at her.

"Zen, calm down and listen to—"

"Stop telling me what to do. I know your life is perfect, Bailey, but in case you haven't noticed, mine isn't. I have a part-time gig that barely pays my bills, the car I'm driving belongs to my asshole of an ex, and I'm freeloading off my best friend. I'm a mess, my life is a mess, and yeah, despite your attempts to make my body as perfect as yours, that's a hot, fat mess too. And right now, I really don't need a fucking lecture from you. So, can you just let me have my doughnuts and leave me the hell alone?"

Bailey took a step back and folded her arms. "Are you done?"

"Yep," I said with as much attitude as she had given me.

"You sure?"

"Yep."

"Good, now put that fucking box down and let's go."

"Go where?" I frowned. If she was about to suggest anything involving any kind of exercise, I was going to have to cuss her out again.

"Well, that's what I was trying to tell you before you threw your little temper tantrum over your doughnuts. Caldwell called. He's at the hospital and wants to see us. He tried to reach you, and when he couldn't, he called me."

"Didn't he have surgery?"

"He had an appendectomy, and he says he's fine. I told him we'd come up and see him for a few minutes, but we weren't staying long. So, come on," she said, glancing down at the Krispy Kreme box. "Unless you'd rather stay here and continue having your pity party. And you already know if that's the case, you'll be having it by yourself."

I put the box of doughnuts in the middle of the kitchen table and walked past her. "Let me get my phone."

"I'll wait for you in the car," I heard her yell right before the front door closed.

I went into my room and grabbed my phone from the nightstand, where it was charging. It took a few minutes to power up and then began buzzing with notifications of three missed calls: all from Caldwell, and a text to both Bailey and me:

Hola, mamis. Don't worry, your boy is alive and kicking. Come and see for yourself at Mercy General room 354. Bring snacks.

I shook my head and smiled, relieved that he was okay. On the way out the door, I grabbed the box of doughnuts, hoping he wouldn't notice the missing ones.

We arrived at the hospital just before visiting hours were over. The lady at the front desk acted like we were breaking curfew and she was our momma. She almost didn't give us a pass. When she finally relented, we hopped on the elevator and went to the third floor to Caldwell's room. The door was open, and he was sitting up in bed, talking and laughing with two other women: one older, and another about our age. I hesitated before knocking on the door. The three of them turned and looked at us.

"I knew my mamis wouldn't let me down. Get in here," he told us happily.

"Hello." I spoke to the two ladies, then said, "Caldwell, what in the world?"

"We were worried about you," Bailey told him.

"I'm fine, I'm fine. You brought me Krispy Kreme? You do love me." He reached for the box.

"No, Jose! You know you can't eat that. The doctors have said soft foods only for two days," the older woman scolded. Caldwell put his hand down and pretended to pout.

"What? He sent us a text asking us to bring him snacks," Bailey told her.

"That doesn't surprise me at all. How are you ladies? I'm Hazel, Jose's mother, and this is his sister, Melody. Jose has told us all about you. Thank you for coming," she told us.

"Nice to meet you," I told her. "And I'm sorry about the doughnuts. I didn't know he wasn't supposed to have them."

"I'll take them," Melody said. "I'm starving."

"So, you're just gonna eat doughnuts in front of me?" Caldwell protested. "That's so wrong."

"Sure am," Melody said, opening the box.

"Melody, that's not nice. Don't do that," Hazel scolded her. "Move over so the ladies can have somewhere to sit."

Melody moved down so that Bailey and I could squeeze onto the small love seat with her. Hazel was seated in a chair beside the hospital bed.

"So, you're feeling okay?" Bailey asked.

"Yeah, I had a rough night, but I'm much better now," Caldwell answered.

"I was so afraid. He called me at, like, two in the morning in so much pain that he was screaming. He couldn't even drive himself to the hospital," Hazel said, reaching over and rubbing Caldwell's hand. "My Jose was dying. That's all I could think about."

"He was not dying, Mommy. You treat him like such a baby." Melody groaned.

"What happened?" I asked.

"My appendix, and she's not exaggerating. I felt like I was dying," Caldwell said. "They took it out, though, so I'm good."

"How long will you be in the hospital?" I asked.

"Until tomorrow."

"Then you come home so I can take care of you," Hazel told him.

"I knew she was gonna say that." Melody told us, "I told you she treats him like a baby."

"He just had surgery. Who is going to take care of him while he's recovering? You?" Hazel asked.

"Oh, no, Ma. You know that wouldn't work," Caldwell said.

"See, this is why I tell you you need a good woman, Jose. And since you don't have one, you come home so you can get well."

"I'll be fine, Ma," Caldwell said, then he looked at me. "I talked to Josh a little while ago."

I swallowed hard, preparing myself to hear that the renovations had been stopped and I was out of a job.

"Yeah, he was the one who told us you were in the hospital," I said, hoping he didn't notice the fear I felt.

"I told him everything was still a go with the remodel and he would be in good hands while I'm out of commission."

"What?" I said, making sure I'd heard him correctly. "How? I'm not a contractor."

"You don't have to be a contractor, Zen. The floors have been ordered, the painter has been scheduled, and you're more than capable of overseeing that. The doctors have said I'll only be out of work for two weeks," Caldwell told me.

"Two weeks? Jose, you need much more time than that," Hazel objected.

"Mommy, please." Melody groaned again.

"You can handle this, Zen. You know what to do," he said.

"I, uh, but—" I stuttered.

"Yeah, she does," Bailey agreed. "When my house was being built, she made sure everything was done. She was so damn bossy that some of the workers thought she worked for the builder. You got this, Zen."

"I promised Mama G that the house would be finished by Ephraim's birthday. She wants to have a get-together, a celebration, and I told her it would be ready. I'm not gonna let her down."

"That house is very important to her." Hazel sighed. "Ephraim was such a good boy."

"Ephraim was a wild boy," Melody said., "But he was cool. His death was a shock to so many people."

I was tempted to ask how he had died, but instead, I said, "I don't know. Josh is still against this. I mean, he unlocked the door for us today, but he still was negative about this entire process."

"I don't think he's gonna be a problem. Trust me. I already talked to him. Ma, can you hand me my bag?" Caldwell pointed to the white paper bag, which held his personal belongings, that was sitting in the corner of the room.

Hazel stood and passed him the bag. He reached inside and took out a set of keys, then fumbled with them until he removed two and passed them to me.

"Here. Now you don't need him to let you in. But I think he's probably gonna be around a lot more, though."

I took the keys and stared at them. As elated as I was to continue working on the house, I was a little hesitant. If I agreed to this, it meant that if anything went wrong, then it was all on me. And despite his being cooperative today,

I wasn't too thrilled at the thought of dealing with Joshua any more than I already had. His negativity regarding the house was just bad energy, and that was the last thing I needed.

Caldwell flinched slightly and closed his eyes.

Bailey stood up and announced, "Well, I think we should be going. Caldwell, I'll check on you in the morning. Call me if you need anything."

"Thanks, pretty girl. Give me a hug." He reached for her, and she grabbed his hand.

"Bye, Caldwell," I said.

"Zen, you know I'm just a phone call away, or a text, or FaceTime. I'm gonna be checking in every day, and you know my guys got you," he told me then closed his eyes again.

"It was nice meeting you both," I said to Hazel and Melody.

We said good-bye, and as soon as we stepped into the corridor, we heard Hazel and Melody talking.

"They're so nice and pretty. So lovely."

"Yes, I see why he likes her. She's cool."

I stopped in my tracks and whispered, "Bailey, Caldwell likes you."

"They aren't talking about me, fool," Bailey hissed.

"They're definitely not talking about me. It has to be you. You're the one he asked for a hug, not me," I pointed out.

"Zen, trust me, the topic of that discussion is not me, and they definitely ain't talking about Caldwell either."

I looked at Bailey, who was staring at me like she was waiting for me to offer an opinion, but I didn't have one for her.

"Don't play dumb with me. You know exactly who they're talking about," she said with a smirk on her face. "Looks like your life ain't as messed up as you think it is. You still have a job, and possibly a new boo."

Chapter Nineteen

To my surprise, the remodel continued to go smoothly, even in Caldwell's absence. I knew it was mainly due to his amazing crew of guys and the power of technology that allowed him to check and make sure everything was up to his standards. One would think the minor imperfections would not be noticeable, especially on his cell phone screen, but he noticed each one and commented on them.

"Why isn't there a tarp on that area over there?" he asked while we were FaceTiming one afternoon. The painters had completed two of the upstairs bedrooms and were about to start on the third, and I was showing him their work.

"Where?" I asked, looking around.

"Over there, near the closet door. They're gonna end up getting paint on the floor," he fussed.

"Tell him we got this."

I turned around and shook my head at Josh, who had walked into the room. Turning the phone so that the camera was facing him, I said, "Can you please tell him he's gotta stop sneaking up on me?"

"Josh, my man. What's good?" Caldwell said.

"How you feeling, man?" Josh asked.

"I'm getting better. Almost back to a hundred percent. The doctor said I'll be good as new by the end of next week."

"The doctor said you are to rest, Jose. You need to heal."
I heard his mother yelling in the background, and Josh
and I began laughing.

"Anyway, like I said, make sure they put the tarp down
where they're painting." He continued giving additional
instructions, and I made mental notes of everything he
said, most of which he'd already gone over with me in
previous conversations.

"Okay, Caldwell, I got it," I told him.

"Josh, how's it looking, man?" Caldwell asked.

"I gotta admit, it's looking great. I'm impressed." Josh
nodded at me, taking me by surprised.

"Jose, get off the phone and lie down!" Caldwell's
mother yelled again.

"I'll check in with you later, Zen. Josh, holla back at me.
Adios," he said, and the call ended.

"So, you came by to check up?" I asked, putting my
phone in the back pocket of my paint-covered jeans. My
shirt and sneakers were just as worn, because I had been
doing a little of the painting myself.

"Something like that." He glanced down at my clothes.
"I thought the painter said he had a crew. Why are you
doing it?" he asked. "Where are they?"

"He has two other guys who are about as old as he is,
and you saw for yourself that he ain't that young," I said.
"And don't get me wrong; they are really good, but they're
a little slow, and I need for this to get done before those
floors are installed day after tomorrow. So, I decided to
help out a little."

"Wow," he said.

"Wow what?"

"Nothing. You're just really dedicated to this, that's all."

"I told you I love this stuff. It's my passion," I told him.
"Plus, believe it or not, painting is very therapeutic and
helps me think."

He looked around the half-painted room and said, "Well, like I told Caldwell, I'm kinda impressed. It looks great."

"I'm glad."

"You're really trying to finish this in two days?" he asked.

I leaned over and dipped the roller into the pan of paint, then ran it against the wall and said, "I'm gonna damn sure try."

The following day, I got to the house early and was surprised to see Josh's truck sitting out front. I let myself in and could hear music blasting from upstairs. As I got closer, I could hear him singing loudly.

"You're the biggest part of me. You're the light that sets me free," he belted.

I stood in the doorway for a few minutes, staring. I didn't know what was more shocking: the sight of him painting in a pair of coveralls and Timberland boots, his awkward dance moves, or the fact that the room was almost finished. As he continued singing and dancing, the laugh that I had been holding back escaped, and he jumped.

"Shit, you scared me," he said.

"If you jump when someone enters a room, then you must be doing something you ain't got no business doing. Aren't you the one who told me that?" I asked.

"True," he said, hurrying to pick up his phone off the nearby ladder to turn off the music.

"So, what are you doing here?" I asked. "Other than singing Seventies rock. What you know about Ambrosia?"

"Oh, you got jokes, huh?" He laughed. "Unfortunately, I know a lot about them. My parents had their album and the cassette, so I was forced to listen at home and in the car. How do you know about them?"

"Same, except my aunt used to play their album all the time. Them and the Bee Gees. I can probably name all their greatest hits." I shrugged, "But you still didn't answer my first question. What are you doing in here?"

"What does it look like I'm doing? Painting."

"I can see that, but why?" I asked, still confused.

He put the paint roller down and said, "Honestly, I don't know. When I left yesterday, I went to a meeting that didn't go so well, and it left me in a really bad head space. I thought about what you said about painting being therapeutic, so I came back and decided to give it a try. You were right. This is hella therapeutic. It really helped me clear my head. So, this morning, I got up and came back."

"You must've stayed hella late and got here hella early, because you got a lot done," I told him.

"I'm an early riser anyway."

"Well, I'm glad it helped you clear your head," I said, taking a sip of my tea and placing it on the window ledge, making sure there was tarp on the floor under it. I wasn't going to chance Caldwell calling and noticing again. Normally, I would be drinking a skinny latte from Starbucks, but I was still making penance after my recent ice cream and doughnut binge days earlier.

"It really did." He smiled, and I noticed he had a deep dimple in his left cheek that I had never paid attention to—probably because he rarely smiled. He really was a nice-looking guy.

I realized I was staring and quickly looked away before he noticed too. "Too bad you didn't wear a pair of your old Timbs, because those are ruined," I said.

He looked down at his feet. "These are my old Timbs."

I went into the bathroom in the hallway, where we had stored the additional paint supplies, and grabbed another pan and roller. When I returned, Josh had turned the music back on. This time he had turned on the Bee Gees.

"Really?" I asked as I poured paint into the pan and walked to the wall opposite the one he was working on.

"It's a playlist, I swear. That just happened to be the song that played next."

For the next four hours, we made small talk as we worked and listened to music. By the time the other painters arrived, we had finished the master bedroom and another room. We actually made a fairly good team. Josh's long, muscular arms were perfect for painting long strokes, and my keen eye for detail worked great for the areas around the windows.

As we worked, I kept pushing out the thought of Bailey's insinuation that Josh might potentially be my new boo. Although he was a little friendlier, he didn't give off any kind of vibe that he was remotely interested in me.

Every now and then he got a phone call and stepped out of the room. Although I wasn't intentionally eavesdropping, I could tell that the first couple of calls were business related from his tone. Then, he got another call, and I knew that it was personal.

"Yeah, I wasn't home when you came through. I stepped out to get some air," I heard him say, and I stepped closer to the doorway to hear. "Now, you know I would've been down for that had I known, boo. Most definitely. I need to get home and take a shower first. Oh, really? Give me an hour."

When he walked back in, I was moving so fast away from the door that I slipped on the tarp and fell on my butt, splashing paint into my hair. "Ugggghhhh."

"Oh, shit. Are you okay?" Josh rushed over to me.

"I'm fine."

He reached down to help me onto my feet. "Is anything hurt?"

I was too embarrassed to look at him, but I did take his hand. "Other than my pride?"

When I got to my feet, our eyes met, and unable to hold it in, we both laughed uncontrollably. Tears streamed down my face and his. He went to wipe his eyes and ended up smearing paint on his cheek, causing me to laugh even harder. When we composed ourselves, we stood staring and smiling at one another.

"What?" I finally asked.

"You got paint on your chin," he said.

"*You've* got paint on *your* chin."

"I'm glad you're okay, but I think that's a sign that it's time for a break."

I thought about the phone call he'd just had and said, "I think you're right."

"I can come back later," he offered.

"No, you're good. I actually have to go to pick out the bathroom fixtures, so I'll be gone for the rest of the day." I started cleaning up my supplies.

"Bathroom fixtures?"

"Yeah, for the master bathroom. We're redoing the entire thing and making it a little more modern," I said. "Sink, toilet, retiling the shower."

"Oh, okay. So, that has to be painted too?"

"Yep." I nodded. "But don't worry. We got it."

"Are you kicking me out of therapy?" he asked.

"Not at all."

"Then I'll be back."

I doubted his boo from the phone call, whoever she was, would let him come back over here anytime soon. "Well, I'm done for the day," I said, trying to let him off the hook.

He was having none of it. "Like you said, we got it."

***

I tried as hard as I could not to think about Josh. Every time he would pop into my head, I reminded myself that he had a midday booty call.

"Am I missing something?" Bailey asked after I told her about the events of the morning.

"I don't think so," I said.

"Who cares if he had a midday booty call? Hell, clearly there's some chemistry there. What you should've done was planned on being his late-night snack." She laughed.

"Eww, that's nasty." I shook my head.

"No, that's real. Don't act like you don't want no dick, Zen. Unless you done got some and ain't told me. Hell, you're long overdue, sis, and Josh may be just what you need. I say go for it."

"You're crazy."

"Welp, just so you know, I'll be gone for three whole days next week. You got the crib to yourself just in case you wanna bring your work home with you," she teased.

"Trust me, I don't."

The next day, when I got to the house, I found Josh hard at work downstairs.

"Good morning," he greeted me.

"Good morning. Uh, we were gonna finish upstairs before we started down here," I told him.

"It's finished."

"What? The entire floor?"

"Yeah, the guys stayed until around seven, and I left at around eleven and came back this morning at about six. I brought you a tea. It's in the kitchen. Four Splenda and a splash of half and half, right?"

"Uh, yeah," I said, stunned that he remembered my preferences. I'd told him when we had a debate over Starbucks coffee versus tea the day before.

"All righty then, let's get to work. Floors are being delivered in the morning, right? We got a lot to do and a short time to get it done," he said. When I didn't move, he asked, "What's wrong?"

"Nothing." I was tempted to remind him that a month ago he was totally against this entire project and felt that it was a waste of time, and now he was acting as if he were the lead contractor while Caldwell was out sick.

It was almost nine o'clock when we finally finished painting. Somehow, we had managed to get the entire house done. I was dog tired, but the excitement of being one step closer to finishing my first major project had me energized. I wasn't by myself.

"We really did it. We got it done," Josh said, looking around the kitchen, the last room we had done.

"We did." I nodded, and we gave each other a high five.

"We should go celebrate."

I looked down at my paint-covered clothes then pointed to his. "Where are we going like this?"

"It doesn't have to be anywhere fancy. We can go grab a drink somewhere nearby," he suggested.

"Aren't you tired?" I asked, suddenly feeling nervous about going somewhere with him. We had been working side by side for two days, but now I felt self-conscious.

"Not really. Are you? You seemed kind of hype a minute ago, so I just figured . . ."

"I was."

"Come on, one drink. We can go to Chubb's. It's right up the boulevard and not far from here."

"Chubb's? That hole in the wall?" I asked, thinking about the run-down bar located in the middle of a strip mall, famous for its fish plates and shootouts.

"My uncle owns that hole in the wall," he told me with a slight smile on his face.

"Oh, I mean, I've never been there personally, but I heard it's got decent fish." I tried to clean it up.

"I'm just playing with you. Come on. I'll drive."

We hopped into his truck and headed over to Chubb's. It was a lot nicer on the inside than it was on the outside, and I wasn't as terrified as I thought I would be when we walked in. We were immediately greeted by a short, stocky man who I instantly knew had to be Chubb.

"Well, look who the cat done drug in," he cackled.

"What's up, Unc?" Josh hugged him, barely able to get his long arms around the man's large body.

"I heard you had moved back, but I didn't believe it. How you been, nephew?"

"I'm good. This is my friend, Zen. Zen, this is Chubb." Josh introduced us.

"Nice to meet you," I said.

"The pleasure is all mine, young lady." Chubb smiled. "Y'all been playing paintball?"

"No, Unc, we've been *painting* painting."

"Really? Now, your daddy would be proud to hear that. You know how he liked doing stuff like that. He loved to build and fix things. Him and your brother," Chubb told him.

"Yeah," Josh said, and I could sense a shift in his demeanor. "Well, we just popped in to grab a quick drink."

"Well, you know where the bar is. Vic!" he yelled to the bartender, "take care of these folks, and it's on me. Give them whatever they want and make sure their fish is fresh."

"Oh, we're not eating," I said quickly.

"What? Nonsense, young lady. You wouldn't dare come into my place and disrespect me by not having one of my fish plates, would you?" Chubb asked me.

I turned to Josh, who shrugged. "You heard him. We gotta get a plate."

We made our way to the bar and took a seat.

"What you having?" Vic asked us.

"I'll have a glass of chardonnay," I said.

"You're kidding, right?" Josh asked.

"What do you mean?"

"Come on. This is a celebration. We need a real drink. Give us two kamikazes, Vic."

"What? Oh, hell no," I objected.

"What? You can't handle it?" Something about the way he said it made me wonder if he was talking about the drink. He smiled again, and his deep dimple caught my eye. "I mean, if it's too much for you to handle, let me know."

"I can handle it," I said, determined not to be intimidated.

"Two kamikazes?" Vic asked.

I stared at Josh and nodded.

Two hours later, we were sitting at a table in the back, eating fish and comparing the miseries of our lives between shots.

"So, your boss hit on you, and you got fired, and you find out your controlling fiancé had a baby by another chick?" Josh slurred as he leaned across the table toward me. "And so then you moved in with your best friend?"

"You got it," I said, feeling unusually giddy as I wobbled in my seat, trying to keep from falling over. "Your life cannot be as bad as mine right now, Mr. Former-NBA-player-who-lives-in-a-posh-condo."

"You think so?" He said, "Well, I was in the NBA and rode the bench for two years. I met this beautiful girl, who said she loved me, and we got married and moved to the city she grew up in. I took all of my money and invested into her lifelong dream of opening her own restaurant. And we opened it and it was a huge success. My life became all about her and her family. I pretty much forgot all about mine."

A look of sadness passed over his face. "And my dad called and told me my brother was sick, but did I care? Nope, because my wife and her fucking dreams were more important. Then my brother died, and then my dad, within six months of each other. And my wife was still bitching because according to her, I was distracted and not focused on our future. So, then guess what happened?"

"What?" I asked, my eyes wide with anticipation.

"She tells me she's fallen in love with someone else and she's leaving me." He slammed his hand on the table for emphasis.

"Shut the fuck up," I said, the alcohol loosening up my language. "That cheating bitch! I'm glad you left her ass."

"I didn't leave her; she left me for her head chef—who is also her best friend since middle school," he said.

"No!" I gasped. "That bastard."

"Nope, nope, nope." Josh shook his head at me. "Her best friend is a *woman*!"

"Oh, shit!" I said. Then, I couldn't help it; I started giggling, "Your life is just as fucked up as mine."

"I told you." Josh laughed, picking up his shot glass and holding it up. "To us, the losers."

"The biggest losers." I laughed and picked up my own glass to join the toast.

"A'ight, you two, where are your keys?" Chubb came over and said, "It's time to go."

"Don't look at me. I ain't drive," I said to Josh.

"Um, oh, here they are." Josh held up his set of keys, "Tah-dah!"

"I don't think you should drive. You're drunk." I reached for the keys.

"You're drunk too," he said, holding the keys away from me.

Chubb took the keys and said, "You're both drunk. Vic is gonna drive you home. Let's go."

Chubb led both of us to the door, where Vic was waiting for us. He took the keys, and when he pulled to the front of the club, Josh helped me get into the back of his truck and then climbed beside me. The temperature had dropped, and I began shivering.

"Are you cold?" Josh asked, putting his arm around me.

"A little," I said, and he pulled me closer to him. I enjoyed the feel of his body beside mine. I looked up at him and said, "I can't believe that heifer cheated on you with her bestie."

He looked into my eyes and said, "I can't believe that motherfucker cheated on you and had a baby by some random."

I smiled, and he leaned down and kissed me. It was a sloppy, drunk kiss, but it was still warm and tantalizing and left me wanting more.

"Where to first?" Vic asked.

Neither one of us answered. We were too busy exploring one another's mouths to respond at first. He asked twice more, until finally, Josh gave him his home address.

Chapter Twenty

I woke up to the sound of a doorbell ringing. At first, I was confused and unsure of where I was, until I closed my eyes and bits and pieces of the night before began to fill my head: drinking at Chubb's, kissing in the back of Josh's truck, and being dropped off by the bartender, who had helped us stumble onto the elevator just before giving Josh his keys and telling us an Uber was waiting for him and we were on our own. Then, more kissing and groping on the elevator ride, and finally getting to Josh's apartment, where we didn't waste any time taking off our clothes as soon as we got inside the door.

"Your fucking body is amazing," I remembered saying as I ran my fingers along his chiseled chest and down his washboard abs.

"No, you are fucking amazing," he said, snatching my bra off, cupping my full breasts in his hands, and kissing my neck.

I remembered him pinning me against the hallway wall and moaning as his fingers entered my throbbing wetness, and then we were on the cold, hard floor, where I lay back as he sucked and licked my sticky sweetness until I couldn't take it anymore, screaming out his name as I climaxed from the pleasure of his tongue. I don't know when we went into his bedroom, but I know that when we got into his bed, the sex we had was hot, passionate, loud, and satisfying.

Again, there was the sound of a doorbell ringing. I opened my eyes and rolled over in the bed. Josh wasn't there. I heard his voice coming down the hallway.

"Who is it?"

I couldn't hear who answered on the other side until the door opened.

"What the hell is going on? I've been waiting since five-thirty, and I've been calling you for an hour," a female voice said, full of attitude.

"Shit, my bad. What time is it?" Josh groaned.

"It's damn near seven o'clock. Oh my God, Josh. Are you hung over? Were you drunk?" she demanded to know.

"I had a couple of drinks. My bad. I forgot," he mumbled.

I quickly sat up and scanned the room for my clothes, but they weren't anywhere to be found. The last place I remembered having them was the hallway. I scrambled out of the bed, wrapping the sheet around me, praying that whoever this chick was, she didn't see my belongings.

"I can't believe you. Do you know how pissed I am right now? I could've—"

"I know, and I'm sorry. I'll give you a call later today."

I heard the door closing, and I felt horrible—not only because I was hung over and nauseated, but also because I was embarrassed. I had gotten drunk and slept with my boss. Well, technically he was my boss's son since it was his mother who paid me, but still, it was inappropriate and unprofessional. The only thing that made me feel slightly better about the situation was the fact that I vaguely recalled a brief conversation about condoms and Josh reaching into his drawer and taking one out. So, at least the sex was protected.

"Good morning." He walked back into the room, wearing only a pair of basketball shorts.

"Good morning," I responded, avoiding eye contact while trying not to stare at his sexy-ass body at the same time.

"Sorry about that. My, uh, that was my neighbor. I was supposed to meet her in the—"

I held up my hand and said, "No need to explain. It's all good. I'm just trying to get myself together right quick."

"Are you okay? I mean, how are you feeling?" he asked.

"I'm okay. I, uh, I need my clothes," I mumbled. "Have you seen my phone?"

"Your clothes are out there." He pointed toward the hallway. "I can get them for you. I haven't seen your phone. You want some coffee or water? I got some juice or Gatorade."

"No, just my clothes," I said, wrapping the sheet a little tighter.

He walked out and a few seconds later came back with my clothes in hand. "Here you go. I didn't see your phone out there. Sorry. But I did see your keys and wallet."

I took the clothes from him and said, "Where's your restroom?"

"Right through there." He pointed. "You sure you're good?"

"Yeah." I nodded.

"There's towels and washcloths in the small closet to the left," he told me.

I quickly walked into the bathroom, holding the sheet around my body as tightly as possible. Clicking on the light, I caught a glimpse of myself in the mirror. I looked horrible. Not only was my hair standing all over my head, but there were several bruises on my neck and chest. I sat on the commode and saw that there were even small bruises on my inner thighs and calves where, apparently, Josh's hands had gripped them. *Damn*, I thought, *that shit must've been incredible.*

I took a quick shower and tried to tame my hair the best I could, then slipped my clothes on. When I came out, Josh wasn't in the bedroom. He had gotten dressed and was standing in his living room, watching Sports Center on his huge-ass TV and drinking a Powerade.

"Can I use your phone?" I asked. "I need to call an Uber. The floors are being put in today, so I need to get going."

"Zen, you don't need to do that. I can take you to get your car," he said.

"You don't have to, really—"

"Come on," he said, finishing the rest of his juice and grabbing his keys off the table. My wallet and the keys to my car were sitting on the same table, but my phone was still missing.

We rode the elevator to the parking garage of his building. For a second, I stopped, and he turned and looked at me.

"What's wrong?"

"How do you know where your truck is?" I asked.

He held up his phone and said, "Find My Car app."

The app led us straight to his truck, and we drove in silence to the house, where my car was still parked out front. He had barely put the car in park before I thanked him and hopped out.

I had just gotten into my car when I heard tapping on my window. Josh stood smiling, holding my phone.

"Where did you find it?" I asked, rolling down the window and taking it from him.

"On the floor in the back, under the seat. You must've dropped it."

"Oh, thanks," I said.

"Well, I'll see you later I guess," he said nonchalantly.

My phone began ringing, and I saw that it was Bailey. I knew she must've been worried sick, especially since

I hadn't come home the night before. I looked at Josh and said, "I gotta take this. Thanks again." Then, without waiting for a response, I answered the call. "Hey, Bailey."

"Girl, what the hell is going on?"

I made sure Josh had moved away from my car before I answered her. "Bailey, I fucked up. Like, really fucked up."

"How? What happened?"

"You're not going to believe this. Hell, I can't believe this," I told her.

"Are you still with Josh?" she asked.

"Wait, how did you know I was with him?"

"You both drunk-dialed me from your phone. You made him ask permission to take you home." She laughed. "Once I found out that neither one of you was driving, I was cool with it."

"Shit, I don't even remember that," I admitted.

"What do you remember?" she asked. "Did anything memorable happen? Do tell."

"I'm on my way home. I'll be there in fifteen minutes. Can you leave work?"

"For this? Hell, yeah. See you in a few," she said.

I was laying across my bed, wishing my growing headache would go away and contemplating whether a batch of chocolate chip pancakes would help more than the two Aleve I'd just taken. Bailey walked through the door carrying a tray of drinks and a bag from Starbucks.

"Hey, bestie." She smiled. "I brought you a latte and a bagel."

"Really?" I sat up. "You actually brought me coffee and carbs? You must already know how bad I fucked up."

"You're really gonna have to give me the details and tell me everything that happened." She sat on the bed beside me and passed me a cup.

I took a long sip and told her everything I could remember, even pointing out the hickeys on my neck. By the time I finished, I could see her amusement.

"I'm glad this is so entertaining for you," I said, taking the bagel out of the bag and biting it.

"You're so damn dramatic, Zen. You haven't told me anything you did that was fucked up. You got drunk and you had sex. That shit happens all the damn time. Was it consensual? Did you want to fuck him?"

I glanced over at her. "Yeah, I did. But isn't that ironic? The last guy I worked with who came on to me was unwarranted and cost me my job. And here I am screwing the next guy I'm working for. If that's not fucked up, then I don't know what is."

"It's not fucked up, Zen. You wanted some dick, you needed some dick, you got some dick. What happened between you and Josh was nothing more than what happened that weekend we went to Cabo junior year," Bailey reminded me. "What was that guy's name again?"

"Terry, I think. Or was it Tony?" For a second I was amused, remembering that wild weekend, but I was an adult now, and that kind of behavior was not in my best interests if I wanted to build a career. "But this is different. I haven't seen Terry or Tony or whatever since that weekend, but I have to see Josh, at least until the house is done. And then his girlfriend showed up at his door." I sighed.

Bailey's eyes widened. "Did he say she was his girl-friend?"

"Well, no, he said it was his neighbor. But it's the same chick I overheard him talking to on the phone, and I know they're fucking," I told her.

"But you don't know for sure that it's his girl."

"This whole thing is just messed up all the way around. I should not have slept with him. Now shit is gonna be awkward between us. It already was when he took me to get my car. He was mad quiet and was so . . . uncomfortable."

"Maybe you should talk about what happened."

"Hell, no. I wasn't about to bring it up, and I'm not going to. I'm gonna pretend like it never happened," I told her. In that moment, flashes of Josh and me rolling naked in his bed popped into my head. I shook it away.

My phone rang. It was Georgette. I thought about ignoring her call but didn't want to risk pissing her off. I answered nervously. "Hello?"

"Zen, good morning. Are you at the house?"

"Um, no, ma'am. Not yet. I'll be headed over that way in a little while. Is everything okay? Did you need something?"

"I talked to Josh, and he told me what happened," she said, and I swear it felt like my heart stopped beating for a second.

I felt the nausea from that morning returning. I couldn't believe this was happening. "Oh, he did? I . . . we . . . "

"Yes, you and he finished painting the downstairs just in time. He seemed quite pleased with the job you guys did. I think he's coming around. I was a little nervous when Jose became ill, but he was right when he told me you would be able to handle everything. I'll have another check for you next week."

"Thank you so much, Georgette. I'm just glad we were able to get it done too," I told her, feeling my panic subside slightly.

"Well, either I can meet you somewhere and give you the check, or I can give it to Josh."

"I can meet you and get it. It's no problem," I said hurriedly.

"Well, it's up to you. Let me check my schedule and see what day works best for me," she said.

We made plans to meet the following week. I took another shower, changed clothes, and went back to the house just in time to meet the installers with the floors. It took the entire day for them to be put in, and I kept wondering if Josh was going to show up, but that never happened. When I checked in with Caldwell, I waited for him to mention Josh's name, but he didn't.

Later, while I was lying in bed, I scolded myself for even thinking about sending him a text. What was wrong with me that I couldn't get him out of my head? It wasn't just the sex that I kept thinking about; it was also the things he had shared while we were drinking. The hurt, the betrayal, the heartbreak: it was all too familiar. Despite him looking like he had it all together, his life was just as much a mess as mine was, and something about that drew me to him.

Chapter Twenty-one

"You are doing an incredible job, Zen," Georgette said. We were at the same Starbucks, sitting at the same table where we had originally met nearly a month ago. "Josh sent me pictures of what's been done so far. The floors look amazing, and so do the walls. I can't wait to see the finished product."

I tried to act nonchalant, but I was surprised to hear that he had sent her pictures of the floors, since I hadn't seen or talked to him in over a week; not since he dropped me off at my car. It was clear that he was avoiding me as much as I had been avoiding him.

"Yes, things are coming along great. I'm glad that you and Josh are satisfied," I said, trying to focus on her and not the thoughts of Josh that were distracting me.

She handed me the check, and I put it in my purse without looking at it. I had no doubt that it was the same amount that she had given me last time, and I was fine with that.

"So, do you think everything will be finished by the thirtieth of next month?" she asked.

"I don't see why not. Is that when you want to list it?"

"List it? That house isn't being sold. That was Ephraim's pride and joy, and he and his father worked hard to build it," she said with certainty. Then, with tears in her eyes, she said, "Ephraim's birthday is the thirtieth of next month, and I would like to host a party there in his honor."

I reached across the table and said, "I understand, and I think that's a beautiful idea."

"Thank you, Zen. I appreciate you and all of your hard work, and so does Josh." She smiled.

I wasn't so sure if her son appreciated me as much as she thought he did, but I wasn't about to say that to her.

After we parted ways, I sat in my car and swallowed the lump that had formed in my throat. I thought about the date that Georgette had talked about. It was a date that I had been dreading for months. The thirtieth of next month. It was the date that I had anticipated my baby being born, had I still been pregnant. My due date that now would never happen.

I got myself together and headed over to the house. I was inspecting the work they had started doing in the kitchen when Josh walked in the front door. He looked just as surprised to see me as I was to see him.

"Oh, hey," he said awkwardly.

"H . . . hey." My voice was shaky, and I had to clear my throat.

"I thought you were meeting my mother for coffee," he said.

"I did."

"Oh, okay. Well, uh, how've you been?"

"Good, and you?"

"I'm good," he said. "The kitchen is coming along nice."

"Yeah, they're doing a great job. We're actually ahead of schedule, believe it or not." I couldn't believe we were standing here making small talk like we hadn't been rolling around naked together just a few weeks ago.

"What about the upstairs bathrooms?" he asked, continuing our effort to avoid the uncomfortable and embarrassing truth.

"Almost finished."

Breaking the strained mood a little, he gave me a comical look and asked, "What kind of shower head did you get?"

I shook my head and said, "One that makes the water beat on your chest."

"You better not have," he said and headed up the stairs with me following behind. When he walked into the master bathroom, he exclaimed, "Oh, wow."

I could tell by the look on his face that he liked what I had decided to do in the master bathroom. When I had told Caldwell what I wanted to do at first, he balked, but eventually, he gave in. The shower was tiled in mosaic stone and had a spa feel to it. I had taken a chance, and it paid off, because it turned out better than I expected.

"And it has a detachable head," I said with a wink, surprising myself. His enthusiasm for the design had me feeling a little more relaxed, I guess.

Josh laughed and turned to me. "Zen, this is incredible. You really did the damn thing in this bathroom."

"Thanks. I'm really glad you like it."

"I really do." He looked down at me, and our eyes met. I could feel the connection with him that I hadn't felt until that night at Chubb's. I was drawn to him.

"You are amazing," he said. Apparently, he was drawn to me too.

He took a step closer to me, and I waited for my nerves to kick in, but they didn't. I anticipated his touch, and when I felt his fingers touching my cheek, I didn't pull away.

"This house is special, Josh," I told him.

"You are—"

"Hello? Josh?" A female voice drifted up the stairs. It was the same voice I'd heard that morning at his apartment. He looked at me for a second, and then his hand dropped. I stepped away from him, now realizing that the reason he had come to the house was because he thought I would still be with his mother. He hadn't expected me to be there, especially since his girlfriend was coming.

"Zen, wait," he said as I turned and walked out of the bathroom.

"Josh, are you upstairs?" the female yelled.

I could hear her climbing the stairs, and by the time I made it into the hallway, she was there. I stopped, and we stared at one another for a moment. There was something familiar about her. I knew her from somewhere but couldn't place her at first.

"Zen?" she asked, looking surprised.

I stared at her, dressed in form-fitting designer jeans, a cute top, and a pair of heels that I had been eying for the past two weeks at Zara. Her flawless makeup only accentuated her perfect image. I could tell that her hair weave had easily cost her eight hundred dollars. In her hand was a Balmain bag. This chick had money and plenty of it. I had already assumed that she did, based on the fact that she lived in Josh's building, but now it was confirmed. I suddenly felt self-conscious about the oversized white button-down I wore, along with my baggy jeans and paint-covered Nikes. I rubbed my hand over the wild, top-knot ponytail that I wore daily.

"Have we met?" I asked her.

"Zen, it's me, Tam." She smiled, and her porcelain veneers sparkled. "From the job."

I thought about everyone I had ever worked with but couldn't place the model chick who was standing in front of me.

"You two know each other?" Josh asked.

"Yeah, we used to work together at Graves Realty last year," she told him. "Wow, Zen, you look good. You lost a lot of damn weight, girl."

"Tamela?" I suddenly realized who she was, but she looked totally different from when we worked together.

"Yeah, it's me, Zen." She laughed.

"You look . . . I mean . . . I didn't rec—"

"You didn't recognize me, huh? I get that a lot. I had a little work done." She adjusted her perky breasts that were peeking out of the top of her shirt, then flipped her long hair over her shoulder.

"I see," I told her. "You still working over there?"

"Girl, no. I left there a little after you did," she told me.

"Zen is the designer handling the house," Josh told her.

"Really now? That's interesting. Well, I'm glad things worked out for you." Tam smirked. "It was a pretty big deal when you left."

"Well, wherever you are now, it seems to be working out for you too." I ignored her comment and pointed to her bag.

"To be honest, I'm in between jobs right now. I'll find something else eventually. I came through to check out this house my boo has been spending so much time working on." Tam grabbed Josh by the arm. "Can a sister get a tour?"

"Uh, yeah." Josh looked uncomfortable, but she didn't seem to notice.

"You guys can start up here. I have some work to take care of downstairs," I told them.

"We'll chat some more before I leave, Zen. We need to catch up," Tam said. Either I was hiding it really well, or she was oblivious to the tension between me and Josh.

"Sure," I said flatly and walked back downstairs into the kitchen. I couldn't believe Josh was dating Tam. She was such a skank. The only thing I could think about was how loud and unprofessional she and her friend Danay would be in the office, especially in the staff meetings. What did he even see in her? I knew exactly what he saw:

her ass, hips, and now her new breasts. After all, he was a man, and a good-looking one at that.

I could hear her laughing loudly and easily imagined her groping and touching on him. Wait, was I jealous? Hell no, I couldn't be. Josh wasn't my man, and I didn't even really like him, I reminded myself. The more I thought about the two of them, the more they seemed like the perfect match. She was a loud-mouth barracuda who liked attention, and he was an arrogant asshole. Any slight connection I might have felt with him was now stuffed deep down inside of me, and I sure didn't plan on ever acknowledging it again. From here on out, it would be purely business until I finished this job, upon which I would never have to see his ass again.

"This place really is better than what I expected," Tam said as they walked through the downstairs rooms. "I was not expecting it to be this modern and fancy, especially considering this area and how it looks on the outside."

"What do you mean? This is a nice neighborhood. These families have been living here for years." I became defensive. "This is why Josh's brother picked this area to build the house. It's their family's land."

"Zen and Caldwell made a lot of updates on the house that my brother wanted but didn't get the chance to do," Josh added. Tam just gave him a blank stare.

Josh's phone rang, and he excused himself, leaving Tam and me alone. I felt uncomfortable as hell, but self-involved Tam still seemed totally oblivious.

"Josh wasn't lying. You hooked this house right on up. He's gonna get some dough for this place," Tam said.

"He's not selling it." I frowned. "His mom just told me that this morning."

"She don't want him to sell it. But the bottom line is this is Josh's house. It's in his name, and the reason I came to see it is because he wants my sister to list it. You know she's one of the top listing agents in the city. That's how I got the job at Graves for real. She pulled some strings for me."

Her explanation answered the question that I had always wondered about her employment in a place where she was truly unqualified to work. Aside from that, I was bothered by the fact that she said Josh was selling the house. I couldn't believe he would trash his family's legacy so easily.

"Oh," was my only response. She said something else, but I was too busy thinking about how elated Georgette had been earlier in planning the housewarming in honor of Ephraim and how devastating this would be for her.

"After you left, I decided to use that situation to my advantage, and it paid off. So, I owe you a thank you, girl," Tam said.

"Huh? What?" I turned my attention back to what Tam was saying.

"I was saying I owe you a thank you because you helped me secure the bag, literally." She patted her purse and laughed.

"And how did I do that?" I asked, confused about what she was talking about.

"I filed a sexual harassment suit against Graves and got a hell of a settlement check," she said proudly.

"You did what?" She now had my full attention, and I was hanging on to her every word.

"I filed suit against those motherfuckers and won. I didn't even have to go to court." She laughed. "I hired a lawyer and told him that Lloyd displayed inappropriate behavior toward me in the workplace."

"Wow, Tam," I said, shocked.

"Yeah, got a check for over two hundred and fifty grand."

"Shit." The word escaped my mouth before I could stop it.

Tamela began to laugh. "That's right. See, here's where you went wrong. Instead of going to Priscilla's two-faced ass, you shoulda hired a lawyer and told him what was happening. My lawyer is the truth, and she's a woman, so she was not playing with they asses. When they heard about all the nasty shit that motherfucker was saying to me; then we had e-mails and text messages too? They were begging to settle."

"I can't believe Lloyd. I mean, he crossed some boundaries with me, but he never sent me e-mails or texts," I told her. "I'm sorry you had to deal with that. At least you didn't have to deal with them accusing you of lying. They didn't believe me at all."

"I know, but the gag is that I really fucked him with his fine ass!" she screeched.

I stood staring at her with my mouth open. I shouldn't have been shocked by her sleeping with Lloyd. As soon as she said it, I quickly recalled the comments she had made regarding him. I then thought about Priscilla telling me that other employees had heard comments that I made concerning Lloyd. Here this chick was bragging about her settlement check that she was awarded based on a lie, and I was fired for telling the truth. It was unfair, and I was livid.

"Ain't that a bitch," I said. The longer I stood there, the angrier I became. I could feel the tears beginning to form in the corners of my eyes and the desire to punch Tam right in her collagen-enhanced face. I needed to get out of there quickly. I heard the front door opening, and I passed Josh coming in as I walked out.

"What's wrong?" he asked, but I didn't answer.

By the time I made it to my car, the tears were falling. I sat behind the steering wheel, crying in frustration. I had just started the car to leave when I noticed a black Mercedes S550 parked directly behind me, so I couldn't back out. It had to be Tam's, because the other two vehicles parked in front of the house belonged to Josh and to Caldwell's workers. The sight of the gorgeous car angered me even more. I was stuck and couldn't go anywhere until she came out and moved.

Luckily, it didn't take long for them to come out. They both walked over to my car and waited for me to roll down the window.

"Is everything all right, Zen?" he asked, his voice full of concern.

I glanced over at Tam, who stood beside him looking innocent as hell, when in reality this was all her fault. Okay, I knew technically it wasn't her fault, but she wasn't blameless either.

"Yeah, I need to get out, though. I have to go. Can you move, please?" I asked without looking at either one of them.

"Oh, sure. No problem. It was good seeing you, Zen. You look really good, and you've worked wonders on the house," she said. I was waiting for her to get the hell away from my car, but first, she reached in her purse then handed me a small card. "You should call her."

I hesitated before taking it, but she seemed like she wasn't going to move until I did. I took it, and she finally got into her car. I tucked her stupid card into my visor, not even bothering to see whose it was.

"Zen, are you sure you're okay?" Josh asked again.

"I'm fine," I said, then asked, "Does your mom know you're listing the house once it's done?"

"Huh? I . . . who . . ."

I shook my head, not bothering to hide my disgust. "That's fucked up, Josh. I hope you know that. That's just wrong." I glanced in the rearview mirror and saw Tam had eased her car out of the driveway and was waiting on me to move. I shot a disgusted glance at him and, without a word, drove away.

Chapter Twenty-two

"Zen, where are you?" Caldwell called me just as I pulled into the crowded drive-thru at the bank. I still hadn't deposited the check that Georgette gave me the week before.

"At the bank. Why? What's up?"

"Which bank? Where? I need you to come and get me right now."

"Citizens Bank in midtown. Why do I need to come and get you? From where?"

"My crib. I got a call from Home Depot, and I gotta get over there ASAP. My mama got my truck parked at her crib. You gotta come," he said.

"Who called you from Home Depot and why?" I asked, rummaging for the check that I had dropped in my purse when she gave it to me.

"Stop asking so many questions and come and get me. Hurry up," he said.

"Caldwell, I don't even know where you live." I sighed. "And can't this wait until I finish at the bank? I'm already in line."

"No, get out of line. And I'll text you the address."

When I didn't find the check, I pulled out of line. I would come back later and go pick up Caldwell now.

When I got to his house, he was already waiting out front, moving slower than usual, but he looked fine.

"Are you supposed to be out of the house?" I asked him.

"Yes, I am. My doctor cleared me yesterday. I'm fine. I just don't have my truck because it's still at my mother's house. She was supposed to come and pick me up, but she's still at the hair salon, and I gotta go meet this guy right now," he explained. "He's been waiting almost an hour."

"What guy? I'm so confused."

"I got a hookup that I'm trying to make happen if you hurry up," he told me.

"What kind of hookup? On what?"

"Will you stop asking so many questions and drive?" he said, taking out his cell phone and dialing a call.

"Hey, Josh, you get my text? Okay, cool. I'm headed there now. Cash only, though. All right. See you in ten minutes."

I tensed up when I realized he was talking to Josh. He was the absolute last person I wanted to see. "If Josh was going to meet you, why didn't you just get him to pick you up?"

"Because he's all the way on the other side of town. You were closer. What's the problem?"

"There is no problem. I'm just saying. I stopped handling my business to pick you up to help him handle his. I have a life too," I snapped.

"Okay, I don't know what that means, but damn, Zen, you coulda just said you were busy. A simple no woulda been fine." Caldwell looked at me like I was crazy.

"You were talking so fast that I didn't have a chance to say no. You always do that. It's like I don't have a chance to comprehend what you say sometimes," I complained, not even caring if I was making sense.

"Well, excuse the hell outta me. I didn't know I was so inconsiderate with my conversation. And as far as I was concerned, we were both working as a team on the same project, which meant going to meet this guy was your business. But, trust me, I understand exactly how you feel."

I knew that what I said was wrong and out of line, not to mention disrespectful. I was taking my disappointment and frustration out on him, and he wasn't the one who was causing it. Still, I was too caught up in m hurt feelings to apologize just yet.

My cell phone vibrated. I looked down and saw that it was from the last person in the world I felt like being bothered with: Var. I hit IGNORE the same way I'd been doing since the day he gave me the decals. I glanced over at Caldwell, who was texting on his phone with a big frown on his face. I had hurt his feelings and felt bad.

"Caldwell, I'm sorry," I said as I pulled into the store parking lot. "I didn't mean that. You're right; we are a team. I'm just bugging."

"Pull around to the side of the store," Caldwell said. He didn't even react to my apology.

"The back? Why? This better not be illegal, Caldwell," I warned him.

"Oh, so you think because I'm Hispanic and a fast talker this gotta be illegal, huh?" He glared at me.

"You know that's not what I meant. Don't be like that." I sighed, feeling even worse. I pulled around to the back of the store where there was a box truck parked.

"Park behind that truck," he directed.

I looked at him briefly then followed his direction. When I put the car in park, I reiterated, "I apologize, Caldwell. I was wrong."

"I heard you the first time. It's all good. Look, I don't know what the hell is going on with you and Josh . . ."

"Wait, what is that supposed to mean? Has he said anything about me to you?"

"Not directly, but y'all were cool, and now there's this weird vibe whenever I bring either one of you up.

The other day, he asked if you had a regular schedule. He's tripping, and so are you, but I'm gonna tell both of y'all you either need to fight, fuck, or figure it out. This may be fun and games for him, but this is my damn livelihood." He opened the car door and said, "I'll be back."

He slowly eased his way out of the car then closed my door with a little more force than necessary. I could tell he was trying to get his point across. I sat speechless, watching him greet the driver of the truck. They talked for a few minutes, then he opened the back of the truck, and they both climbed in.

A store employee walked out, and I started to panic. Even though I knew there was no need, I said a quick prayer, asking that whatever this "hookup" was, it was on the up and up. He walked to the back of the truck and climbed in. A few minutes later, the three of them came out, all smiling, and Caldwell got back into the car.

"Everything good?" I asked.

He held up a shiny black square and said, "Everything's great. Check this out."

"Is that marble?" I said, taking the beautiful block of stone from him.

"That, my dear, is granite for the countertops." He smiled.

"What? It's gorgeous. Okay, I get that there's no budget, but this is way more than Josh is probably willing to spend. Especially since—" I wanted to say that he was selling the house, but I didn't. That would be Josh's mess to deal with when the truth came out and he broke his mother's heart.

"Man, when I tell you I got a deal, I got a deal," Caldwell said. "Pull around front."

"How? And what about the granite we already ordered?" I said as I turned my car around.

"Some rich guy ordered this and decided he didn't want it. He can't return it because it's special order, so my boy called me, and we struck a deal. Since what we ordered is standard, the guy here is gonna let us cancel and let them use our store credit. I'm about to go in and handle the paperwork as soon as Josh gets here with the cash."

I pulled to the front of the parking lot, but Josh was nowhere to be seen.

"Well, I'm gonna let you out and go ahead and park, because I need to look at some other stuff while we're here anyway," I said. He got out of the car, and I whipped into a parking space.

"Zen."

When I stepped out of my car, I heard someone calling my name. I turned around and saw Var walking toward me. Could this day get any weirder?

I waved and said, "Hey, Var."

"What're you doing over here?" He smiled. "Damn, you looking better and better every time I see you."

"Thanks, Var," I said, wondering why he was commenting on how I looked, since I had on leggings and an oversized shirt, an outfit he would normally complain about.

"I was at the light on the boulevard and thought I saw you," he said, explaining the coincidence of both of us being in the Home Depot parking lot at the same time. Well, I thought, at least he wasn't stalking me.

"I tried calling you, but I guess you still got me blocked," he said with a laugh.

"No, I don't have you blocked anymore. I was on the phone," I lied.

"Uh-huh. Looked like you had a dude in the car with you, Zen."

"It's not like that, Var." I sighed.

"I ain't tripping. All I'm saying is I thought we were better than that." He shrugged.

I stopped just as we got to the entrance of the store. "Better than what? What are you talking about?"

"I'm saying if you got a man, then just say it. I already know you do."

"Bye, Var." I turned to walk off, but he grabbed my arm.

I looked at his hand on me, then my eyes traveled up to meet his. His grip softened, and so did his eyes.

"Zen, why are you doing this? You know how much I love you."

"Hey, Zen, what do you think about this?" Caldwell was so busy looking at whatever it was he had in his hand that he didn't realize Var was standing with me.

"Well, damn." Var frowned. "You gotta be kidding me."

"Oh, hey, Var," Caldwell said.

"This is the nigga who was in my car? You fucking the handyman now?" Var sneered. "I guess I see why you lost all that weight. You left me to be with the fucking help. Ain't that a bitch."

"Var!"

"Hold up, man. There's no need for all that," Caldwell told him with extra bass in his voice.

"Don't tell me what there's a need for. You been plotting on Zen for a while now, Caldwell. I ain't stupid." Var stepped past me and toward Caldwell.

"I don't know what you're talking about, but you need to calm down, man." Caldwell stood firm.

"Var, please don't do this. Just go away," I pleaded.

"Don't tell me what the fuck to do," Var said.

I tried my best to grab hold of Var, but he snatched away. Tension was thick, and I knew if the two of them came to blows, it wouldn't be a fair fight, not only because Var was taller and bigger, but because Caldwell was recovering from surgery. Var normally didn't have a temper and he wasn't a fighter, but he enjoyed being able to intimidate people with his size and have them back down from him. Caldwell seemed as if he wasn't going to back down.

"Don't do this, man," Caldwell warned. "You don't want it."

Before I could stop him, Var shoved Caldwell, and he stumbled backward. Luckily, he didn't fall. He grimaced in pain, and I jumped in front of him.

"Var!" I yelled.

"Get out the way, Zen." Var took another step forward.

"What the fuck is going on?"

We all looked at Josh, who had walked up on us.

"Var, please leave," I said between clenched teeth.

"This ain't got shit to do with you, playa. Move on," Var growled and lurched at Caldwell again. He was stopped by Josh, who snatched him back.

"What the fuck?" Var yelled, seemingly just as surprised by Josh's actions as I was. "Get the fuck off me, you pretty-boy motherfucker."

"You need to walk away now, bruh. It's over," Josh told him.

"Man, shut the—" Var said, now surrounded by me, Caldwell, and Josh.

"LeVar, stop it!" I screamed as I held onto Caldwell, who was leaning on me. "You need to leave. Someone is gonna call security."

He turned and looked at Josh, then he turned to me and said, "Fuck you, Zen. You know what? Give me my fucking car."

"What?" I couldn't believe he was behaving this way. I had never seen him so angry.

"You think I'm gonna let you drive another nigga around in my car? Especially that nigga?" he yelled at me.

"Are you serious?" I said, shocked by what he was saying.

"Dead-ass. Give me my fucking keys," he said.

"Come on, man. Don't do this. It ain't what you think," Caldwell told him.

I looked at Josh, who looked confused by the conversation but was eyeing Var like he was ready to give him a beatdown.

"Shut the fuck up," Var said, then looked me right in the eye and said, "I want my fucking keys now, or when security does show up, I'm filing a police report for theft."

"Var . . ."

"Give him the fucking keys," Josh told me.

"What? No. He—"

"You heard the man. Give me my fucking keys," Var said.

A small crowd had started to form around us. I was embarrassed and didn't even try to stop angry tears from falling as I took the keys from my purse.

I tried to reason with Var one final time. "Var, let's go and talk somewhere."

"Oh, now you wanna talk? Naw, Zen. No need for any further conversation. We've both said all we need to say," Var answered.

Josh walked over and took the keys that were in my hand and tossed them at Var, who caught them. He looked at me one final time before walking off.

"That's one bitch-ass motherfucker." Josh shook his head.

I thought about running after him and demanding that he give me the keys, but I knew it wouldn't do any good, and even if there was a small chance that he would listen to me, my pride wouldn't allow it.

"Zen, don't worry about it. It's gonna be okay." Caldwell rubbed my back.

My heart sank as I recalled loving, accepting, and supporting the man that I had once loved and still cared about, who had now publicly humiliated me for no reason whatsoever. I stood there in front of Home Depot as I watched him get into a car that he had given me and drive away. I had officially hit rock bottom.

Chapter Twenty-three

"Are you sure you're gonna be okay?" Josh asked for what seemed like the hundredth time since we'd left the store.

"I'm good," I told him. We had just dropped Caldwell off at his mother's house. His truck was parked outside, and he offered to take me home, but Josh told him to go inside and get some rest, and I agreed. Although he hadn't mentioned being in pain, I could see that he was moving slower and wincing a lot more since Var shoved him.

"Did you need to stop anywhere?" he asked.

"No, you can just take me home." I gave him the address, and we spent the twenty-minute ride to my gated community listening to Mary J. Blige's "My Life." I was tempted to ask him if he was trying to be funny with his selection of music, but based on how he sang along with MJB, I got the sense he listened to it often. Plus, I didn't feel like making small talk with him. He had helped me out at Home Depot, but that didn't mean I was over everything else that had happened before. Besides, he insisted I give the keys back to Var, so in the end, he didn't really help me all that much.

I gave him the code to enter the subdivision. When we pulled up to the house, I was expecting to see Bailey's car in the driveway, but it wasn't there.

"Damn it."

"What's wrong?" Josh asked.

"Bailey's not home, and I don't have a key." I reached for my phone and dialed her number, which I'd done several times already on the drive over here. She hadn't responded to any of my texts either. I leaned back and put my hand across my forehead in frustration.

"No worries. I'm starving," he said. "Let's go get some food and maybe she'll be home in a little while."

I really didn't have a choice, so I said, "Okay."

"What are you in the mood for?"

"It doesn't really matter," I said with a big sigh.

Not knowing what else to do, I decided to reach out to Var and try to reason with him. I called him, but he didn't answer, so I sent him a text, hoping he had calmed down.

Josh was sitting there watching me, still trying to figure out what I wanted to eat. "You feel like fish? We can go to Chubb's." He gave me a weak smile.

"Uh, no." I shook my head. I really could've used a drink, but going back to the scene of our crime would be dangerous.

"Not in the mood for kamikazes, huh?" he joked. I was too pissed about my car to even be annoyed by his silliness right now.

"Honestly, I probably could drink a few of them," I said, "but I'm gonna have to decline."

"A'ight, drinks it is!" he announced happily, purposely ignoring my wishes. When I glared at him, he shrugged and said, "They don't have to be at Chubb's, and they don't have to be kamikazes."

"Good."

"Unless you want kamikazes from Chubb's." He raised an eyebrow.

Even though I still felt overwhelmed, I couldn't help but smile. Josh smiled back and seemed relieved as he drove out of the neighborhood.

We ended up at Cheesecake Factory. I hadn't realized I was hungry until we walked in and my stomach instantly started growling. My mouth watered as I stared at the cheesecakes on display, and I decided that I was going to get a slice, whether or not I had room for it after dinner. After the day I'd had, I deserved it.

Not long after we ordered drinks, Bailey finally called.

"I'm locked out," I told her, deciding to spare her the horrific details of the afternoon until later.

"What? Where are you?" she asked. I could hear a lot of noise in the background and knew she wasn't home.

"I'm out with Josh getting something to eat right now. What time will you be home?"

"Shit, Zen. I'm at the conference in Baltimore," she told me.

"What? You're not supposed to leave until tomorrow night," I said a little louder than I should have. Two ladies who were seated in the booth across from us looked over, and I mean-mugged them so hard that they immediately looked away. Josh smiled in amusement.

"I know, but my regional director wanted to meet with a few of us, so he had us come in a day early. Where are your keys?"

I closed my eyes and shook my head. My day was getting worse by the minute. I had no car, and now nowhere to go.

"I lost them," I told her.

"Lord have mercy, Zenobia." Bailey groaned. "I guess you're gonna have to call a locksmith."

The waiter brought our drinks, and I gulped down my entire glass of wine without caring.

"Don't worry. I'll figure it out," I told her. "Go enjoy your trip. I'll be fine."

"If you don't figure it out, call me back."

I hung up the phone and tried texting Var again.

"Zen," Josh said, startling me a little. I'd been so caught up in my dilemma I'd almost forgotten where I was.

I looked up from my phone. "Yeah."

"I need you to do me a favor."

"What?"

"Breathe."

"What?" I repeated.

He reached across the table, took the phone from my hand, and before I could protest, he looked at me and said, "Stop and breathe."

My eyes met his, and I said, "I told you my life was an even bigger mess than yours. Believe me now?"

"Your life is fine. What that chump did today was not a reflection on you. That was his bitch-ass-ness, not yours. I mean, I know you told me he was a jerk, and Caldwell had too, but damn."

"I've never seen him act like that, though. What happened today, that was something different." I sighed.

"Don't make excuses for bad behavior. He's a grown-ass man who threw a temper tantrum in the middle of the store like a toddler, then demanded that you give him his toy back." He took a sip of his beer.

"You're right. That was inexcusable."

"So stop feeling bad about his bullshit."

"Right now I'm not feeling bad about his bullshit. I'm feeling bad about my keys because I can't get into my house," I told him. "This is the worst."

"Nonsense. It could be way worse than this."

"Really, how?" I looked up at him.

"You could still be standing out in front of Home Depot instead of enjoying a nice meal and glass of wine with a handsome gentleman."

"Caldwell would *not* have left me at Home Depot," I said.

"Okay, you could be at Caldwell's house, listening to him and his mom argue," Josh retorted, and I couldn't help but laugh.

"You're right. This is better than that."

We ordered our meals, and I finally felt relaxed enough to make small talk while we ate. By the time they brought our dessert to the table, I felt brave enough to ask the question I had been holding in all evening.

"Why are you so anxious to sell your house?"

He looked up from his slice of cheesecake and said, "Because that's not my house."

"I'm confused. Whose house is it? Everyone keeps saying it's your house; even your mom."

"Well, technically it's mine. The deed is in my name, but that house was my brother and my dad's thing. Building and fixing stuff, that was Ephraim and my dad. They would spend every free moment they had working on it. I remember inviting them to basketball games and tournaments, even offering to pay for them to come out, and they couldn't come because they were working on the house. Getting them to come to a game was like pulling teeth. My mom would come and support, but the two of them . . ." His voice drifted off, and the pain in his face matched the sound of his voice.

"I'm sorry. That's messed up, Josh."

"It's cool. And I know that for my mom, that house is sentimental because it was something Ephraim and my dad worked hard to complete; but for me, it's a reminder that as hard as I tried to make my dad proud, even making it to the league, I could never compete with that house."

I thought about what he said for a second, then offered, "Maybe the competition wasn't about you."

"What do you mean?" he asked.

"Maybe they were competing with time. They both died right after that house was finished, right? Maybe their determination was because they were on a deadline, like the one we're on, but they didn't know it. Before she died, my aunt used to say she was on borrowed time. Your brother could have easily left the house to your mom or your dad because he was still living at the time. But he left it to you. Look at is as a gift they wanted you to have."

He didn't respond at first, and then simply said, "I guess I never thought about it that way. I just always felt like the odd man out when I was around them."

"Did they ever invite you to come work on it with them?" I asked.

"Sometimes," he admitted.

"And did you?"

"Nope, because I guess I figured that was their thing."

"Looks like you chose to be an odd man sometimes, huh?" I suggested.

Josh nodded. "You make a good point."

Conversation after that point was exceptionally pleasant, instead of strained and awkward. We laughed and talked, and things seemed to be back to the way they were before the night of drunken sex.

He paid the check, and while he went to get the car, I excused myself, went into the bathroom, and tried calling Var again. He still didn't answer. I decided the only thing I could do was get a rental car and hotel room for the night. As I walked out of the restaurant to meet Josh, I began searching online package deals on my phone.

"Damn it," I said as I climbed into his SUV.

"What's wrong now?" he asked.

"I was in the middle of making a stupid room reservation, and my phone died."

He reached into his console and handed me his phone charger. "Here. Charge your phone. But why are you getting a room?"

I looked at him out of the corner of my eye. "Because I don't want to sleep in a homeless shelter."

"Zen, you know you can stay at my place. It's not a problem at all," he said.

"No, I can get a room. Thanks for the offer, but I don't think your *neighbor* would appreciate that at all."

"You're funny, but my *neighbor* and I aren't like that. Tam and I are just cool. Nothing more."

"You don't have to explain anything to me, Josh. And besides, I got a deal on a room and a rental car, so I'm good," I said, trying to find the deal I had located a few minutes earlier.

"Put the phone down, Zen. You're not getting a room. You stayed at my crib before, and you can stay again." He reached over and took the phone from me. His hand lingered on mine a few seconds longer than necessary, and I felt the hairs on my arm stand up.

"I was drunk, and so were you," I said. "Neither one of us was thinking straight."

"I was thinking fine. You don't think I wanted you to stay?" he asked.

"In that moment, you probably did."

"And you didn't want to?"

"I did."

"So, what's the problem now? And don't get it twisted. I'm not inviting you to stay over because I'm trying to do the same thing we did last time," he said adamantly.

Hearing him say that made me feel a little slighted, mainly because I wasn't sure if he was showing the level of respect he had for me, or he ultimately didn't want to sleep with me because he wasn't attracted to me.

"There isn't a problem, Josh," I said, "but can you just take me to pick up a rental car, please?"

"Zen, you don't need to get a rental," he insisted.

"I have to be able to get around until I figure out this car situation with Var."

"Didn't I tell you to stop worrying?" Josh turned down an unfamiliar street, and we arrived at a storage facility.

"What are we doing here?" I asked.

He entered a security code, and the gate opened. He drove through and went all the way to the back, where he parked in front of a unit.

"I wish you would just trust me and stop asking so many questions. One thing you're gonna learn about me, Zen, is that when I say I got you, I got you. Do you trust me?"

I hesitated for a second and finally said, "I guess."

"You guess?" He looked surprised and offended.

"Okay, okay, I do."

"Great. Now, get out and come on." He hopped out of the truck, and I followed him to the door that he was unlocking. I waited as he pulled up the door, stepped in, and turned on the light. I gasped when I saw that it was filled with furniture and boxes.

"Whoops, this is the wrong one," Josh said. He reached for the light, but I stopped him.

"Oh my God, is all of this yours?" I squealed and began searching through the contents of the unit.

"Sort of. It's the furniture that came out of the house."

"This is a lot of stuff. It's really nice." I ran my hand along a framed poster of Josh in his college basketball uniform. "They might not've come to your games, but they were definitely your fans."

"My mom probably had that made," he said.

"But your brother had it in his house."

"Come on. What I'm looking for isn't in here."

He opened two other storage units, both filled with furnishings and personal belongings.

I asked, "What are you looking for? Maybe I can help find it."

"A'ight, it's gotta be in here. This is the last one," he said as he approached another unit. He pulled the door up and said, "Finally. Here it is. I told you I got you."

I stood beside him and stared at what was inside. "What the hell? Whose is this?"

"It was Ephraim's, but now you can use it," he said, pulling a brown tarp off of what I now saw was a black Honda Accord that looked practically brand new.

"I can't use this," I said, still stunned that Josh would even be willing to do this.

"Why not?" he asked with a puzzled look.

"Because it's not . . . I can't . . . this isn't . . ." I didn't have an exact answer, but I knew I couldn't use that car.

"You sound ridiculous, Zen." He opened the car door and got in. "The key is right here under the seat somewhere."

"You keep the key in the car?"

"Yeah, so I won't lose it," he said, just before the engine started up, letting me know that he had found the key. "I start it up once a month so the battery doesn't go dead."

I shook my head. "Thanks, but no thanks."

Josh got out of the car and asked, "What's the problem now? You don't have to get a rental, and you can use it as long as you need to. The car just sits here covered. It's no big deal."

"Because I'll still be back at square one driving someone else's car."

"Trust me, I would never pull a bitch-ass move like your ex did."

"I'm not saying that you would do that, but you would still have the ability to. It's time for me to position myself so that I will have my own. You know what I mean? I appreciate the offer, Josh. Really, I do. But I can't."

He looked disappointed as he turned the engine off and covered the car again. "Well, in case you change your mind, it's yours to use. I'm just trying to help, that's all."

"I appreciate it, but you can really help by taking me to the airport to pick up this rental."

He finally agreed and took me to the rental car agency, where I picked up a car to use for the next week. When I came out with the keys, he looked at me and said, "You sure about this?"

"Yes." I nodded. "I really appreciate you."

He stepped out of the car and gave me a hug. I enjoyed the feel of being in his arms a little more than I wanted to, and based on the length of time he held me against him, he enjoyed it just as much.

"You don't have to get a room, Zen. You can stay with me," he said, leaning his chin against my head. "I want you to."

I stepped back so I could look at him. "Josh . . ."

"And this doesn't have shit to do with your being locked out of your house. I want you to stay with me because I enjoy talking with you and being with you." He pulled my face close to his and kissed me, softly at first; then when our lips parted, his intensity increased. His mouth was as warm and inviting as I remembered from the first kiss we'd shared. He wrapped his arms around my waist and held me closer. When he finally released me, he smiled and said, "And I enjoy kissing you."

"I see."

"Stay with me, Zen."

Chapter Twenty-four

I stepped off the elevator and continued down the corridor until I got to room 1521. My hands were full with bags of items I'd purchased from Walmart to get me through the weekend: toiletries, a phone charger, socks and underwear, pajamas, two pair of leggings, and a couple of cute T-shirts. I fumbled with the bags and my purse as I used the keycard to open the door.

The Westin was one of my favorite hotel chains, and the king-sized room was spacious. I put my bags down on the dresser and closed the curtains, pausing to take a view of the city lights. It looked so peaceful. I sent Josh a quick text, thanking him again and telling him I would talk to him in the morning, sent Bailey a text telling her where I was, and then I took a much-needed, long, hot bath.

I had just climbed into bed and was searching for something to watch on television when Var called my phone. My first instinct was to cuss him out as soon as I hit the ANSWER button, but I was the one who had tried calling him earlier, so technically he was just answering my call.

I quickly counted backward from five before saying, "Hello."

"Hey, Zen. I got your text."

"I sent several texts," I said, not trying to hide my attitude.

"Well, you can come over and get your stuff. I ain't realize I had your car keys. Sorry about that. You wanna come now?" he asked as if he were doing me some kind of favor. "Or I can come to you. I don't have the code to get into—"

"Var, I'm not even home. I couldn't get into the house because you have my fucking keys and Bailey is out of town," I snapped.

"Oh," was his weak response.

"Oh," I repeated mockingly.

"Well, where are you? Are you with that dude?" he snapped.

"I'm not dealing with this tonight, Var. I'll come by in the morning and get my stuff."

"You're acting like this is all on me. All I'm asking you to do is be honest with me. If you got somebody else, then just say it."

"Good-bye, Var." I hung up the phone. It rang again, and thinking it was him calling back, I answered, "What?"

"Damn, I'm just making sure you're okay. Calm down." Bailey laughed.

"I thought you were Var. My bad."

"Var? What the hell does he want?" she asked.

I lay back on my comfortable pillows, grabbed the jumbo bag of M&Ms that I'd gotten from the store, and shared the details of the day.

"He offered you a fucking car? And you didn't take it?" she gushed.

"No, I didn't take it. Are you crazy? Why would I put myself in the same situation and risk the car I'm driving being taken away by a dude with a bruised ego?" I asked.

"Well, you do have a point. But I would've taken him up on his offer to stay at the crib. Especially after the great time y'all had the last time you ended up over there," she said playfully. "So, where are you staying?"

"I'm staying at the Westin. I sent you a text telling you where I was and my room number a little while ago. Are you drunk?" I laughed.

"I didn't get a text from you. The last text I got was the one you sent earlier, asking where I was," she said.

I looked at my text messages and realized what I'd done. "Shit."

"What?"

"I sent Josh both texts. The one for him, and the one for you." I groaned.

"That's funny as hell. Are you drunk?" She laughed.

My phone beeped, and I saw Josh's name on the screen. I told Bailey I would talk to her later and answered the phone without even saying hello.

"I'm sorry. I meant to send that text to Bailey."

"Oh, damn, so that wasn't an invitation? I was on my way," he said.

"You were not," I said; then added, "Were you?"

"No, I wasn't. But I'm glad you're safe and sound."

I didn't know if I believed him, because I could tell that he was in his truck.

"Where are you going?" I asked.

"Nowhere, really. I was bored, so I decided to ride out. You wanna join me?"

"No, I'm in for the night. Thanks for offering. I'll give you a call tomorrow," I told him.

"A'ight. Talk to you then. Enjoy the rest of your night, Zen."

"Josh?" I asked, hoping he hadn't hung up.

"Yeah?"

"Thanks for everything. I really appreciate it."

"Naw, I should be thanking you," he said then ended the call.

I put the candy away, put my phone on the charger, and pulled the covers around me; then I tossed and turned for about an hour, unable to sleep. Every time my eyes closed, I thought about Josh and the kiss we'd shared. I rolled over and reached for my phone, only to put it back down.

What are you doing? Calling him would be insane. Things just became normal between you. Do you want to mess that up? What is wrong with you? I tried to reason with myself, and again asked, *What is wrong with you?*

I sat up, and this time when I picked up my phone, I didn't put it back down. I dialed Josh's number. When he answered, I simply said, "Come over. I want you to stay with me."

Fifteen minutes later, I heard a knock at the door. As soon as I opened it, he pulled me to him and kissed me as he walked inside. I tore at his clothes, pulling his shirt over his head as he stopped in the middle of the floor to take off his pants and shoes. He kissed me as we continued the remaining ten feet across the room until we reached the oversized bed.

He went to lay me down, but it was my turn to take control. I pushed him down on the bed and then kneeled in front of him. We smiled at one another just before I took his hardened manhood in my mouth. A groan escaped, and his fingers softly entangled my hair as my lips went back and forth, sucking and teasing the tip of his slightly curved penis, taking it farther and farther into my mouth until I nearly gagged. The sound of him moaning my name over and over caused my already moistened pussy to become even wetter.

"Stop," he said, then pushed me away gently and stood up. He reached for his pants and took out a condom, then slipped it on. He walked back over to the bed and lay on his back. "Get on top."

I smiled and obliged, straddling him and guiding him into my welcoming wetness. It was my turn to moan now, enjoying the feeling of him inside me. I rode him, slowly at first, as his fingers teased my clit. Then his hands made their way around my body and gripped my ass, encouraging me to go faster. I leaned over, and he took my nipples into his mouth and sucked them, driving me closer to climaxing.

"Oh, shit," I panted. "That's my spot."

"Damn, Zen," he said, smacking me on the ass.

I felt myself getting wetter and wetter, and then he gripped me so tight that I knew he had arrived at the same destination I had, and we released simultaneously. I collapsed onto his chest. He kissed my collarbone and moaned my name again.

"Holy shit," I whispered, exhausted and satisfied.

"That was fucking amazing," he said.

We lay for a few more minutes, both of us hot and covered in sweat and enjoying the moment, until he finally got up and went into the bathroom.

"Hey, Zen," he called out a few minutes later.

"Yeah?"

"Can you come here a sec?"

Thinking something was wrong, I walked to the bathroom door. "What is it?"

He opened the door and pointed to the steam-filled shower. "Can you come in here and scrub my back?"

I laughed, and he pulled me into the bathroom with him. We showered, then had another round in bed, leaving both of us satisfied and exhausted. I fell asleep with my head on his chest and his arm around me.

"Did your family come to your wedding?" I asked the next morning while we lay in bed.

"Huh?"

"Did they come to your wedding?" I asked again.

"Oh, yeah, they did. But it was like this whole production, so big that I can't even remember them being there. I mean, they were in the pictures, but for real, it didn't even feel like a wedding. Shit, it didn't even feel like a marriage." He sighed.

"Why? Weren't y'all together for a while before you got married?"

"Yeah, we were, but, man, most of the time while we were dating, I was on the road. We dated two years before I proposed, but I didn't really know her. I don't think I ever did.

"Don't get me wrong, she was cool, but I think I loved her ambition more than I loved her. This chick was determined and driven. I liked that about her. And she made me feel like we were gonna be this amazing team. She had the plans, and I had the finances. It made sense. So, we opened Amelia's, and she was right. It was a hit," he said.

"*The* Amelia's?" I asked, realizing he was talking about one of the hottest restaurants in the Southeast, where the "who's who" in sports, music, and media dined.

"Yep, that Amelia's."

"Wow."

"So, I poured everything into making her dreams come true, and she shitted on me. Now she's about to open her second location with the divorce settlement and marry the love of her life. And I have . . . nothing."

I touched the side of his face and said, "That's not true. You have a life and the same opportunity to live your own dreams and make them come true. Her leaving you was probably the best thing that happened to you, because you don't have to live on her terms or follow the plans she has. You can make your own plans."

As I said the words, I realized that they weren't just for him, but for me too.

"Remember when I told you that Var and I broke up when I found out he had a baby with someone else?"

"Yeah." Josh nodded.

"I found out right after I'd had a miscarriage. It was the most heartbreaking moments of my life, and I felt like I had nothing else to lose. Until I lost my job," I said.

Josh kissed the top of my head and said, "Zen, I'm so sorry."

"But now I realize that if all of that hadn't happened, I would be married and have a baby with a cheater, working at a job I hated because he wanted me to work there, living in a house I didn't want to live in. And knowing me, I probably wouldn't want to leave because I would have stayed to keep my family together."

"That's deep. So, I guess we should both be glad that we're losers, huh?" he asked.

"The biggest." I laughed and kissed him.

Later that day, I drove to Var's house to get my keys. I sent him a text to let him know I was there, and then waited by the car for him to come out of the house.

"You could've come inside, Zen," he said.

"I'm good," I told him.

"Whose car is this?"

"It's a rental. Can I get my keys, please?" I stood straight with my hand held out.

"You didn't have to get a rental. You know I'm not keeping your car. You can take it."

"It's not my car, Var. It's yours. You made that clear yesterday, and you were right. I should've given it back to you a long time ago. I don't know why I didn't. Wait, that's a lie. I do know why."

"I know why too, Zen. It's because you know deep down we're supposed to be together," he said.

I shook my head. "No, that's not why. It's because I was too afraid to let go of you, of us, completely. I think that having this car was like a security blanket that made me feel like I still had you if I needed you."

"You know I'm there for you, Zen."

"No, Var, you're not. You proved that yesterday. And I'm glad you did, because you know what I realized? I was miserable for a long time when I was with you. I thought going back to school and taking that job and putting away those things that I loved to do was important because, as you put it, you were helping me be the best me I could be."

"And that's right. You know I encouraged you to be better, Zen, because I love you."

"No, you controlled me. You never supported me and the things I wanted to do. Never. But this isn't about you. It's about me. Because despite not having what you call a good job, and living with my best friend, I am the happiest I've ever been. I'm finally able to follow my dreams and pursue goals that I know will make me the best me I want to be, not the me someone else wants. So, Var, you can keep your car. But first, give me my keys so I can get my stuff out," I told him.

"So, it's like that?" He shoved the keys at me. I ignored his hostility and thanked him as I took them out of his hand. I cleared everything that belonged to me out of the car and then took his key off and gave it back to him.

"It doesn't have to be like this, Zen. I swear, I'm sorry," he pleaded.

I looked at him and smiled. "It's okay, Var. Like I told a friend of mine, God has a way of taking things away from us to make room for something better. We'll both be fine."

Var sat in the driver's seat and pulled down the visor. A card fell out, and he handed it to me. "You forgot this."

I looked at the card and saw that it was the number of an attorney. It was the card Tam had given me, encouraging me to call. I assumed it was the lawyer who had helped her win a settlement from the realty firm. I took it from him and tucked it into my pocket, just in case someday I decided to give her a call. After all, I didn't have anything to lose, did I?

Epilogue

"Zen, I gotta say, you outdid yourself with this house," Bailey said as she walked into the kitchen where Georgette and I were taking tops off trays of appetizers that the caterer had dropped off.

"Isn't everything gorgeous?" Georgette grinned. "I walked in, and it took my breath away. She and Josh refused to let me see it until today."

"Well, it wasn't just me. It was Caldwell too," I told her.

"Where is Caldwell? I didn't see him," Bailey said.

"He's in the backyard with Josh. They're grilling," I told her.

"You guys need any help?" Bailey offered.

"Sure, wash up and grab a tray and bring it on out," Georgette told her, picking up a tray of fruit and heading to the backyard, where a tent and tables had already been set up, along with a deejay. It was a gorgeous day, and people had already started arriving.

"Well, she sure is pleased. I'll bet you a hundred bucks you're gonna get a hefty bonus. You did a hell of a job on this house—and her son," Bailey teased.

"Stop it. I'm just glad we got everything finished in time."

"I don't know why you were worried. Y'all have been working nonstop. Unless y'all were working on something else that you ain't tell me about." She winked.

"Shut up. And Caldwell was putting in just as many hours here as we were. We all wanted to make this party happen for Georgette."

"Well, bestie, it looks great, and you did an amazing job. I'm proud of you," she said, picking up a veggie tray.

"I'm glad you think so, considering that now that it's finished, I'm back to working at Loehmann's. So, I'm gonna have to have my rent reduced until I come across another design job." I laughed, picking up a tray, and we both headed in the same direction as Georgette.

"Hey, pretty lady." Josh greeted me when I stepped out the back door.

"Are you speaking to me or her?" I teased, winking at him.

"Clearly, he's talking to me," Bailey said. "Hey, Josh. The house looks great."

"*Hola, mami. Qué hace una estrella volando tan bajo?*" Caldwell winked at Bailey.

"I don't know what the hell that means, Caldwell. It better not be nasty or I'm gonna punch you in your throat," she warned him half-jokingly.

The party was a major success, and I was able to meet lots of Josh and Georgette's family members and friends, many of whom were excited that Josh was home.

"This is more like a welcome home party for you than a housewarming for the house," I told him as we danced. "For someone who didn't wanna be back here, it looks like you're enjoying yourself."

"I am," he said happily. "I think that has a lot to do with you, too. But we'll discuss that later. I've got a surprise for you."

"What is it?"

"You'll see."

I became nervous, wondering what the surprise could be.

"Josh! Hey there." Tam sauntered over and hugged him. Another woman, looking like her minus the plastic surgery, stood nearby. "This is my sister, Jeri."

"Nice to meet you, Jeri."

"Same here. My sister was right. This place is incredible. I love what you've done with it."

"That wasn't me. That was Zen. She's the designer." He walked over and stood beside me, "Oh, and Caldwell, the contractor, is over there."

"Well, kudos to you all. I'd love to sit down and discuss some business with you when you get a free moment. I know Tam has told you I'm interested in listing the property when you're ready," Jeri said.

"Yeah, we talked about that, but I actually already have a realtor I'm working with right now," Josh said.

My jaw dropped, and I was unable to move for a second, stunned. I excused myself and went inside, going up the stairs into the master bedroom, where I sat down and cried. All the work we had done, the time we spent, the progress we made, and Josh was still selling the house. And he hadn't even mentioned it, not one word. Something told me he hadn't mentioned anything to his mother, either.

"Zen, are you okay?" Georgette tapped on the open door.

"Oh, I'm fine," I said, wiping my tears.

"What's wrong?" she asked.

I was about to say "nothing," but instead, I told her, "He's selling the house."

"Who's selling what house?"

"Josh. He's selling this one. He's already working with an agent to list it. I tried to talk him out of it, and I thought he changed his mind, but he didn't."

The look of concern turned to one of pain, and now, she began crying. I hugged her, and we cried together.

"What the hell is going on? Why are y'all up here crying?" Josh walked in.

"Don't use that language with me, Joshua," Georgette snapped at him and stood up.

"I'm sorry, Mom. But what's wrong? What happened?"

"I can't believe you," she whispered.

"What is she talking about?" He turned to me.

"I told her about you selling the house."

"What? Why would you tell her that?" he asked.

"Because she needed to know. I didn't want her to drive over here and see a For Sale sign in the yard. I have too much respect for her, unlike you, so I told her what you're doing," I snapped.

"Okay, I don't know where all of this is coming from, but I think there's been some kind of mix-up. I'm not selling this house."

Both Georgette and I stared at him, now even more confused.

"You're not? But you told Tam's sister that you're working with a realtor already."

"I am. I'm buying another house."

"Another house, Joshua? You're going to have that expensive apartment and this house already."

"An investment property that I'm going to remodel." He smiled at me. "I'm gonna live here in this house while my team and I flip the other one."

I smiled at him and said, "You and your team?"

He nodded and pulled me up off the bed. "Yeah, I got an amazing team that I work with. Caldwell, of course, and a talented young designer that I came across."

"Oh, Joshua, that's wonderful news." Georgette clapped. "Your father would be so proud. And Ephraim."

"Yeah, I think they would." He nodded. "I guess it took losing the both of them to show me what I really needed. So, you ready to work?"

"I can't think of a better loser to work for than you," I said, feeling full of joy and hope.

Lusting for a Big Girl
A Full Figured Story

By

C. N. Phillips

Girls with the most beautiful hearts always seem to have the most insecurities. They say that it is about what's on the inside, but how can that be true when the outside is what the world sees first?

Chapter 1

Teeka

The soft crooning of Eric Bellinger filled a large, candlelit bedroom, and soft moans acted as ad libs to the music. Clothing was strewn about the floor like bread crumbs leading to the king-sized bed, taken off by someone in a rush. The bed was moving in a way that only a man making love to a woman could make it move. One final scream of pleasure entered the atmosphere before the bumping and grinding stopped.

Teeka Smith lay on her back and tried to catch her breath after the ride Keelan Metoyer had just taken her on. She swore she could see stars—or maybe that was just the shadow of candle flames dancing on the walls. Her eyes locked with his as he lay nestled between her legs, trying to steady his breathing. Her soft hand found its way to his cheek, and she stroked it tenderly.

"I love you," she said, staring intensely at him. "The things you do to me, and the way you made me feel . . . I don't want to get that anywhere else."

Tiny beads of sweat rested at his temples. His hair was cut into a brush cut with waves so deep that Teeka wanted to dive in them. She was addicted to everything about him, from his mind all the way down to his sexy, muscular body. He had a tattoo across his chest of a brick underpass with graffiti spray-painted all over it. She traced it with her fingers every time they made love. In that moment, she used it as a getaway from his gaze.

She'd finally done it. She'd finally told him how she really felt about him.

She heard him sigh and felt him remove himself from inside of her. The bed dipped beside her, and he lay on his side, facing her. His hands fondled her D-sized breasts and pinched her brown nipples.

"I thought we said we weren't going to do that," he said. "That catching feelings would make things complicated."

"But that was seven months ago." Her voice was soft when she spoke.

"And I still feel the same way now as I did then."

She honestly hadn't known what kind of response to expect from him. She had hoped for something good, though. His bluntness almost made her speechless, but she still wanted clarification.

"So, you don't feel the same way?"

"I mean, we're cool," he said. "The sex is great and we vibe, but I never really thought about making you my girl or nothing. If that's what you're asking."

"Oh."

"I'm sorry, T. K. I'm not trying to hurt your feelings or anything. I just thought we both understood what this was. I'm about to hop in the shower, all right?"

"Okay."

She didn't know what else to say. She watched him get up from the bed, watched him go to his closet to grab towels, and she watched him head toward the master bathroom. Her eyes scanned over his body—his in-shape body. Fitness was a big thing to him, and he was cut everywhere that he could be. Teeka blinked, coming out of her daze, and sat up on the bed.

"Keelan," she said right before he shut the bathroom door.

"What's up, T. K.?" he said, looking back at her.

"Is it . . . is it because I'm a big girl that you won't be with me?"

"What?"

"I know what our arrangement was, but after all of this time, you mean to tell me that you don't feel anything for me?"

"Of course I do, but why complicate things?"

"What would be complicated? We're both adults, we both make good money, and like you said, we vibe. The sex is great. Everything is there. The only thing that could possibly stand in the way is my weight. I'm good enough to fuck, but not be with. Is that it?"

Keelan sighed, and his eyes graced the ceiling before he turned them back on Teeka. He opened his mouth to speak, but then stopped, seeming like he changed his mind.

"I don't want to hurt you, Teeka."

"I want you to be honest with me," she said, clutching his burgundy satin sheets to her chest. "You speak your mind any other time, so why not now?"

"Okay then," he said. "Here it is. You are a pretty woman, but I like my women fit and smaller. I want my woman to be a reflection of me because I want her to look good by my side. I don't care to hear people saying 'Keelan got himself a big girl." And I also think it would be selfish of me to ask you to change yourself for me. So, to answer your question in your own words . . . yes. Yes, you are good enough to fuck but not be my woman. But that does not mean you aren't a good woman. After tonight, and after me saying all of this, I completely understand if you don't want to see me at all anymore."

Teeka had wanted him to be honest, but she didn't think his honesty would crush her the way that it did. She was sure that her hurt read all over her face, because she had felt it drop, but she held in her tears.

"Thank you for your honesty," she whispered and lowered her eyes to the bed. "You can get in the shower now."

"T. K.—"

"You've said everything that you needed to say. Now please, shut the door so that I can get dressed. I don't want you to have to look at any of my rolls. How rude of me would that be?"

She heard Keelan groan, but he must have known not to say anything else because the next thing she knew, she heard the door shut. She was glad, too, because she couldn't hold the tears back any longer. Her brown cheeks were wet, and her eyesight was blurry as she hurried to get dressed. The shower water hadn't even been on for a full two minutes when she made a beeline for the front door of his condo.

She could still feel the moistness between her legs as she made her way to the elevator that led to the parking garage. Her shirt was on backward, but she didn't care. It was almost midnight. She doubted anyone would see her leaving.

Ding!

The elevator doors opened up, and she instantly spotted her cherry red 2008 Ford Focus a little ways away. All she wanted to do was get home and soak in the tub. She knew it wouldn't wash her hurt away, but it would soothe the pain a little. She hoped so, anyway.

He doesn't want to be with me because I'm fat, she thought on the ride home. *Why does this always happen to me? Why come onto me in the first place? I was the same size back then that I am now.*

The reason it hurt so bad was that it was an already existing wound cut open all over again. For as long as she could remember, Teeka had been bigger than most of the women around her. When she was younger, she was a round, plump girl. When she became an adult, her mother would always say that she wasn't fat, she was a full-figured woman. Although her body had an hourglass shape and she had a big bottom that sat up, Teeka weighed a little under two hundred pounds. Her stomach didn't poke out too much anymore, but there was definitely still a pouch there. She had a pretty, heart-shaped face with full lips and doe-shaped brown eyes, with eyelashes so long that they looked like extensions. Men often told her how beautiful she was to them, and she believed them—until they got between her legs and stopped calling. No matter what, things always ended the same. She was the girl no one wanted to take home to their parents and friends.

There was one thing that Keelan had said that was correct, though. Despite her horrible dating track record, she was happy with her life. She loved everything about herself, including every roll and every curve. There had been times where she hit the gym and tried to lose weight, but whenever she looked in a mirror, there was nothing about herself that she wanted to change. She accepted who she was inside and out.

Still, that didn't make Keelan's words hurt any less.

When she finally got home to her one-bedroom apartment, she stripped out of her jeans and blouse so that she could take a shower. At first, she wanted to take a bath, but there was something about feeling the hot water spilling down her body that calmed her nerves. The sound of the water running and the steam building up around her made her get lost in her own mind. She thought back to when she'd first seen Keelan at her job, and how handsome he was. He was an executive at the law firm where she was a secretary. She hated that the memory was still so fresh in her mind—so fresh that she could still smell the cologne he was wearing. . . .

***

"Acqua Di Gio?" Teeka's voice came out confident as she stood behind the new guy.

"Excuse me?" He turned around to face her.

Teeka had just entered the large breakroom to grab a water bottle and some coffee the way she did at the beginning of every work day. She was wearing her best cream-colored, skinny-leg pantsuit with a pair of three-inch red pumps. The room was usually empty because she was often the first one in the office, but that day, she was surprised to see a tall figure looming over one of the Keurig machines. He was wearing a crisp navy blue suit and rocking a fresh haircut. When she approached the counter, she got a whiff of his cologne, and she instantly smiled because it was one of her favorites.

"Your cologne. It's Acqua Di Gio, right?" she repeated herself with a smile. "I'm sorry, it's just one of my favorites."

"No, you're good," he said, returning her smile. Lord, was that man fine. "But yes, you're correct. It was a gift from my parents last Christmas. I just found it, actually, in the move."

"Oh, that's right. I heard Mr. O'Brian saying that you weren't from Chicago," she said, mentioning her boss's name.

"Steve is your boss?" he asked. "So that must mean you're a—"

"Secretary," she finished so he wouldn't guess incorrectly. "I was on my lunch when you started on Monday, so we weren't properly introduced. Keelan Metoyer, right? I'm Teeka."

She held her hand out so that he could shake it. One thing that Teeka had never been was shy. She used to get picked on a lot in school, but she figured a way to get a grip on it was communication. She made sure that she was friendly with everyone. That way, no matter what *happened, she was never the bad guy in any situation. Right then and there, she just saw a fine man who she wanted to talk to, so she did. She wouldn't let her physique stop her from doing anything that she wanted to do.*

She liked how his eyes stayed on her face instead of roaming her body. She was all too used to that when it came to men. She was voluptuous; she knew that. But she was still a person, not an object.

"Well, it's very nice to meet you, Teeka. Now that I'm seeing you, I wish I would have met you on Monday."

Teeka wasn't sure what he meant by that comment, but she didn't think he was flirting. Or maybe he was and she was just being naïve about it. His eyes may not have trailed her body, but the moment he turned his attention back to the Keurig machine, Teeka's eyes were all over him. Her eyes stopped at his ring finger, and she smirked to herself when she saw that nothing was there.

"Something funny?"

Dammit. He'd caught her staring at him.

"Oh, no." She shook her head and walked over to the stainless steel refrigerator. "I was just thinking to myself."

"What were you thinking?"

She grabbed one of the many water bottles on the fridge door before closing it. She tried to form her thoughts to words, but when she looked back at him, she had nothing. He was watching her curiously, waiting for her next move. She wondered if he'd seen her staring at his tight butt.

"I was wondering where you came from and . . . and if you left a family behind, I guess. I'm sorry if that's overstepping my boundaries. I know you don't know me like that."

"No, it's fine. You'd be surprised how many times I get that inquiry, actually." He chuckled. *"No, I am not married, and no, I don't have any children. I'm twenty-nine, from Milwaukee, but after receiving this job offer, I realized it was time for a fresh start somewhere new."*

"Well, we're all glad to have you here, Mr. Metoyer," Teeka said and started out the door. *"Have a good day! I need to go get started on some of Mr. O'Brian's files before he gets here."*

"All right. And, Teeka?"

She paused to look over her shoulder. *"Yes?"*

"You can call me Keelan."

Teeka snapped back to the present and realized that her trip down memory lane had lasted longer than she thought. The hot water that had once spouted from the shower head was now barely warm. She washed up and got out of the shower. The silk sheets on her queen-sized bed were calling her name. She dried off and applied lotion to her body before climbing nude into her bed.

The clock read a little before two in the morning, and she had half a mind to call her best friend, Lynne, and wake her up. Teeka decided to wait to bother her with the tea tomorrow. All she wanted to do then was close her eyes and pretend that nothing bad had happened that night. Of course, it was easier said than done, because Keelan Metoyer plagued her dreams all night long.

When you break someone's heart and destroy them on the inside, you lose the right to say that you care about their well-being. You don't get to wonder how they are doing now and if they are okay, because if it was genuine, then you would not have hurt them in the first place.

Chapter 2

Keelan

He couldn't get the look on Teeka's face out of his mind when he shut the bathroom door behind him. She was sitting on his bed, not even looking at him. He could tell that she had been biting back her tears, and he fought the urge to go and console her. Things were complicated, and he didn't want to make them any more so.

She didn't need to tell him that she loved him. He already knew that. He could tell by the way she let him fuck her however he liked. He could tell by the way she always checked on him mentally, physically, and emotionally. Not only was she his friend, but she was his confident, and he felt like the lowest piece of shit on the earth.

He stood in the bathroom, knowing she was right outside the door dying inside. He stared at himself in the mirror and felt shame. How could he have made her feel that way about herself? Who was he fooling? He loved everything about that woman. From the first day he met her, the confidence she had turned him on in ways unimaginable. She was everything that he wasn't, and normally that would make them polar opposites, but it actually acted as the glue between them. He'd never laughed so hard in his life than when he was with her. Nor had he ever cum so hard when he had sex with anyone else.

At first it was only about the sex. He was new in town, and he just wanted a body to keep him warm at night. If he had known that he was going to fall in love with her, he would have left her where he found her.

Of course, he'd noticed her size, but that didn't change how he felt about her. Now, when she brought it up, he used it as his way out. He needed a way out. Things had gotten too deep. That night, for example, he'd gone out of his way to make her a candlelit dinner and made love to her using only the flames as light. Why wouldn't she tell him she loved him? He had gone out of his way to be romantic, and he didn't even have to. A piece of him wanted her to say it, but why, if he knew that she couldn't have him?

He turned on the water to the shower, and not even two minutes later, he heard the front door slam shut.

"Shit," he cursed himself.

He wished he would have just been honest with Teeka from the beginning. Instead of striking a deal to not catch feelings, he should have just told her why he couldn't. He should have just told her the truth about himself.

One of the first questions she'd asked him when they first met was if he had a wife, and he said no. That was the truth. He didn't have a wife . . . yet. He did, however, have a fiancée. Alecia Clout had been his college sweetheart, and the two of them had been together for so long it seemed like marriage was the only step in their relationship to conquer. He loved her, and for the most part, she fit his life perfectly. She was gorgeous, smart, fit, and shared a lot of the same goals and aspirations as him. Right before he left, the two of them had gotten into a big fight because she felt he wasn't applying himself.

"What did you go to school to get your master's degree for, Keelan? To be some white man's flunky for the rest

of your life?" she said when she found out that he was thinking about accepted the job in Chicago. "What about the job offer here? The one my daddy offered you at his firm downtown? You'd be making twice as much as you would in Chicago. Think about our futures for once."

"I don't want to live my life chasing money," he told her. "I want to chase happiness. Yes, I would have a big office overlooking the city, and the money would be great, but the stress of that position would make me hate getting up in the morning every day. We aren't hurting for money right now. We don't have any children yet. I just want to enjoy the next few years of my life, because when we get married, it all stops."

That was the mistake he'd made.

"Oh! So, when we get married you're not going to enjoy your life anymore? Is that what you're telling me?"

"No! That's not what I meant."

"Well, that's what you said."

"Alecia . . ."

"Don't Alecia me! Especially when you keep doing things to upset me!"

"So, me wanting to be happy upsets you?"

"Yes! I mean no! The way you're going about it upsets me. Daddy keeps telling me I'm making a mistake marrying you, but I keep telling him how much of a standup man you are."

"I don't give a damn what your father thinks about me. And I don't need you to defend me to him either. I just need you here by my side because I've already made up my mind. I'm taking the job in Chicago."

"And that's it? No discussion, no nothing. What about me? Did you think about the life I would have to pick up here?"

"You, too, went to school to get your masters, didn't you?" Keelan asked. "And now you're comfortable

working for your father's Fortune five hundred company. Well, I don't want to work for your father, so that's not an option for me. You act like you couldn't find work in Chicago."

"He's my father, Keelan!"

"And I'm your man. But the next move is yours, because like I said, I've already made my decision."

"Then I guess you'll be going to Chicago alone."

It wasn't what he wanted. He wanted Alecia to come with him so they could start a new life together, but she was so wrapped around her father's finger at the time that she hadn't seen the good in the opportunity at hand. The two never officially broke it off, and neither had cancelled the wedding, but Keelan felt as if they were on a much-needed break. And that's where Teeka came into the picture.

He had never been the player type, nor did he ever expect himself, of all people, to be in love with two women at once, but here he was. Then, when Alecia told him that she was ready to make the move to Chicago to make it work between them, he knew the right thing to do was to cut things off between him and Teeka. Still, why did he feel so bad about it? He figured either way, Teeka would be hurt, but telling her the truth was just too hard to do.

He stayed in the shower, trying to level his thoughts for almost an hour. When he got out, of course Teeka was gone, but the smell of her sex still lingered in the air. He went to lock the front door and thought about calling to make sure she'd gotten home okay. His plan had been for her to stay the night, but after what he'd said, she probably couldn't wait to get out of his presence.

He put on a white wife beater and a pair of Ralph Lauren briefs before he fell into his bed. His nose instantly smelled the Carol's Daughter hair milk that he'd just bought Teeka in his pillowcase. He made a mental note to wash his bedding before Alecia—

Bzzzzz! Bzzzz! Bzzzz! Bzzzz!

His phone vibrated violently on the mahogany nightstand next to his bed. He hoped that it was Teeka calling him, but of course it wasn't. After all, what could she have to say to him?

"Hey, baby," he answered after checking the caller ID. "I would have thought you'd be 'sleep by now."

"Hi, lovebug." Alecia called him the nickname she'd given him in college. Her voice was sweet as honey, and she sounded genuinely happy to talk to him. "I couldn't sleep. I'm surrounded by all of these boxes, and I just keep thinking about how excited I am to see you, baby. I can't wait for my life to go back to normal. This house has been so empty without you. Seeing you two times a month just doesn't suffice."

"I know, baby. These two weeks are going to fly by."

In two weeks, Alecia would be moving to Chicago. In one month, the two of them would be married. The reminder made him feel even more like shit because he was truly living a double life. Teeka had thought that the monthly trips to Milwaukee were to see his family. What she didn't know was that that was only partly true. He and Alecia had been working on mending the broken pieces of their relationship and had decided to go forward with the wedding. For a month, he had been trying to figure out how he would break things off with Teeka, but it had been so hard. Now, he didn't have a choice.

"So, about that . . ." Alecia's voice carried on mischievously, and Keelan raised his eyebrow.

"About what?"

"The two weeks thing. I can't do it. I decided that I'm coming tomorrow!"

"T–tomorrow, tomorrow? As in the day after today?"

"Well, technically today, since it's past midnight. I was going to surprise you, but I couldn't hold in my excitement. Plus, I need you to pick me up from the airport."

She giggled in Keelan's ear, but he barely heard it. He was at a loss for words. *Tomorrow?* He thought he would have two more weeks to prepare. Guess not.

"That sounds good, baby," he replied quickly so she wouldn't think anything was wrong. "What about your things, though?"

"Oh, my daddy is going to have it all sent. I'll bring what I need until then. I can't wait to see your place and for you to show me where you work."

"Where I work?"

"Yes! I want to see the company you love so much! ETCO Enterprises has definitely made some waves on the market. I'm so sorry that I didn't support your business venture, baby, but I promise to do so from here on out."

"You want to see where I work?" he asked again just to make sure he'd heard her right.

"Yes, silly! I guess I'll have to wait until Monday, since tomorrow is Saturday, but yes, I want to know all about your Chicago life."

Damn, he thought.

If Teeka thought he was a dog after that night, she would definitely think he was one after Monday. Oh well, though. She was his past, and she would have to stay there in order for him to have a real future with Alecia, right?

Lying is often done with words, but it can also be done with silence.

Chapter 3

Teeka

"He said *what*?"

Lynne's voice was so loud that Teeka had to look around and make sure no one saw her on the phone at her desk. Most of the executives were at a meeting, so her floor was pretty much vacant. Lynne's outburst was over the top, but she had a reason to respond the way she did. Teeka had finally caught her up on what transpired on Friday, and she didn't leave out any detail.

"He basically told me that I'm too fat for him to be with," she confirmed.

"But, bitch, you've been the same size since he met you!"

"Exactly, girl. My feelings were so hurt. Still are, to be honest."

"And you have to work with that greasy motherfucker. You want me to come put some detergent in his tank? He still drives that nice Mercedes, right?"

Teeka found herself smiling. She and Lynne had been best friends since elementary school, and Lynne did not play when it came to her. She definitely had that no-nonsense Chicago attitude, and she was about it. Granted, they were adults now, but Lynne would throw down with anyone for disrespecting her, and Teeka had yet to see her lose a fight. She fought most of Teeka's battles growing up whenever kids teased her. Honestly, if it weren't for Lynne, the teasing probably would have never stopped. They were ride or die, and Teeka would go around the world and back for their friendship.

"Yes, he still drives the Mercedes, but no, I don't want you to put anything in the tank. I am not trying to use my savings to get your ass up out of jail."

"You're right, but hey, if you change your mind, the offer is still on the table."

"I just can't believe he said that to me. I mean, I know we agreed to not catch feelings, but come on. The man has been basically wining and dining me for seven months, and we've just been masking it as friendly outings. Still, what did we expect to come from it?"

"I don't know. Something isn't adding up. I think he's covering up something, girl. What made him say that in the first place?"

"Well, like I said, I finally told him I loved him, and he basically brushed that off."

"So, he didn't say that he *doesn't* love you?"

"I mean, basically. And then I asked him if the reason why he won't be with me is because I'm fat."

"See, that's the problem."

"What do you mean, that's the problem?"

"You gave him an option. Girl, you know these men blame their stupidity on any and everything, and you gave him a scapegoat. Shit, if that's what you already think the problem is, why not just go with it?"

"So, are you saying that my weight isn't the problem?" Teeka asked, growing more confused by the second.

"What I'm saying is I've seen the way that man looks at you. He doesn't care about them extra pounds. He probably got a bitch somewhere in the cut."

"No." Teeka shook her head, dismissing the possibility. "That's not possible. I'm literally with him five days a week, and whenever I call him, he answers. Whenever I need him, he's there."

"Okay, let's back up a second. Y'all both agreed to not catch feelings, right?"

"Yes."

"But everything you've told me shows that there are feelings on both sides. I think he's just scared. You know how men get when they get something real. Their first thought is to run. Most of them say hurtful things to push you away. That way they don't have to be held accountable for a failed relationship. It's hard for men to let women be close to them. Just like we are scared to get our hearts broken, they are the same way."

"Look at you," Teeka joked, playing with one of her long, natural curls. "Sounding like you know what you're talking about!"

"I grew up with all boys. I learned a li'l something by being around those idiots all day." Lynne and Teeka shared a laugh. "But no, seriously, sis, I think you need to put that shit he said to the furthest part of your mind and figure out what the real issue is, because it's not your weight. Girl, you may not be small, but you got it going on. I would love to have your hips and ass, okay?"

Teeka heard the elevator opening down the hallway, and she knew someone was coming. She didn't know who it was, but the last thing she wanted was for Mr. O'Brian to see her taking personal calls while still on his clock.

"Girl, somebody is coming," she said in a hushed tone. "I'm going to call you back on my lunch break. Actually, I'm just going to stop by when I'm off. You're off at five today, right?"

"Yup. Just stop on by."

"All right. Love you! Bye."

Teeka disconnected the call just as she heard heels stabbing the marble floor. She looked up not to see Mr. O'Brian, but a woman so beautiful it was like she'd just stepped off a *Vogue* cover. She was slender, with a Coke bottle shape and golden brown skin. Her face was beat to the gods, and her hair extensions had pretty curls that bounced when she walked. She wore a red blazer over a white blouse and rocked slightly baggy navy blue trousers. Teeka's eyes set on the Chanel bag resting on her arm, and she admired it for a second before the woman stopped at the front desk. She gave Teeka the brightest smile that she could with her perfect teeth and raised cheekbones.

"Good afternoon. Oh, my goodness! I love your hair. I wish mine would curl like that," the woman said to Teeka, who was still stuck wondering who the model in her lobby was.

"T—thank you! I just throw water on it most of the time." Teeka returned the woman's smile. She had a familiar accent. "Do you have an appointment for a consultation?"

"No, I don't actually. I came up here to have lunch with my fiancé. He told me he would be outside at noon, but here we are ten minutes past that. I was just making sure everything was okay."

"Oh, no worries," Teeka said, checking a few things on her computer monitors. "The executives are upstairs in a meeting, and sometimes they run a little longer than usual. If you'd like to, you can wait in the lobby. I'm sure they'll be right out."

Teeka motioned to the lobby, where a few other clients were waiting. The woman glanced quickly over in the direction that Teeka was pointing before turning her attention back to Teeka's desk.

"Thank you so much—Teeka? Did I say that right?"

"Yes, you did."

"Perfect. I'll wait for him. Before I do that, is there a little girls' room that I can use?"

"Yes, right down the hall you came from, but to the right. You can't miss it."

"You are a doll. Thank you!"

Teeka smiled to herself when the woman walked away. She wished all women were as pleasant when she first met them. She wondered who the lucky man was. The woman looked like she was rolling in money.

A few minutes later, Teeka heard the chatter of a big group coming from one of the back meeting rooms. She instantly sat up straight and pretended to be doing something. Mr. O'Brian paid her well, more than what a secretary should make, and she didn't want to seem like she was slacking. He'd been good friends with her father before he died of colon cancer five years ago. His wife and Teeka's mother were the best of friends as well. When Teeka graduated college and couldn't find a job in her career field, Steve gave her a job at his company making the same amount she would have if she had gotten a job with her degree. He always said it was the least he could do. The only thing he asked of her was to perform well and call him Mr. O'Brian at work.

"Teeka, you look lovely today. Yellow has always been your color. Hard at work as usual?" His pleasant voice boomed as he approached her desk.

"Yes, of course!" She smiled up into his pale face and winked. "Aren't I always?"

"Uh-huh." He chuckled. "Silly, just like that dad of yours. But as long as you get your work done, I don't care how you do it. Did you tell your mother what Sandy said?"

"Yes, I did," Teeka said and shook her head. "I don't see why they make us play messenger when they're together like four times a week."

"That has been a mystery to me for years now," Mr. O'Brian said. "I think they're both just trying to make sure that the two of us are really at work."

"That must be it." She giggled. "But your twelve o'clock has been in the lobby waiting for you. Here is his casework. I think he's just here to sign off on some paperwork about his settlement."

"Perfect. I'm going to my office. You can buzz him on back."

"Great," Teeka said and activated the buzzer in the man's hand once Mr. O'Brian walked away from the desk. When the redheaded man brought the buzzer back to her, she took it and stood up. "Right this way. Mr. O'Brian apologizes for the delay, Stanley, but he's been looking forward to seeing you."

She used her access badge to take him through a door behind her desk that led them to a long hallway filled with the offices of the higher-ups. Mr. O'Brian's was at the very end of the hall, and of course, was the largest. The door was already open, and when Stanley walked through it, she shut it behind him.

On her way back to her desk, she hoped that she had missed Keelan and that he'd made his way to his office. Normally, he would stop at her desk around that time and ask if she wanted to get a bite to eat, but hopefully he knew not to do that today. But of course, that was too much like right. When she opened the access-only door, sure enough, there he was.

"Look, Keelan. I—"

She stopped mid-sentence because as she got closer to him, she could see that he was not alone. He was having a conversation with someone in front of her desk. That someone happened to be the woman who had been looking for her man.

When they heard her voice, they both stopped and glanced over in her direction. Once the woman saw Teeka, she gave her a big smile. "Teeka! I came back to ask you what it is you use in your hair. My honey here"—she placed a hand casually on Keelan's arm—"has been trying to talk me into going natural for months, and

I've been thinking about it, but I want my hair to look as lovely as yours."

A fist closed on Teeka's chest and stopped oxygen from getting to her lungs. Not really, but that's what it sure felt like. Keelan avoided her eye contact. He stood there in his tan Tom Ford two-button suit that she loved so much, looking as guilty as a kid who'd just been caught stealing in a candy store.

He is her fiancé? Fiancé? He had a woman the whole time? She took a deep breath and tried to save face.

"C–Carol's Daughter," Teeka said and cleared her throat. "A really good friend of mine bought it as a gift, and I've been using it ever since."

"Thank you!"

"You're welcome—I'm sorry, I never got your name."

"Alecia Clout, soon to be Alecia Metoyer." She smiled big and threw her hand out so that Teeka could see her ring. "We're making it official next month."

"W–wow." Teeka's eyebrows raised at the size of the ring. "That is a gorgeous rock. And next month? How long have you two been together?"

"Since our college days." Alecia leaned into Keelan and kissed him on his cheek tenderly—the same way Teeka would when she sat next to him while they caught up on their favorite shows. "He moved to Chicago almost eight months ago for work, and I've finally made it out here to join him. My father is the CEO of a firm similar to this one in Milwaukee. He's looking into buying shares at ETCO and maybe even start a merger."

"So, you two were college sweethearts," Teeka said out loud, more for herself than anyone else. "Wow. That is a beautiful story. I wish you both . . . the best of luck. Any man would be lucky to have someone as beautiful and *fit* as you to be their wife."

"Thank you. Come on, honey, I'm starving! Plus, I wanted to show you a few venues I have in mind for the wedding. Have a good day, Teeka!" she said.

"You too." Teeka clenched her jaw and sat back at her desk. She refused to look at him. How could he do that to her? How could he lie to her about something so big and for so long? She was surprised by how well she had handled the situation, because her insides were telling her to blow up and cause a scene. She kept her eyes on the computer in front of her and waited for them to leave. The tears were coming, she could feel them. She just needed to hold them for a few more minutes.

"Go pull the car around front, baby. I'll be out in a second. I need to grab something from my office," Keelan said.

"Okay, but hurry."

There were a few seconds of silence, and then Teeka heard the elevator ding. She could feel his eyes burning a hole in the side of her face.

"Teeka . . ." he started.

"I have those caseloads for you, Mr. Metoyer. They'll be on your desk when you come back."

"Teeka, please let me explain."

"I'm sorry." She blinked the tears in the corner of her eyes away to nonexistence. "Explain what? How to print out the cases? I know how to do my job, Mr. Metoyer."

"Don't be like that. I didn't mean for any of this to happen, and I didn't want you to find out this way."

"Find out what? That you have a beautiful, *thin,* and rich fiancée?" She laughed to herself. "I can't believe I—"

Fell for you, she finished in her head.

"I wanted to tell you, but I didn't know how."

"I don't see how hard it could have been. Especially if you wanted things between us to be just sex. That was a sure way to keep it like that or end things completely."

"It's complicated ,Teeka."

"Obviously not too complicated. You got what you wanted from me for seven months. I was just the fill-in girl until your princess got into town. It all makes sense now." She shook her head.

"T. K."

When she heard him call her by her nickname, she couldn't stop the surge of anger that overcame her. "Don't." She put her hand up, finally looking at him. She glared into his eyes. "Don't call me anything but Teeka. Honestly, you don't even need to speak to me. And if it is about work, you can e-mail it. I never knew you, and you never knew me, okay?"

"No, not okay," he said with a clenched jaw. "I want to explain everything to you, and you're going to let me. I'll be at your house at eight o'clock tonight. Please be there."

"Bye, Keelan. *Baby* is in the car waiting for you."

"Eight o'clock, Teeka."

He didn't wait for whatever smart remark was bound to come out of her mouth next. He turned and walked down the hallway, leaving Teeka more confused than she was before.

Know this: I am addicted to you. I have tasted your mind and cannot forget its flavor.

Chapter 4

Teeka

Trying to work when her heart was in one million pieces may have been the hardest thing Teeka had ever done. She was happy that she didn't see Keelan the rest of the day, because she may not have been able to hold in her emotions. When five o'clock rolled around, she jetted out of the office as fast as she could. She was not in the mood to deal with anyone's last-minute requests, and if Mr. O'Brian needed anything from her, he would have to wait until the morning.

When she got home, she contemplated calling Lynne and telling her what had transpired after the two had spoken earlier. She changed her mind once she sat on her sofa in the living room. She was still trying to grasp it all, and she didn't want to voice thoughts that weren't all the way formed in her mind.

She tried to think back to see if Keelan had given off any signs of being taken. No, not that she could remember. He had always pegged her as a man who was on the dating scene. She didn't recall him ever acting suspicious when they were together, or even giving her a reason to think that there was any other woman in his life. He told her that the reason he wanted things to stay the same between them was that he was focused on his career and didn't want anything to get in the way of that. Now she knew the truth.

She sat cross-legged on the couch in front of the television for so long that she didn't even realize that multiple episodes of *Will & Grace* had gone by. The television just served as background noise, and before she knew it, the time read eight o'clock on the nose.

Knock! Knock! Knock!

The sound of knuckles hitting her door made her jump. She looked down at herself and saw that she was still in her work clothes. Her pumps were on the floor in front of the sofa, and that's how she knew she was distraught. Shoes were not allowed in her living room. They got taken off at the door. She had really been sitting there thinking for hours.

"Just go away," she said in a barely audible voice. "Just leave me alone."

Knock! Knock!

Turning off the TV, she got up and stepped quietly to the front door. Standing on her tiptoes, she looked through the peephole, and sure enough, there was Keelan standing on the other side. He was dressed like he was either going to or coming from the gym, and he wore a look of anticipation on his face.

She lowered herself and leaned into the door. She didn't want to open it, but then again, a piece of her did. The door was cold against her forehead, and she wished she could rewind time to when she saw him in that breakroom. If she could do it all again, she wouldn't have said a word to him. If she had the opportunity for a redo, she would act like she didn't even notice him. He would be just another man who worked at the same place she did. The only thing was, none of that was possible. She was where she was, and there was nothing that anyone could do about it.

"Teeka, I know you're there. I can hear you breathing." There was that voice, the one that just last week sent chills down her spine. "Teeka, please listen. I know I've caused you depths of pain that I myself wouldn't be able to handle. I can't get the look of your face out of my mind. Please just open the door."

"Why? So you can look me in my eyes and lie some more?"

"I never lied to you."

"So, what do you call not telling me you were next in line to tie the knot?"

"Please open the door so I can explain."

"I don't want to. You don't deserve to be in my presence, let alone my space. Go home. Go home to your future wife, Keelan. Does she know you're here, or does she think you're at the gym?" Silence. "Exactly. So, you're lying to her too. You are a real piece of shit. Do you know that?"

"Yes. I do know that."

"I'm glad you do." She rolled her eyes and stepped away from the door. "Now, get the hell away from my door before I call the police and report you for harassment."

She walked through the dining room and down the long hallway that led to her bedroom. If he was going to keep knocking, she didn't want to hear it. She was going to shut the door and drown him out. Eventually he would get the point. After all, he still had to go home to his woman.

She was almost to her room when she heard the front door unlock and open.

"I tried to give you the option to let me in yourself, but since you want to be stubborn, I guess I'll let myself in," Keelan said.

Teeka whipped around to see him standing behind her, holding up his keychain. "You gave me your spare key when you asked me to check on your spot when you and Steve went on that business trip, remember?"

"And you were supposed to give it back."

"Well, I'm glad I didn't." He tried to offer her a small smile, but she wasn't going for it.

"You can set my key down on the table and leave the way you came."

"Not until you hear me out, Teeka." He advanced on her.

She tried to will her feet to move as he walked toward her, but she couldn't. Just like always, he had this spell over her body. Why? Why, even after what he had done, was she still a victim to his charm? He stopped when he was directly in front of her.

"First I want to apologize for the other night. Your size plays no part in the way I feel about you. I enjoy every piece of you, Teeka, and if a man ever truly makes you feel like you aren't good enough because of something that you are happy with, then leave him where you found him."

"Why did you say it then?" she asked.

"You told me you loved me, and I was shocked."

"So, to counter my words, you hurt me with yours? And why did you lie to me?"

"I'm stupid; I know." He grabbed her hands and put them to his chest. "I didn't lie to you, or at least I didn't try to. At first this was just sex for me, but then I got to know you, and after all of the time we spent together, I guess it was inevitable."

"What was?"

"Me falling in love with you."

Teeka froze for a second. Had he just said what she thought? He loved her? She let the initial shock fade before she snatched her hands away and scoffed up at his six-foot-five frame.

"You're doing it again. Lying. How can you love me when you have a whole fiancée, Keelan?"

"When I moved here, Alecia and I were on the fritz. I honestly didn't even know if we would be together, let alone get married. She didn't support my dreams the way that I would hope. I come from nothing and had to grind for everything that I have. She, on the other hand, comes from a wealthy family and has had everything handed to her, so there were some aspects of my life that she didn't understand. This move to Chicago was one of them. When I came here, it was a fresh start and I was able to reinvent myself.

"And then I met you, Teeka. You were everything that I didn't know existed in a woman. The moment I felt myself falling for you was the moment I told you that we should keep things as just sex. I know sometimes I came off as a complete asshole, but that's because if you got too close to me, I would hurt you. Who was I fooling? We still ended up here, right?"

"So, where does Alecia come into play again?" Teeka asked but then decided to answer her own question. "All of those trips to Milwaukee weren't just to see your parents, were they? You were rekindling what you had with her."

"I did go to Milwaukee to see my parents . . . but I also went to see her. You are right. She apologized for everything that had happened and said that the time apart had made her realize that she didn't want to live without me. What was I supposed to do, Teeka? Throw eight years away because I'd been feeling somebody else for a few months?"

"Wow. Get out of my house." Teeka tried to turn away from him, but he stopped her by grabbing her arm.

"You're not listening to me, T. K. I'm saying that was my thought process back then."

"What about now? Do you love her?"

"Yes," he said. "I think so."

"You think? Why are you here, Keelan?"

"Because I know that I love you."

Teeka shook her head at him. She couldn't believe his nerve! Had he really come to her home to tell her to her face that he was in love with two women?

"Well, she can have you. I don't want anything to do with you, and I won't give you the opportunity to hurt me anymore."

She felt the hot tears on her face and became angry with herself. She was so vulnerable, and the only one who could fix the ache in her heart was still causing it. Why did she even think that someone like him would go for someone like her? Especially now that she knew what kind of woman he liked. Alecia was everything that she wasn't, and she could see why Keelan proposed to her.

"I don't want to hurt you anymore," he said.

"Then leave."

"I can't." He cupped her chin and pulled her close to him. "Because I don't want to." He kissed her juicy lips, sucking on the bottom one before drawing back. "Tell me to stop." He kissed her again, this time plunging his tongue in her mouth before pulling away. "Tell me that you don't want me."

"I–I can't," Teeka murmured.

"You want me?"

"Yes . . ."

"I don't think that it's you that wants me." He pushed her backward until she was against the hallway wall. Hiking her leg up, he let his right hand travel underneath her skirt and cup her second set of lips. "I think she does. Am I right?"

"No."

"I'm not?" He immediately removed his hand, and that caused her to suck air through her teeth.

"I mean . . . yes. No. I don't know, Keelan," she pouted. "Why are you doing this to me? You've hurt me so bad. I can't even think straight."

"Come here," he said and lifted her up like she weighed fifty pounds.

He wrapped her legs around his waist and locked lips with her once more. She kissed him back with vigor, letting all her emotions seep out through her lips. Somehow, they ended up in her bed with their clothes off and thrown on the floor.

"Unhh!" She moaned out loud when his lips found their way to her nipples. "Yes, suck them like that, baby."

She didn't need to tell him twice. She knew that he loved her round, natural breasts, and she enjoyed the extra attention he always gave them when they had sex. That night, though, it was like he was making love to them. He sucked, licked, and nibbled all over them until a puddle had formed between her legs. She parted them, giving him the signal that something else needed attention immediately.

"Fuck me."

"Not yet," he responded and then disappeared underneath the covers.

Not needing to ask what he was about to do, Teeka felt his tongue on her clit before she had a chance to catch her breath.

Teeka, what are you doing? He has a woman at home! Tell him to stop right now! She thought. *But it feels so gooood! I can't make him stop. Fuck her!*

She didn't know if it was the pleasure he was giving her or what, but suddenly she didn't care that he was engaged. All she wanted was for him to get her to where she was going, and if that meant wetting his face up with her juices, so be it. Her hands slid down the comforter until she found his head. She mushed his face into her pussy and ground her hips in an upward motion.

Keelan didn't miss a beat. He stopped licking and put her whole clit in his mouth, sucking away as she fucked his face.

"Keeelan! I hate you!" she yelled out when she felt the first wave of her climax coming. "You stupid-ass nigga! I hate you—ahhh!" Her back arched and her legs shot up in the air from the power of the orgasm that had overcome her. Her screams were so loud she was sure the tenants next to her knew what was going down in her bedroom.

"You hate me?" Keelan asked when he finally came up for air. He positioned himself between her legs and looked down in her face. "Huh, Teeka? Do you really hate me?"

"I–I hate you for making me love you if I can't have you. What about me, Keelan? Am I just supposed to forget about you? Am I just supposed to let you go?"

"I don't want you to," he said, and she felt the tip of his manhood at her opening. "I want you to love me."

"That's not what you said Friday."

"Fuck what I said Friday. I was trying to push you away, but when I realized that meant you would be out of my life . . . it wasn't worth it.

"You can't have her . . . and me," she whispered.

"Then—" He forced himself inside of her and gasped at how wet she was. "Then tell me not to get married."

"Keelan!"

"Tell me!" he said, thrusting inside of her with more power.

"Oh, Keelan!" She wrapped her arms around his shoulders and rested her cheek on his shoulder. "Please don't get married! Be with me."

"Okay," he said and continued to touch her in places he never had before. "Just don't leave me. Don't give up on me. Please, T. K., I don't even want to think about another man inside of this pussy. Not my pussy."

He sexed her for another hour and kissed her all over. She lost count of how many positions they did that night, but it still wasn't enough. He brought her to four more orgasms before finally letting off his own nut.

When he pulled himself out of her, he fell on the bed next to her and caught his breath. She scooted as close to him as she could and rested her head on his shoulder. Her chest heaved as she, too, tried to get a grasp on what had just happened. The two lay in the darkness without saying a word for what seemed like forever. Teeka was almost certain that he had fallen asleep, but then he spoke.

"I was serious," he said.

She felt the vibrations from his voice under her face. She swallowed the saliva in her throat and tried to find the words to say. When nothing came, she decided to pretend she didn't know what he was talking about.

"Serious about what?"

"About not getting married. She wants it to happen next month, and honestly, all I've done these past seven months was get used to the thought of it not happening."

"What about her?"

"I love her," he said, and Teeka stiffened where she lay. "But the love I have for her is different now. I don't feel the same that I did before. I mean, I want to settle down, just not with her anymore."

"Why? And don't say because you met me."

"Well, that is one of the big reasons, but . . . I don't know. We just don't mesh the same. Like, she wants money over happiness, and I'm the complete opposite. She doesn't want kids, and I do. She wants me to be the kind of man her father is, and I can't be that for her and still be the same man that I want to be for myself. I don't know. . . . It's complicated. I thought that maybe I could go through with it, but her being here over the weekend reminds me of why I can't. Of why we were apart in the first place. I'm sorry if this is stuff that you don't want to hear."

"Don't be sorry. I just wish that it was something you told me when we first met. I would have understood, and maybe we wouldn't be here right now," Teeka said and sat up. "But you took that choice from me. I'm not mad at you anymore, Keelan. I sympathize with you. No, I don't want you to get married, and yes, I want you to be with me . . . but what will that cost me?"

"What are you saying, Teeka?"

"I'm saying . . ." She sighed. "I'm saying that I love you, Keelan, but I think you should take some time to yourself and figure out what you really want in life, because we only get one of those. Go home, Keelan. I'll be all right."

"T. K.—"

"Thank you for giving me the best dick I've ever had, and showing me that I do know how to love somebody. Before you came here tonight, I'll be honest, I was a complete mess. While you were fucking me, I was completely vulnerable. But now? Now I see things for what they really are, and I refuse to be the other woman while you decide what you want. That's not fair to me, and no matter how much I care about you, I have to care about myself more. This can't happen again, Keelan. I think it's time for you to go home to your fiancée before she starts to wonder where you are."

Teeka's eyes had adjusted to the dark, so she could see the shock on his face. She wanted to take back every word she had just said, but she knew that she meant them. What would she look like carrying on any kind of relationship with another woman's man? True, before Keelan, her dating record had been pretty much nonexistent, but she would be damned if she settled for the situation at hand. She wasn't *that* desperate.

"This isn't what I want," he said.

"I don't think you know what you want."

"I want you."

"Then why is another woman living in your house?"

He was silent. He sighed big and got up from Teeka's bed to gather his clothes. When he was fully dressed, he turned back to face her.

"Okay, I'll go. For now. Will you at least speak to me at work?" he asked.

"Of course."

"Are you going to walk me to the door?"

"Nope, because I didn't open it for you," she said, and she could have sworn a look of sadness washed over his face. "Oh, and Mr. Metoyer? Leave my key on the dining room table before you leave and lock the bottom lock. I'll see you at work tomorrow."

No matter who and where you are, time always discovers the truth.

Chapter 5

Keelan

He didn't know what he was playing at, going over to Teeka's place like that. Did he really think that she would be okay with the fact that he had a whole relationship he'd kept hidden from her? He had hoped that when he told her his true thoughts, she would . . . what? Be with him?

"Shit!" he said to himself as he drove his SL Benz on the highway.

With what he'd said on Friday, mixed with what had happened not even thirty minutes ago, he probably seemed like one confused man. As he drove home, he could still smell her scent on him. He could still feel the softness of her skin on his body. Little did she know he hadn't even had plans to go home that night, especially after being inside of her again. He had wanted to wake up to her and even cook her breakfast in the morning before they both went to work. His overnight bag sat packed and unused in the backseat. He would have come up with something to tell Alecia the next day, but all he wanted to do was be with Teeka.

He wished that he'd never agreed to make things work with Alecia. He wished that he had just told her he was content with life without her; but then her father would pull out of the deal with ETCO. It was the same deal that was going to make him vice president of the company. It was all such a sticky situation. So much was riding on the merger between Clout Enterprises and ETCO that the last thing he wanted to do was anything that would upset Alecia.

He couldn't get the tone of Teeka's voice or the last words she'd said to him out of his head. She sounded definite in her decision. If there was one thing he knew about that woman, it was that she knew her worth. They both knew that she was too good to come second to any man and that she deserved everything he wanted to give her. Except he couldn't. Not while, as she had so nicely put it, he had another woman living in his home. Teeka was done with him, and the only way for him to get her back would be to cut things off completely with Alecia, but that was something he couldn't do either.

"Fuck!" He banged on the steering wheel as he parked his car in the parking garage of his condo. He reached in the gym bag and pulled out some Axe so that he could spray it on himself. He smelled like Teeka's perfume, and Alecia was sure to smell it on him as soon as he stepped foot in the house.

Once he felt as though he'd masked the scent, he grabbed the bag and got out of the car. Teeka was on his brain the whole walk to his unit. Before he stuck the key into the lock to open the door, he took a big breath and tried to pull himself together.

"Hi, baby!" Alecia gushed as soon as he opened the door. "I was literally just wondering when you'd be coming home from the gym."

She had been in the kitchen pouring herself a cup of orange juice when he walked in. She was wearing nothing but a robe and underwear underneath. Her hair was pulled back, and the makeup that she wore daily was completely wiped from her face, showcasing her natural beauty. She eyed him seductively, and it seemed as though she'd forgotten all about the orange juice.

"Hey, Leesh," he said, completely disregarding her getup and the fact that she was staring at him like a hungry tiger. He started toward the bedroom. "I'm about to hop in the shower and go to bed. I have to get up early."

"You want to go to sleep"—she came and blocked his way—"when I'm trying to let you dig into me any way that you like?"

She reached down and rubbed his crotch. Keelan's dick reacted to her touch, but he knew that it probably still had Teeka's dried secretions all over it. He pulled away just as she tried to take it out. Her eyebrow raised, and he could tell instantly that she was suspicious.

"I just came from the gym. I'm worn out and feel disgusting. Plus, didn't I give you enough last night?" he asked.

"Enough is never enough." She grinned and reached for him again. "Plus, a little sweat has never scared me, baby. You know that."

"I know a lot that doesn't scare you." He grabbed her hands and kissed her quickly on the lips. "But right now, I just want to soak in some hot water. You can join me if you'd like."

"You're no fun tonight," she pouted and moved out of his way. "Go on and take your stupid shower."

He smiled and walked around her, continuing his journey to the bedroom with his gym bag on his shoulder. All he wanted to do was be alone, and he knew he wouldn't be getting a lot of time to do that anymore.

"Oh, and honey?"

"Yeah?" He stopped, turning to face where she stood in the dining room with a raised eyebrow.

"I've been meaning to ask you: Why do you have Carol's Daughter hair milk in your bathroom cabinet?"

"What?"

"The hair lotion in the bathroom. It's for natural hair. I was wondering why it was there."

"Oh, that," he said, thinking quick on his toes. "That's the brand Steve's secretary suggested for you, isn't it? I thought I'd grab you some just in case you were serious about trying it."

"Oh, yeah, that's right. Teeka, wasn't it?"

The way she asked didn't really sound like a question. Her eyes watched his face like a hawk for any sudden change. His heart was racing, but he played it cool by shrugging his shoulders.

"Yeah, I think so."

"Think? You've been working there for how long and don't know the secretary's name?"

"I mean, yeah, her name is Teeka." His heart was thumping through his chest.

She stared at him for a few more seconds before her eyes lowered slightly. "Are there any other good-looking black men that work in your job?"

"I don't really look at other men like that. And I'm not sure why you're asking me this," he said.

"I'm just saying she's pretty—I mean, if you're into bigger women. But she's cute, and I hope she has other eye candy to focus on besides you. I'm used to women ogling over you like a piece of meat, just not any so close to you and for so long in the day. I saw the way she looked at you at the office. I would hate to have to come up there and . . . regulate. You know Daddy hates to see me unhappy."

"You're tripping, Alecia." Keelan shook his head at her.

"So, she doesn't like you then?"

"What?"

"She's never tried to flirt with you or anything? I mean, I know you wouldn't talk back to her. She's not your type at all. But still . . ."

"Still what?"

"When I showed her my ring, I swear it was like her face dropped. I swear it's like black women can't be happy for other black women in better positions in life than them. Maybe if she lost a few pounds then she could find a man, too."

"I'm about to get in the shower, Alecia," he said, brushing her off, and he saw the unsatisfied look on her face. If she was unhappy, then he knew that he would be unhappy too. "Will you be in bed when I get out?"

"I suppose," she said and clicked her teeth.

"Good," he said and grinned at her. "Make sure you have nothing on when I'm done. You said enough isn't enough, right?"

She smiled big at what he was proposing and nodded her head. "Hurry up, babe. I've been horny since I saw you leave in those gym clothes. Oh, and thank you for the hair products. You're so thoughtful. I think I'll try it out tomorrow when I take this weave out."

He winked at her and went to the room. He felt bad for lying to her about Teeka and the hair lotion. He even felt bad about the fact that he was going to sleep with her after he'd just slept with another woman, but he figured that it would be the last time—especially since he was pretty sure that he and Teeka were done.

It's time to let him go. The way he kissed, smiled, and smelled, you have to let him go. The way his hands felt on your waist, the way he said your name, you have to let it go. Because that's who he was . . . not who he is.

Chapter 6

Teeka

"Mama, I have to get off this phone. You know I'm at work!"

"Girl, now you know Steve ain't gon' be mad at you for talking to your mama, so don't start."

Teeka rolled her eyes to the high heavens, knowing her mother, Rashanda Smith, wasn't going to let her get back to work without saying what she needed to say. When she'd first called her daughter, Rashanda had asked what was going on in her life. Well, Teeka made the mistake of telling her the truth, and now she was paying for it. It was a Tuesday, and it had been two weeks since Keelan had been to her house. For the most part, Teeka was doing okay, but until then, the only person she'd talked to about it was Lynne. Suddenly she remembered why.

"I told you to leave that boy alone. Any man trying to remain friends with benefits for as long as he was is always up to no good."

"It's not like that, Mama. He didn't think they were going to get back together, and now that they are, I'm just going to let it be."

"As you should. I didn't raise you to be nobody's side chick. Lordy, your daddy would turn over in his grave if you even thought about doing something as silly as that."

"Well, I'm not, so can we just drop it?"

"Mm-hmm, I told you that those honey-roll thighs were going to attract some bears. Nuh-uh, not today! I'll punch that motherfucker in his face if he even thinks about playing games with you!"

"Mama!" Teeka laughed so hard in her computer chair that she rolled backward. She scooted back to the desk and looked around to make sure she wasn't disrupting anyone. "I can't believe you just said that!"

"I'm serious, too! I was wondering why I hadn't heard from you as often. Mm-hmm, I said something is wrong with my baby. You usually call me every day and stop by at least three times a week. I can't remember the last time I saw you."

"Mama, I was over there yesterday."

"I was in the bed when you came over. I didn't even have time to make you nothing to eat, so that doesn't count, girl."

"I'll come over tonight then."

"Nope, that ship has sailed. You know I play Bingo on Tuesdays with Sandy. We're up against those cows Sheena and Alise tonight. I'm going to shout Bingo so loud in those tramps' faces they'll be hearing my echo for days."

"Okay, Mama." Teeka laughed again. "Well then, I'll come by this weekend."

"That's perfect, baby. While you're at work, do me a favor. Tell Steve I said thank you. Tell him that I got the letter from the bank in the mail."

"What letter from the bank?"

"The letter saying that my house is paid off. That letter!"

"What? Steve paid off you and Daddy's house?"

"That's right. He said it was an early birthday present, and I said well, that's some present. There was still twenty thousand some-odd dollars left to pay on it. That man is truly heaven sent."

"Wow! That was so nice of him," Teeka said, genuinely shocked. Steve had always treated them as family; he was honestly like the uncle she never had, but that was definitely a blessing for her mother. "I will tell him you send your love. But I have to go, Mama. I'm trying to work here."

"That's fine. And all right, but don't let me hear about you talking to no Keelan Metoyer. Hear me?"

"How old am I again? I love you, Mama. See you later."

She disconnected the phone because she knew that her mom would just keep on talking if she let her. She shook her head at her mom's last words as she focused back on the computer screen. No matter what she did, it was like she couldn't evade Keelan. Of course, she had to see him at work, she had even had to speak to him a few times. She was doing a great job at saving face because just like before, no one knew about anything that had transpired between her and Keelan.

"Teeka!"

She was sitting at her desk, typing up an important e-mail for Mr. O'Brian when he popped out from his back office. As usual, he was wearing a suit. That day, he had opted for gray, and his white hair was combed back. Looking at him, you wouldn't be able to tell that he had a thing for sistas, but his wife, Sandy, could tell you different. The two had been married for over twenty years, and Mr. O'Brian hadn't gotten enough of her chocolate yet. When Teeka looked up, she saw the older man's smile was brighter than she'd ever seen it before.

"Oh, wow, did Sandy make that casserole that you love so much last night or something? Because you seem to be in a great mood!"

"No, she didn't make the casserole yet, but I really wish she would. I am, however, in a great mood. Ask me why," he said with a smile.

238 C. N. Phillips

"I'm almost afraid to," she teased. "But anything for you. Why?"

"We're sealing the deal with Clout Enterprises on Friday. And in honor of that, we will be having a banquet downstairs in the dining hall on Saturday. I hope you can make it."

"That's amazing!" Teeka grinned. "I know you've been working on this deal for some time now. I'm so glad it's finally coming through for you."

"Yes, the contract is just for a year to see how things go, but I'm very confident in this business venture. Edward Clout will be flying in on Friday to have a look around and see firsthand how we do things around here."

"Clout?" Teeka asked, trying to remember where she'd heard that name before. "That sounds so familiar, but I can't seem to place why."

"Probably because this whole place has been gushing over Keelan and his bride to be! Alecia Clout is Edward's daughter. If it weren't for him, this deal wouldn't have even been made possible. He came to Chicago and made things shake, didn't he? And have you seen Miss Clout? Beautiful young woman—not as beautiful as you, of course," he said.

"Yeah, yeah. Whatever. You're only saying nice things because you know I'm typing this letter up to Candace over in finance." Teeka giggled. "She wants to know where the charge for twenty thousand dollars on the company's Master Card came from. What should I say?"

"Tell her that the charge came from me, and she needs to mind her damn business," he answered with a twinkle in his eye.

"Well, all righty then." Teeka raised her brow. "You want me to say it just like that, or spruce it up a bit?"

"Just work your magic like you always do, of course," Mr. O'Brian said and turned to head back to his office. He paused and looked back at her. "Why are you still here, Teeka?"

"It's only ten o'clock. My lunch isn't for a few hours."

"No, I mean why are you still my secretary? You have a business degree. Why not apply it? Shoot, I can create you a new position if you'd like. I just know Thomas would want you to be happy."

Teeka smiled sadly at the mention of her father's name, and she felt a rush of fondness go through her at the concern in Mr. O'Brian's voice.

"I am still your secretary because you would lose your mind if I wasn't here to help you find it," she told him. "I am happy, and you pay me so well I don't think I want for anything. Except maybe a new car, but that will come in due time."

"Indeed it will." He patted her on the shoulder.

"And Mr. Steve?" She stopped him right before he disappeared, calling him by the name that she used when she was just a kid. "What you did for my mama . . . thank you. My daddy would be so grateful to you for taking care of us the way you have all these years. You didn't have to do any of the things that you've done for us. And . . ." Something dawned on her. "Is that where the twenty-thousand-dollar charge came from?"

He winked at her. "Never thank me for taking care of my family. It's my pleasure."

And with that, he was gone. Her dad had always said that Steve and Sandy took to her the way they would have their own child if they could have any. In that moment, she thanked God to have a man like Mr. O'Brian in their lives.

After their exchange, she figured that she would have a pretty good day, and she was right. She dived into her workload, and the time flew right on by. By the time she had made her last reminder call and put her last notes in the system, the clock read ten minutes to six.

"Oooh-wee, look at this fly girl!"

Teeka would recognize that voice anywhere.

"Girl, what are you doing here?" she said to Lynne.

"I wanted to surprise my best friend in the whole wide world. Duh!"

"Uh-huh."

"And I wanted to check on you. I know this might have been a hard two weeks for you. Has he tried to say anything to you?" Lynne asked.

"Not anything that isn't work related." Teeka shrugged, knowing exactly who she was referring to. "I think I made myself pretty clear the last time we talked."

"Girl, I still can't believe you put the pussy on him and made him bounce. That was gangsta!"

"Well, I wasn't trying to be *gangsta*. It was just something that had to be done. But, wait. Hold up." Teeka looked Lynne up and down, finally noticing her outfit. "Lynne, why are you dressed like you're about to be wined and dined by somebody fine and divine?"

She was wearing an off-the-shoulder black dress that stopped just above her knees and a pair of peep-toe sheer black booties suitable for the fall. Her hair had long, lustrous wand curls that bounced with each step that she took. Lynne was very pretty in the face, with hazel-colored eyes and lips so full they looked puffy. She was what men would call a slim-thick redbone. She didn't have much in her chest area, but baby had back for days.

"I wanted to surprise you. Duh! And I'm dressed like this because I have a date with a tall chocolate dream named Tony," Lynne told her.

"Tony? Oooooh, he must be new, because I haven't heard about him."

"He is new. I met him three days ago."

"Three days ago?" Teeka's eyebrows raised.

"Girl, yes. Three days ago. It's 2017, girl. I don't have time to be texting these men for weeks before I decide whether or not I'm going to go out with him. I need to know if he's worth my time, and the only way to determine that is if he is in my face."

"I feel you," Teeka said, not noticing that Lynne had something in her hands. She shut down her computer system and began to gather her things. "Just be safe, girl."

"Oh, I will," Lynne said, giving her a devilish smile. "Because you're coming with me. He said he's bringing his friend Vic along since I'm bringing you."

"Excuse me?" Teeka scrunched up her face. She pulled her phone from her purse and pretended to look for something in her text messages. "When did I say I was going on a double date with you, so that I can try and recall that conversation?"

"You didn't, but I figured it wouldn't be a problem."

"Lynne, you know I just got out of a situation."

"Girl, boom. You act like he was your man or something. Plus, the best way to get over somebody is to get under somebody *neeeew*." She rocked her shoulders the way the rapper Lil Uzi Vert did in his videos, and Teeka couldn't help but to crack a smile.

"You're a damn fool, do you know that? And even if I did go on this date, you're dressed like it's almost time to go already."

"Yeaaah, about that. They're picking us up from my place in an hour, but I already stopped at your house and grabbed you some stuff." Lynne held up the pink bag in her hands. "That sexy champagne-colored velvet dress and those nude ankle-strap open-toe shoes. You know the ones with the thicker heel that you like? And, of course, some panties and a strapless bra. So, what do you say?"

Teeka opened her mouth to tell Lynne that she really didn't want to go, but the two women were interrupted when Keelan rounded the corner.

"Be nice," Teeka warned her friend, knowing that her mouth could be like a cannon sometimes.

"Hello, ladies." Keelan addressed them both with his award-winning smile when he got to the front desk.

"Hey, Keelan," Lynne said so sweetly. You couldn't even tell that she'd told Teeka she was going to smack him on sight. "That's a nice suit you're wearing. Blue is definitely your color."

"Thank you," he said, smoothing out his tie. "You look lovely yourself. What's the occasion?"

"Oh, noth—" Suddenly her eyes flashedm and she shot Teeka a cunning grin. "I'm actually about to go out on a date. That's why I'm here, actually. Teeka asked me to stop at her house and grab her a few things because it's actually a double. A double *date,* that is."

The smile on Keelan's face disappeared, and his shoulders slumped noticeably. "A date?" he asked as if he hadn't heard her correctly, and then he turned to Teeka. "Is that right?"

"Umm . . ." The way he was staring at Teeka almost made her want to tell him that Lynne wasn't telling the truth. But then again, the sadness in his eyes at that very moment didn't change the fact that whatever was between the two of them was over. "Yes. I need to hurry up and run over to her house really quick to get dressed. What time were they picking us up again, Lynne?"

"At seven," Lynne answered. "So, hurry up! I'll pull the car up."

When Lynne was gone, Teeka zipped up her Coach tote bag and stood to her feet, ignoring Keelan's gaze.

"Who is he?" he mumbled.

"Huh?" she asked, pushing in her chair.

"The guy you're going on a date with. Who is he?"

"His name is None of Your Business." She began walking to the elevator, but he was right on her heels.

"Oh, really? Just a few weeks ago you were in my bed with my dick inside of you, telling me that you love me. Now you're going on dates with guys?"

"What is it to you? Aren't you getting married next month? The entire office is raving about this amazing wedding you're supposed to be having," she snapped.

When they got to the elevator, he grabbed her hand as she reached for the button. "You're the one who left me alone, remember?" he said. "All you had to do was tell me not to go through with it."

"Psssh! Boy, please. You don't have a choice in that matter, do you?" She looked him square in the eye. "Edward Clout is merging with ETCO, and a lot of that is riding on how happy you can keep his princess, isn't it?" When he didn't say anything, she shook her head. "Look, Keelan. I don't want to cause you any trouble in your relationship. I'm moving on with my life, and it's clear that you are too. Don't make things more complicated than they have to be."

She whipped her curls at him, turned to the elevator, and tried to press the button, but he stopped her again. That time, he pressed his body against her backside and placed his lips close to her ear.

"I don't want things to be complicated. I love you, Teeka. In a perfect world, I would choose you ten times, but the merger—" He let out a frustrated breath. "It would be a good move for the company, and Steve is so happy about it. He's talking about making me vice president. I'm just stuck right now. If you would just wait for me, just until I can get everything in order . . ."

His voice trailed off. Even though he was behind her, she could still smell the cologne on him. It was the same cologne he had been wearing the day they met. He'd never acted that way with her at work, and she could hear the desperation in his voice. She wanted to turn around and kiss him deeply, maybe even let him unbutton her blouse right then and there, but she couldn't. It was over.

"Maybe . . . maybe you should fall out of love with me, Keelan," she said, keeping her voice as even as possible as she lied through her teeth. "This time that we've been apart, I have had time to think about our arrangement. I just got lost in the moment, that's all. I was *dick-matized*. I don't love you, Keelan. I mean, you're cool and we vibe, but I never really thought we would be together."

She used his own words against him. Well, kind of. She felt him grow stiff behind her, and she stood still as well.

"Have a good time at your date, Teeka," he said after a minute and released her hand.

She reached for the elevator button, but the elevator dinged before she could even press it. Keelan stepped back just in time as the elevator doors opened.

"All right, Daddy. I'll let him kn—"

Alecia stopped mid-sentence when she saw Teeka standing in front of her and Keelan not even five inches behind her. Her brow furrowed instantly, and Teeka knew what it must have looked like to her. But Alecia's suspicions were the last of Teeka's concerns. All she wanted to do was get downstairs to her own car and follow Lynn back to her house. At first, she had just been trying to grind Keelan's gears about her possibly going on a date, but now she really wanted to go. She needed to do something to occupy her mind, and maybe meeting a new face wouldn't be so bad after all.

"Have a good night, Mr. Metoyer," she said and stepped onto the elevator when Alecia stepped off.

"Daddy, I'm going to call you right back. I just found Keelan," Teeka heard her say as the elevator doors began to close. Her last sight was of Keelan's sad puppy-dog face turning away from the elevator.

They asked, "Where are you moving to?" She said, "Onto better things."

Chapter 7

Teeka

Okay, breathe, Teeka. You act like this is the first date you've been on. She coached herself as the waitress led the foursome back to their table. The restaurant was an upscale soul food joint in downtown Chicago called Just Eat. It was a black family–owned business, and Teeka felt welcome from the moment she stepped inside. When they were seated, Teeka sat next to Lynne's date, and Lynne sat next to hers. That way, she could be across from Vic, and Lynne could be across from Tony.

Vic was very handsome to say the least. He was tall and had an athletic build about himself. He kept his hair cut low and had a mustache that led into his well-managed beard. He had a caramel complexion with the eyes to match, and Teeka couldn't help but wonder what he looked like with his shirt off.

"So, Teeka, tell me what you do," Vic asked after they ordered their food.

"Oh, wow, you just jump right in, don't you?" she teased.

"I'm a very forward guy," he said with a smile. "I mean that is, unless you don't like forward guys."

Teeka laughed.

"No, you're okay. Well, I'm a secretary at a company called ETCO."

"That's located here downtown, isn't it?"

"Yup, not too far from this restaurant, actually."

"That's cool, but"—he raised his eyebrow—"I thought Lynne told me that you have a business degree. I'm not tripping on where you work or anything, so don't think that. I guess that I'm just wondering why someone with a business degree would want to be someone's secretary."

"No worries. I understand. After college it was hard to find work. The owner-slash-president of ETCO and my dad were best friends before he died, so he gave me a job making what I would make if I had found a job with my degree."

"Word? That's dope," he said and smiled genuinely. "I'm happy that all worked out for you."

"Yes, eventually I'll branch out and find something else, but for now it works. What about you? What do you do for work?"

"I'm the manager of a construction company, but I'm in school to get my degree in computer science."

"Nice!"

"Thank you. I know you probably can't tell by how fly I am," He played with the collar of his Ralph Lauren sweater for effect. "But I'm a closet nerd."

"If you didn't just pop your collar like that, I would have never been able to tell!" The two of them shared a laugh.

Lynne and Tony were lost in their own conversation, and that was just fine with Teeka. Throughout the date, Vic kept complimenting her on how beautiful she looked and telling her how happy he was that she had decided to come out. At the end of the night, Teeka could honestly say the same thing. Vic had been a perfect gentleman.

When they arrived back at Lynne's house, she announced that Tony would be spending the night there. Vic offered to take Teeka home, and she kindly accepted his offer.

"I really appreciate you for the ride," she told him from the passenger's seat of his all-white Dodge Charger. "I would have hated to catch a Lyft ride this late."

"No problem, beautiful," he said, taking his eyes off the road to glance at her briefly. "Dammit, girl, I know I keep saying it, but you sure are fine."

"Thank you."

"No, for real. I have never really been into big chicks like that, but you got it going on."

There it was. Normally men weren't as blunt as Vic about her size, but he did say that he was a forward guy. She was at a loss for words for a moment. She didn't know what he had expected her to say, because his comment wasn't a compliment. Suddenly, she was embarrassed for eating her ribs the way that she had. At the end of the night, everyone except her had taken home boxes. He didn't even realize it, but he had just ruined the night, and she was no longer interested in his conversation.

"Big chicks?"

"I mean no disrespect, but you're just bigger than the women I would normally go for. When Lynne told me at first, I was like nah, I'm cool. But now I'm really glad that I came out."

By that time, Teeka was wishing she had caught the Lyft ride. Her head was turned toward the window, and her eyes were on the scenery that they were passing by. They were a few minutes away from her apartment complex, and she couldn't wait to get there.

"Did I say something wrong?" Vic asked, noticing her sudden quietness.

"I'm just tired," she said. "It's this next right coming up . . . yup, right here. You can stop at the door to that first building right there. Thank you for the ride again, Vic."

"You're welcome," he said, putting his car in PARK. "Hey, do you mind if I call you sometime?"

Teeka was already out of the car and shutting the door when he asked his question. She didn't even give him the satisfaction of an answer. She just kept on walking to the door.

"Teeka! Did you hear me?"

She was unlocking the secured entry door when she turned around and saw that he'd rolled his window down. She sighed and rolled her eyes at him.

"Yes, I heard you, Vic. I would have given you my number had it not been for the *big girl* comments that you made. Let this be a lesson that not all things need to be said out loud. Have a good night."

She opened the door and left him sitting in the parking lot with his mouth open. She hadn't even made it to her floor before her phone was out.

Bitch don't you ever set me up on a blind date again. And you prepped Vic about me being a bigger woman? What kind of friend does that? No matter what size I am, I am still just a woman, like you. The fact that you felt you needed to do that lets me know what you really think about me. Don't even text back.

She pressed the SEND button on her cell phone right as she walked through the front door of her apartment. She couldn't believe her friend, but as much as she wanted to say fuck you in the message, she knew deep down that Lynne probably hadn't meant any harm.

Teeka kicked her shoes off and unzipped the tight dress from the back as she walked to her room. The only light in the whole apartment was coming from the nightlights she had throughout her home. She was afraid of the dark, and Keelan used to make fun of her whenever he was over there.

Keelan . . .

Why did he always find a way to run across her mind? He was probably laid up with his fiancée, doing to her body what he used to do to Teeka's. She crawled into her bed wearing nothing but her panties and bra so that she could curl up underneath her covers. In a matter of weeks, her life had changed so drastically. She should be laying up under him right now, getting on his nerves. She should be poking his cheek and whining about him always falling asleep on her. She should be listening to his light snores and feeling his random forehead kisses throughout the middle of the night. Why her? Why was she left to deal with the pain from his absence? Why did she have to pick up the shattered pieced of a love story that would be left untold? The emotions coming over her were so overwhelming, and there was only one way to let them out. She cried. She buried her head in her soft pillow and cried so hard her chest heaved. Teeka didn't know how to un-love Keelan, because she didn't want to, and because of that, she needed him. The only thing was she couldn't have him. He belonged to somebody else.

If you are busy pleasing everyone, you are not being true to yourself.

Chapter 8

Keelan

"So, are we going to talk about it?"

Keelan had just climbed into the bed beside her. Alecia's voice stopped him as he was reaching to shut off the lamp on his nightstand, and her tone let him know that he wouldn't be going to sleep anytime soon.

"What was that about?"

He had hoped she would leave him alone once they reached his condo, but she hadn't let up at all.

"You made it seem the other night like you barely knew the girl. Now today it looked like the two of you were hugged up. Now, I'll ask again. What was that about, Keelan?"

She had been following him around his bedroom like an annoying puppy dog as he stripped out of his work attire. All he wanted to do was take a shower and go to bed. All her questions were doing was making him think about the one person he would like to forget. Alecia kept trying to get in front of him and make him look at her face, but he kept turning his back to her.

"All hugged up? Now, why would I do that, especially with you popping in every other day?" he argued, still keeping his back to her in the bed.

"You know that's just so I can be my father's eyes and ears until he gets here this weekend. But now I can see what makes that a problem for you. How long have you been fucking her, Keelan?"

"I don't know what you're talking about."

"Look me in my eyes and tell me you're not sleeping with her."

Keelan prepared to face her and lie to her about what he'd been doing while they were apart. All he had to do was tell her that nothing had transpired between him and Teeka, and she would leave him alone. When he finally faced her, he saw a look of determination on her face, and suddenly he didn't see a point in telling her anything other than the truth.

"I can't," he said. "Because I am sleeping with her."

Alecia's face fell, and her shoulders caved inward. It was like watching as her life completely shattered in front of her. Keelan felt like the worst person in the world hurting her like that. Still, she deserved to know the truth.

"I was . . ." She paused and took a breath to hold in her tears. "I was afraid that something like this might happen. I knew that it must have already happened when I laid in your bed and your pillows smelled exactly like that Carol's Daughter you supposedly bought for me. I thought at first that I was tripping, but I remembered that's the same product that Teeka said a *really* good friend bought for her. Seeing you at the office with her and the way you looked at her when she got on the elevator was all the confirmation I needed."

"I never meant to hurt you," Keelan said. He was prepared to hear her announce that it was officially over. "We've just been through so much. I didn't know if we would really make it."

"Okay," Alecia said and took a deep breath. "Just one question before I do anything else. Was it just sex between the two of you, or are you in love with her?" She searched his face for an answer. When she found it, she stared at him in disbelief. "Oh my God. You love her."

"I'm sorry, Alecia."

"Did you even want me to move down here?"

"I wanted to try to make things work," Keelan told her. "But it's like, after all of this time, things are still the same."

"And when were you going to tell me that? After my father signed the contract and you didn't need me anymore?"

"Alecia . . ."

"Do you even love me anymore, Keelan?"

"Of course I love you."

"But are you in love with me? Do you still want to be my husband?"

"I . . ." He sighed and shook his head. "I don't know, Alecia. I just need more time."

"What about Teeka? Are you still going to be seeing her?"

Keelan reflected on his conversation with Teeka and Lynne. Teeka had gone on a date, which meant she was officially moving on with her life. Of course, when they were doing their thing, Teeka would always make it seem as if she were still on the market, but Keelan knew deep down that she wasn't dealing with anyone else. She was the type of woman who liked to focus on one person and one person only. His jaw threatened to clench at the thought of someone else touching her, but it was a thought that he would have to let go of.

"Teeka and I are done," he answered finally. "That's not something you have to worry about."

"Then we can push the wedding back and go from here. But I will let you know this, Keelan Metoyer: I have invested my blood, sweat, and tears into this relationship with you. I dropped everything I had going for myself in Milwaukee to come here and be with you. Now, I will accept my fault in pushing you into another woman's bed, but that will never happen again. I love you, Keelan, but we have more riding on this relationship's success than just love."

"Okay." He kissed her on the cheek and then turned off the lamp on his nightstand.

Alecia's words lingered in the air, or maybe they were just echoing in his mind. He felt relieved to have gotten a weight off his chest, but now he feared that he'd opened up a new can of worms. He didn't believe Alecia would just let it go the way she was making it seem; however, the only thing he had control over was the moment that he was living in, and in that moment, the only thing he wanted to do was sleep.

Letting go doesn't mean you stop caring. It means you stop trying to force others to.

Chapter 9

Teeka

Wrrrt! Wrrrt! Wrrrt!

"Mmmm!" Teeka groaned with her face in a pillow.

Wrrrt! Wrrrt! Wrrrt!

She smacked her lips and threw the covers from over her head. She didn't need to check the digital clock on her nightstand because the sun wasn't even out yet. It felt as though she'd only been sleeping a few hours, and the events from the night before were still fresh on her mind.

Wrrrt! Wrrrt! Wrrrt!

Her phone vibrated again next to her pillow, and she snatched it up. Checking the screen, she saw that it was Lynne calling her at four in the morning. Teeka tried to clear the sleepiness from her throat before she answered.

"Lynne?"

"Don't Lynne me! I have been calling you for hours. Why aren't you answering?"

"Umm, I don't know. Maybe because it's four in the morning."

"That's not the point!" Lynne's voice sounded shrill and alert. "I haven't slept a wink. You don't get to send me messages like that and then not answer your phone."

"You had Tony there to keep you company. You could have waiting until at least eight o'clock to blow my phone up instead of waking me up out of my sleep."

"Girl, I made Tony's ass hit the road when I got your text. Teeka, I don't know what you're thinking I said, or what Vic told you, but I never *warned* him that you were a big girl. Now, I might have told him you were probably a little thicker than the women he was used to, but I didn't think that was a bad thing. Hell, you have more ass than a lot of chicks!"

The more Lynne rambled on, the sillier Teeka felt for even sending the message in the first place. She had just been stuck in a moment of anger, and she needed someone to take it out on. Lynne wasn't the problem, and neither was Vic. She was her own problem. Teeka rolled over so that she was on her back and the phone was pressed to her ear. Her eyes adjusted to the darkness in the room and focused on the lines on the ceiling.

"Lynne, my bad, girl. You know I'm just going through a lot. I thought I would have a good time going on a double date with you, but all Vic did was remind me of how much he wasn't Keelan. I wasn't ready to step out with anyone else, and I honestly don't know when I will be."

"No, it's me who should be saying sorry, girl. Not just as your best friend, but as a woman. I should have known that you weren't over that whole situation or even close to it. I could tell by the way you look at that man that love is still running through your veins."

"I don't know what to do, Lynne. Not only do I work with the man, but his fiancée comes into the office multiple times a week."

"That son of a bitch. I still can't believe he did this to you."

"The sad thing is, I truly don't feel that hurting me was his intention. I believe him when he says that he didn't know where they were going in their relationship. What I do know is that he still chose her over me, and even if I don't want to, I have to let him go. But I don't know how."

"You just have to take the situation for what it is and realize that you were never the problem. In all my time of dealing with the opposite sex, I have learned that men are just selfish. If they can have their cake and eat it too, they will. I just want you to know I'll be one thousand percent by your side. But wait—do you think the girl knows about you? Maybe that's why she keeps popping up at the office," Lynne suggested.

"I don't think that's why she keeps popping up," Teeka replied. "Her father is Steve's latest business venture. They're in the middle of a merger."

"Do you think that's why Keelan chose her over you?"

"That and the fact that they have years of history that I'm not even going to try and compete with."

"Girl, I feel you. I wouldn't either. You're doing the right thing."

Then why do I feel so empty? Teeka thought.

"I'll let you know when I start feeling the same," she said. "But, Lynne, I have two more hours of sleep. I'm going to talk to you on my lunch break or something."

"All right. Love you, boo."

"Love you too," Teeka said and disconnected the call.

She tried to fall back to sleep, but there was no point. She was already wide awake. She lay in bed for a little bit longer before she decided the get a super early start on the day.

Teeka was showered and dressed and ready to leave by six thirty and decided that she might as well head out to work early. Before she left, she made sure to secure the diamond-studded hair pin neatly in the tight bun on the top of her head.

Before she got to work, she stopped to grab herself some breakfast and some coffee. When she finally arrived, she parked her car in the parking garage and made her way inside the large building.

"Good morning, Walter." She greeted one of ETCO's security guards at the entrance as she walked through.

Walter was a married man in his late forties; however, that ring on his finger never stopped him from flirting with Teeka whenever the two crossed paths. He was handsome and muscular, with chestnut-colored skin, but still, he was nowhere near Teeka's type. She always wondered why he didn't just go bald since the hair at the top of his head was thinning.

The bright smile on his face told Teeka that that morning would be no different.

"Mm-mm-mmm! Your bed must be made out of clouds, because whenever I see you, it's like you fell from the sky, girl! You're looking good today, Miss Teeka. Is that a new coat?"

"No," Teeka said and glanced down at her plum-colored hooded pea coat. "I just haven't worn it in a while. Thank you, though, Walter. You're always so sweet to me."

"I would be even sweeter if you let me take you out to dinner sometime," he said.

"I don't think your wife would appreciate that too much." She grinned at him.

"True that. They would probably find my ass in somebody's ocean with a weight tied to my ankles!" They shared a laugh. "But for real, girl, you got it going on. Don't take this the wrong way, but I have always been a sucker for a woman with some meat on her bones. I'm sure you hear every day what kind of fox you are. Let me stop making a fool of myself. I just wanted you to know how beautiful you are, queen."

She couldn't will away the smile on her face if she wanted to. She said good-bye to Walter and continued her walk to the elevators that would take her upstairs to her desk. Walter would never know it, but he had set the mood for her whole day. He had been a little thirsty, but his thirstiness had made her feel good about herself. By the time she got to her desk, her smile had reached from one ear to the next.

She checked her messages and responded to a few e-mails before diving into her muffin and coffee. It was still early, and most of the executives didn't get into the office until about eight thirty. She figured that gave her enough time to get ahead of her workload and get herself together before the day really took off. She checked to see who was online, and she saw a green dot next to Keelan's name. She swallowed the big chunk of muffin in her mouth and hurried to set her e-mail to offline.

"There," she said, hoping that he hadn't seen the green dot by her name.

Teeka figured the only way to get over Keelan was to take him in small doses—and only in a professional environment. She refused to cry over him ever again.

If you don't follow your heart, then you'll spend the rest of your life wishing you had.

Chapter 10

Keelan

"You, my friend, might just be the stupidest son of a bitch I've ever met."

Keelan groaned. He should have known telling his friend Chauncey what was going on with his life was a mistake. He had been keeping things under wraps pretty well, but with it all unfolding right in front of his face, he had to let it out.

Chauncey Adams worked for ETCO as well, in the accounting department, and he was Keelan's first friend in the city. He was about six feet tall, well dressed, and had good luck with the ladies since apparently chocolate brothas were in style. He sat in Keelan's office, casually brushing the low-cut, deep-sea waves in his thick black hair. He was staring at Keelan in disbelief and shaking his head.

"And I can't believe you hit Teeka's ass before me!"

"Hey, chill out, man," Keelan warned.

"I'm just saying." Chauncey held his arms up and shrugged. "Up until just now, I thought I still had a chance with her. You sure have a way of shattering a man's dreams. I would have never known the two of you were involved."

"We kept things on the hush. We wanted our privacy."

"'We, or you?" Chauncey raised his eyebrow. "You had wifey in Milwaukee, and you were diving in Teeka's pussy at the same time. You are living quite the life, Mr. Metoyer."

"I shouldn't have said anything to you." Keelan put a hand over his face and shook his head. "You aren't helping at all."

"My bad." Chauncey laughed. "I'm just giving you a hard time. What I'm trying to understand, though, is if all is forgiven with wifey, why are you still worrying yourself with it?"

Keelan leaned his head back into his computer chair and sighed. He didn't know how to tell his boy that he still wore Acqua Di Gio cologne every day just in case he ran into Teeka. Or that he missed the way she felt beneath him, trying to squirm away because he was in too deep. And that when Alecia called out his name when he was pounding it from the back that morning, he had wished it was Teeka's voice.

"I want her, man," Keelan told him. "I want Teeka, but—"

"But Alecia is the daughter of the man signing a million-dollar contract with ETCO at the end of the week."

"Bingo."

"Damn, I would *hate* to have your problems. How did you get into some shit like this?"

"I don't know, but like you said, I guess it's over. Alecia pushed the wedding back, so that gives us time to move past this situation."

"If you can."

"What's that supposed to mean?"

"Come on." Chauncey gave Keelan a look of doubt. "Do you think I'm that stupid? It's obvious to see that you, my friend, are in love. And not with the one you're marrying. If nobody else has said it, I will. A million dollars is a lot of money, but not enough to sell your life for. Are you sure that you want to walk down the aisle knowing that you want somebody else? Man! That's a big-ass red flag!"

Keelan let the words sink in while he logged into his computer. The first thing he opened was his company e-mail to make sure he hadn't missed anything. His eyes went to the online users, and he saw the green dot by Teeka's name.

"She's here." He checked his clock and saw that she was early. He wondered if she'd had such a good time on her date last night that it had her at work before her shift started. He shook those thoughts from his mind and looked back to Teeka's name. The green dot next to her name had gone grey.

"You gonna say something?"

"Nah," Keelan said. "I wouldn't even know what to say."

"I feel it, but I'm about to go to my office and do some work." Chauncey reached out and slapped hands with Keelan. "Everything will come together the way that it's supposed to. Don't stress it."

"I hope you're right," Keelan replied.

Chauncey shut the door behind him when he left, and Keelan tried to focus on getting his clients their settlements. Soon enough, his mind was so wrapped in his work that he forgot about the world around him. The next time he looked up, the time read eleven o'clock, and someone was knocking on his door. The morning had flown by, so hopefully that set the tone for the day.

"Come in," he said in his smooth, deep voice, without looking up from his computer. "Shut the door behind you."

"I–I'm sorry to disturb you, Mr. Metoyer."

Her voice froze his fingers above the keyboard.

"Mr. O'Brian asked me to deliver these papers to you," she said.

"You can set them on my desk," Keelan said and watched Teeka enter his office, closing the door.

She was wearing a black sweater dress that clung to her body and accented all her curves. The wine-colored, skinny-heel peep-toe booties made her sit up in all of the right places, and the diamond pin in her bun shone in the light. He noticed she even had a little bit of makeup on, and his eyes went to the plum color on her full lips. His erection grew harder the closer she got to him.

"I think he wants you to look at them before you leave today," she said, avoiding eye contact.

"Okay, thank you, Tee—Miss Smith."

"You're welcome, Mr. Metoyer," she said and finally met his eyes. "Have a good day."

But she didn't leave. She stood there, and they stared at each other. There was nothing to be said, yet so much to say. He wanted to mend the broken piece in her heart, and she wanted him to. That's why she was still there. They both knew that the best thing to do was let it go, but how? They always say a drug doesn't become an addiction until you try to stop using it and can't.

"How was your date?" Keelan finally asked the one thing that was driving him crazy.

"It was fine," she told him. "We went out to dinner, and then he took me home."

"Oh, okay," he said and turned his attention back to his computer. "Thank you for bringing me those papers. Tell Steve I'll get on them as soon as I can."

"You're welcome." Teeka turned to leave, and he glanced up in time to see her round ass switching away from him. When she got to the door, she looked over her shoulder. "Why did you ask that?"

"I can't ask you how your life is?"

"You didn't ask how my life is. You asked how my date went."

"And I don't see how that is a problem." Keelan made a gesture with his head like he didn't know what she was talking about. "I just hoped you had a good time, that's all."

"Well, thank you," she told him and proceeded to leave.

"Will you see him again?"

His voice stopped her.

"I don't know, maybe. Why?"

"I just hope that you're being smart, that's all. You're too beautiful and too good to just be sleeping around."

"You mean like I was with you? Or was that different?"

"That was different, and you know it was."

"Was it? The last I checked, that was a dead-end situation too. But no worries. I'm not sleeping with anyone else yet. I know that's what you really want to know."

"Okay," he said as he felt the wave of relief wash over him. He tried not to let it show on his face. "Your business is your business, though, Teeka. If we want this to work, I want things to be normal between us. I don't want to lose you as my friend."

"Normal?" She looked at him like he was stupid before opening the door to his office. "I don't know what kind of selfish-ass world you're living in, but I see we have two different definitions of normal. Things will never be the same for me. If you could, please limit the weight of conversation between us. If it isn't about work, there really isn't any reason for us to talk, and I need you to respect my wishes. Can you do that?"

He wanted to tell her no, get up from his desk, shut the door, and bend her over his desk. The scene played vividly in his head. He could hear her whining his name, trying to stay quiet so no other employees would hear them sexing. He could feel her wet love canal wrapped around his dick, making the sound that he loved to hear so much. But what would happen after she left his office? She would be even more broken than she was when she had entered, because nothing about his reality would change. Teeka didn't deserve that. She deserved a man who could earnestly return her affection.

"Yeah, you got it, Teeka."

"Thank you," she said and left his office.

When she was gone, he contemplated seeing if he could switch the floor that his office was on. That would be pointless, though, because Steve would still be his boss, and Teeka was still Steve's secretary. Crossing paths with her would be unavoidable. He would just have to fake it until finally the feelings he had for her faded. But would they? Something that Chauncey had said played briefly in his mind:

"A million dollars is a lot of money, but not enough to sell your life for. Are you sure that you want to walk down the aisle knowing that you want somebody else?"

Was he making a mistake by marrying Alecia? The rest of the work day, he thought seriously about his life and where it was going. He tried to pinpoint the reason that he'd agreed with Alecia on trying to fix their broken relationship. There were a lot of perks to being with her, but when he listed them all mentally, he found that none of those reasons were that he loved her. His selfishness had led him to put himself in a sticky situation.

Keelan groaned and hit his desk with his fist. It was his lunchtime, but he had no desire to even leave his office. He had a mini fridge in the corner. If he got hungry, he would just grab a salad or something from there.

Pulling out his phone, he opened Facebook and checked his notifications. There was a pending request from Alecia. When he clicked on it, he saw that she had tagged him in a post, telling their friends and family that the wedding had been pushed back. He didn't even want to go through the comments on the post, nor did he accept the tag. His fingers navigated him to Teeka's page, where he was met with an "Add Friend" prompt, letting him know that she had already unfriended him.

He sighed and clicked on her profile picture. It was from the summer and she was sitting outside of a restaurant, laughing, while her curls blew around her face. Her smile was so big that her eyes lit up, and Keelan felt a tug at his heart just knowing that he was the one who had taken the photo. He had just told her a stupid joke, and she had cracked up laughing. She looked so good in that moment that he'd pulled out his phone and snapped her picture.

"What are you doing, man?" he asked himself and clicked out of her profile. "Let her go. You have to let her go."

"Let who go?"

Keelan had been so into his phone that he didn't even hear his door open. He quickly stuffed his phone back into his pocket and stood up to shake Steve's hand.

"Oh, nothing, boss. I was just thinking out loud. Did you knock on the door?"

"Yes, twice. So, whatever 'nothing' is, it sure had you zoned out. But no matter. I just stopped by to see if you had a chance to look at those papers that Teeka dropped off."

"Yes, I did." He shuffled through the mess he'd made on his desk and found the folder that he was looking for. "Everything is in there. I think Mrs. Jacobs will be pleased with the amount awarded to her. The insurance company should be contacting her soon."

"Perfect!" Steve said and took the papers. "You know, you've been doing a mighty fine job since you started. It's no secret that the board thinks I'm moving a little too fast making you the vice president of this company, but I know I'm making the right decision."

"And I won't let you down, sir. Once we close on this deal with Edward Clout, I'm sure the board will be more confident in my presence at the table. I know my new position is riding on this deal."

"There are a few things riding on the merger with Clout Enterprises." Steve patted Keelan once on the shoulder. "But not this position."

"What? Sir, I thought that the merger was the reason why you offered the job to me."

"I can see why you think that." Steve chuckled. "But no, a little birdie that I would trust with my life told me that you were the best man for the job."

"Teeka?"

"You didn't hear it from me." Steve shrugged his shoulders. "That girl is an angel, and if she thinks you're right for the job, then there is no argument. If you weren't already taken, I would try to hook the two of you up. Thanks again. Will I see you at the banquet on Friday?"

"Uh, yeah," Keelan replied in a stunned state. "Yeah, I'll be there."

"Perfect!"

Steve took his leave, and Keelan stood frozen in place. Teeka was the real reason that he was getting a promotion. Had it been Alecia who had put him in a position to win like that, the entire world would have known. But Teeka hadn't said a word, because it was a genuine act. She had always told him that she wanted the best for him, but he always thought it was just pillow talk. He knew now that she had been serious.

Who did he think he was fooling? Letting Alecia move into his condo had been the wrong move, and so was allowing her to believe that there was a future between them. He had been so focused on trying to do the right thing that he didn't notice that he had spared the wrong person's feelings.

At the end of his day, Keelan looked at the clock on his desk, and it dawned on him that he hadn't left his office all day. It was almost six o'clock, and he figured Teeka had probably already left for the night. He took a big breath and grabbed his phone. He typed out a carefully considered message that would both send the world as it was crashing down around him and put it back together at the same time.

"Fuck it," he said out loud as he hit the SEND button.

Learn to walk away from people and situations that threaten your peace of mind, self-respect, values, morals, and self-worth.

Chapter 11

Keelan

After standing in his own way, Keelan finally knew where he needed to be. Sending his text message made it feel as though a big weight had been lifted off his shoulders. It was a weight that returned, of course, once he got home. He had started to go to a bar, but there was still a situation he had to handle first.

"So, you think that trying to make things work with me was a mistake? For real, Keelan?" Alecia was on Keelan like white on rice the moment he walked through the door. He didn't even have time to take off his tie before she was in his face. She was wearing a pair of jeans, a peach T-shirt, and her long hair shook violently around her shoulders. Her face held the expression of a person who was beyond distraught, but she didn't have a single tear in her eye. Any way that he tried to turn, she hopped in front of him and waved her phone in his face.

"Please don't make this harder than it has to be."

"What the hell are you saying? You sent me a message, and unless I'm mistaken, it sounds like you're trying to break things off with me. Indefinitely."

"If that's what you took from it—" Keelan looked around his spacious condo. "I see you haven't started packing yet."

"So, you're serious? Well, I have a question for you. If that's how you felt, why didn't you just say so last night? Why did I wake up with your dick stuffed inside of me?"

"Last night, I thought that maybe I could do it. That I could be the man for you and that we could live our happily ever after. But today . . . today I gave the situation some real thought. I might be the man for you, but you aren't the woman for me. You want everyone and everything to adapt to you and your way of living, but you don't do the same. You're so . . . *controlling*, Alecia. The fun has been gone from our relationship for some time. Since you've been here, you haven't wanted to do any of the things I like to do."

"Fun?" Alecia scoffed and jerked her head back. "*Fun?* Is that what this is about? Pardon me if I'm an adult trying to solidify her future. I don't have time for fun."

"And that's okay, Alecia. I understand that ever since you started working for your father your career has been put on a pedestal. That's just no life for me."

"But I love you, Keelan." Her voice came out tearfully, even though tears were still not in sight.

"Do you? Because sometimes it feels as though I'm just an object to you."

"Why are you saying these things, Keelan? Is it because you don't think I will really forgive you for sleeping with that fat girl? Because I'm over that, Keelan. I just want to move forward with you. After the merger and our wedding, we will be set for life. We will be the couple that everyone loves and envies. Baby, please don't leave me. I moved all the way here for you and told everyone that the wedding was still on. What will they say if we break up?"

"You know, you have always been so concerned with what others think of you. That might be why you are so controlling. I love you, Alecia, but I'm not in love with you anymore. Marrying you would be the biggest mistake of my life. I'm sorry you moved all the way here to start a new life with me. I should have told you after the first week that this new life is starting to feel a lot like the old one."

"This is because of her, isn't it?" Alecia demanded to know.

He didn't have to ask who she was talking about. The old Keelan might have lied just to put a smile on Alecia's face. Keeping her happy had felt like a job for so long. He understood then that he worked so hard at it because he was frightened of her connections. Now, he didn't care about any of that, because he had made some pretty valuable connections of his own.

"Yes," he told her and looked her square in the eye. "I hurt Teeka with words a few weeks ago. For you. I hurt a woman who would never do a thing to hurt me, because I wanted her to leave me alone. But when you came here, all I think about every moment that I'm with you is how much you aren't her. I'm done forcing anything between the two of us. This relationship died the moment you told me to come to Chicago alone. So, go, Alecia. Go back to Milwaukee. You deserve someone who will genuinely love you the way that you want to be loved."

Alecia looked dumbfounded. Her mouth opened and closed a few times, but when she couldn't find the words to say, she used her hand.

Slap!

Her hand stung against the right side of his face. He gave her that one, but when she tried to hit him again, he caught her hand in midair. She fought against his grasp, trying her best to strike him one more time. Finally, she snatched away from him and spat at his feet. She stormed away to the master bedroom, and Keelan heard drawers slamming and the closet door opening and shutting. He went to the kitchen and poured himself a glass of Remy on the rocks while she packed up her things.

By the time she was finished, he was halfway through his second glass. She had two suitcases and a duffle bag in tow. He stood to help her carry them to the car, but she gave him a look that was so icy, he froze where he stood.

"I will be sure to let my father know about all of this. See if the merger happens now," she said.

"If your father wants to say no to a great business deal, then screw it. Even a one-million-dollar contract isn't enough to buy my soul. Now please, leave." He motioned to the door with his hand.

Alecia clenched her jaw tightly before leaving and letting the door slam behind her.

When she was gone, he let out a huge breath. Surprisingly, that went better than he had thought it would. He was sure that he would have some damaged property, but he didn't. With her gone, there was only one thing on his mind—well, one person, actually.

Without thinking twice, he grabbed his keys and hopped in his car. He didn't even remember the commute or how long it took him to get there. The next thing he knew, he was outside of Teeka's door, trying to get the nerve to knock.

"'I've been thinking, Teeka. And I dumped Alecia for you." He practiced out loud, shaking his head and telling himself, "No. That sounds positively awful. Okay, okay. What about this? Teeka, I've been a mess without you. I'm sorry for being too much of a coward to choose you in the first place. Yeah, that's it. Okay. Here goes."

Knock! Knock!

He heard footsteps approaching the door, and he had half a mind to step out of the view of the peephole. When he was certain that she had seen him standing there, he waited for something to happen. Her breathing gave her position away. He pictured her leaned up against the door, biting her bottom lip the way she always did when she was in deep thought. She hadn't cursed him out yet, so that was a good sign. His heart skipped a beat when the door unlocked and swung open.

There she was, standing barefoot in a red silk robe tied tightly at the waist. It looked as if she had already turned in for the night. Her hair was styled in two Cherokee braids, and clutched in her fingers was a personal container of Ben & Jerry's.

Her mouth said something, but her eyes spoke a language that he understood all too well. He stepped through the doorway and grabbed her gently by her elbows. When he pulled her body to his, she didn't pull back. It was like the fight had left her entire being.

"Why are you here, Keelan?" She breathed up at him. "I thought you said you want things to be normal between us."

"This is normal," he said. All the words he had practiced went out the window. "It took me some time to see, but *this* is where I need to be. With you. So, be with me, Teeka. No more friends with benefits. I want to do it for real."

"But, Alecia . . ."

"Is on her way back to Milwaukee."

"What?"

"I told her that I couldn't do it with her anymore. There is no more relationship, no more wedding, and no more Alecia. There is only Teeka and Keelan. The way it's supposed to be."

"How do I know that you're telling the truth?"

"You won't, unless you let me show you."

"I can't be hurt behind you again, Keelan," Teeka said as a tear slid down her cheek and to her top lip. "I thought that I could get over you. I figured that all I needed was a little time. But every day, you are the first person I think about in the morning and the last thought before I go to sleep. You were my greatest source of happiness for so long and then, poof! Just like that you were gone. I had to go to sleep thinking about you being with someone else. Then I had to wake up and pretend like you and I had nothing. Do you know how that feels?"

"No. No, I don't. But I know how it feels to walk a false truth, and I don't want to do that anymore. We both know that we will never be able to let this thing between us go. It's too strong. I miss you, Teeka. I miss your laugh and the way you poke my cheek when I fall asleep too fast. I miss holding you at night and kissing your cute-ass face. Hell, I even miss waking up to that bush on your head in the morning."

"Hey!" Teeka sniffled.

"I'm sorry." Keelan smiled. "I'm being serious, though. Be with me, Teeka. Be my girl, my homie, my lover, and my friend. You're everything to me, baby. Plus, I have something more comforting than that cookies and cream. I can promise you that."

"What if I say yes? What is on the other side of that answer? Will I have to worry about a crazy ex trying to sabotage my relationship? How do I know that she's really gone?"

"Because Alecia isn't half the woman you are on her best day," Keelan said and let his hands fall to her hips.

"Then why did you choose her?"

"The history—or maybe it was because she was safe—but I see now that our life paths just don't cross any longer. I don't want to talk about her anymore. You have to trust me, Teeka. Please, just let me love you."

"Forever?"

"For as long as you let me." He leaned down and licked her bottom lip. "If God blesses us with forever, then I'm all right with that."

She stood quickly on the tips of her toes and pressed her lips against his. The softness of them felt like heaven on his, and he couldn't stop his hands from exploring her body. He'd been wondering what was under that robe of hers and was pleased when he touched nothing but bare skin. He kissed her deeper and slid his tongue in her mouth so that it could intertwine with hers. He could taste the remnants of Oreo cookies in her mouth, but that didn't stop him.

"It was you," he whispered once their lips broke apart. "You told Steve to promote me."

"Yeah."

"Why didn't you tell me?"

"Because if you were going to come to me, you were going to do it on your own. I wanted you to make your own decision. But honestly, I thought I had already lost you. I didn't see a point, so I just let you think what you wanted to."

"I don't remember the last time someone did anything like that for me. Especially if they didn't get anything out of it," he said.

"That's where you're wrong," Teeka said as she undid the knot in front of her robe. "I did get something out of it."

"Well, what's that?"

"Your smile. You do remember how much I love that smile, right?" She let the robe fall slowly off her shoulders and to the floor. "Especially when you're watching me walk away from you naked. Oh, wait. That hasn't happened yet."

She stepped back and touched her tongue on the front of her teeth. She had a mischievous look on her face, and she turned her head to watch him as she walked away. His eyes watched her ass jiggle down the hallway, and he felt his lips spread into a long smile.

"You're something else, you know that?"

"No, I don't," she said and bent over so he could get a good look at her pussy lips. "What I do know is that you're all the way over there, and I'm almost to the bed. Come on."

"You don't have to tell me twice, woman," he said, loosening his tie.

If you live to be one hundred, I want to live to be one hundred minus a day, so that I never have to live without you.

Chapter 12

Teeka

Pure bliss. That was the only way to describe how Teeka was feeling. It was like every piece in her puzzle had finally come together. When she opened her eyes the next morning, the sun was peeking at her through the slightly open blinds in her room. She looked over to check the clock on her nightstand, and her eyes widened when she saw that it was almost noon. She tried to jump up, but a hand on her arm stopped her.

"I already called the office for you. Told Steve that you would be working from home today, and so would I."

"You did?"

"Yes. I'm sure Steve will have some questions for me in the morning, one of them being about why Edward is pulling out of the deal."

"He's pulling out of the merger?" Teeka propped herself up on her elbow and rested her head in her hand.

"Probably. Especially after Alecia tells him that I left her for another woman."

"This other woman must be pretty important if you threw all of that away."

"She's more important than you'll ever know." He cupped her chin and sat up slightly to kiss her.

"So, what are we going to do all day?" she asked. "Netflix and chill?"

"I was going to say let's go out somewhere, but that actually sounds pretty satisfying."

"Takeout?"

"As long as it's Chinese."

"What about your clothes?" Teeka pointed to the suit she'd stripped him out of on the floor. "Those are probably a little sticky."

"I packed a bag just in case you took me back." He grinned at her. "I had to be prepared. It's in my car."

"Perfect. That means I have you to myself all day." She ran her hand down his chest and didn't stop until it was wrapped around his still sleeping member. Her touch brought it to life, and she felt it grow in her hand. "I wonder how we'll pass the time."

"Oh, I can think of a few ways," he said and touched her lips with the tips of his fingers.

"Mmmm. Oh, is that right?" She smiled and lay back down on the bed.

He leaned into her, and she opened her mouth to suck his bottom lip. Soon they were in a full-on lip lock and running their hands over each other's bodies. When Keelan's hand found Teeka's freshly waxed pussy, he gripped it and let his middle finger slip through the crack. He was met with her already flowing juices, and he moaned in her mouth. He rubbed on her clit until he slid two fingers inside of her. Instantly, he felt her walls contract on his fingers, and that turned him on in the best way. He used his wrist to give his hand power to fuck her, and she stroked his shaft at the same time.

When Teeka swung a leg over to straddle him, he slapped her ass and watched her thighs jiggle. She didn't wait for him to prepare before she brought herself down on his erection. His morning wood slid into her and didn't stop until it was knocking on her cervix.

"Ooooh!" She threw her neck back and brought her hands to her breasts.

Keelan put his hands behind his head and watched as she rode him and pinched her own nipples. Her eyes never left his face. She watched the pleasured expression that came over it while he watched her please herself. He was watching his dick get swallowed by her pussy every time she came down on him. He loved when she worked for her own nut, and this time was no different. She bounced on his stiff meat until she felt her clit swell up, and then she slowed down.

"Ooh, I know what that means," Keelan said, feeling the shift in her rhythm.

His hands flew from behind his head and gripped her waist so that he could pound into her with upward motions. The squishy sound of her wet pussy filled the air, and she fell down into him. Her face was buried in his neck, and her hands held on tight to his shoulders.

"I'm trying to take it, baby," she breathed. "Oh, daddy, I'm trying to take this big dick. She's about to come, baby. All over this fat dick."

She always spoke about her pussy in third person, because she told Keelan that she had a mind of her own. She heard him moan her name softly as she was talking dirty in his ear, and she bit down on his dick with her pussy walls.

"Damn, Teeka! Oooh-wee this is some good pussy. Did you give it away to that nigga?"

"Ahh!" Teeka screamed out because on his last word, he thrust so hard into her that she felt it in her stomach. "No! I didn't, baby! I promise!"

He beat her pussy relentlessly as if he were suddenly angered by her. The thought of her letting someone else inside of her must have made him mad, and he was showing it. She felt him slap her ass with so much force that it made her clit jump.

"You're lying. You gave up this juicy pussy, didn't you? You nasty-ass slut!"

"I didn't! Oooh, Keelan! I'm about to come. I didn't give her away, I swear. Can't nobody fuck me like youuuu!"

It was like an eruption went off between her legs. She screamed Keelan's name over and over as she squirted her juices all over his abs. Her entire body jerked as she climaxed, and she went limp when it was done.

She could have rolled over and gone back to sleep, but Keelan was nowhere near done between her legs. His lips found her erect nipples, and he sucked and nibbled all over them while he worked himself in and out of her love canal.

"Mmm, girl," he said and pulled out of her. "You got me all sticky. Bend over. Let me get it from the back."

Although her legs were shaky from her orgasm, she bent over and arched her back as deep as it would go. He put his dick inside of her pussy a few times to get his shaft wet, before she felt the tip at the entrance of her back door. She relaxed her body and bit her lip, bracing herself for the pain before the pleasure. When his whole shaft was inside, she felt tingles up and down her body. There was something about anal sex that did something to her, and she loved it. Once her whimpers turned into cries of pleasure, Keelan showed her no mercy. She rubbed her clit in a circular motion as he worked his way in and out of her asshole.

"Shit," he said as he slapped one of her big cheeks. "You're such a freak, Teeka. You let me put it anywhere."

Teeka wanted to tell him that she would have sucked him and fucked him any way that he liked, because that's how happy she was that he was back. Instead, she just moaned and enjoyed the ride. He brought her to two more orgasms from anal sex before he pulled out and released his seed all over her back. She felt the warmth of the liquid sliding, but he got off the bed and ran for a towel just in time.

"Oh, my goodness," Teeka giggled breathlessly. She let him wipe her back clean before falling over and watching him wipe the nut from his pubic hairs. "That felt like we were teenagers all over again."

"That's how it's supposed to feel. A timeless love," he told her as he finished wiping himself off. He threw the towel into the dirty clothes bin on the other side of the room and sat back down on the bed. "Like a fairy-tale, only this is one fucked up fairytale."

"No." She grabbed his hand and kissed it. "Sometimes in order for things to fall into place, they have to be ripped apart at once. I'm just thankful that you're here."

"Thankful?"

"Yes, thankful. At first, I was mad at you, but then I put myself in your shoes. If I were you, I would have done the exact thing, except . . ."

"Except what?"

"I don't know if I would have had the courage to follow my heart. So, yes, I am thankful for you, Keelan Metoyer."

"Well, I'm thankful for you too. Because of you, I finally got out of my own way."

The rest of the day, they just got lost in each other. He helped her with her laundry, and after they showered, he rubbed her feet. It felt like they were teenagers playing hookie from school. Teeka couldn't remember a time that she'd laughed so hard. She was sure other women would call her stupid for giving him a chance, but oh well. She was a woman in love.

When opportunity knocks on your door, always be willing to take a chance, because you never know how perfect something could turn out to be.

Chapter 13

Keelan

By the time Friday rolled around, Keelan was still all smiles. He made it to the office early, since he hadn't really done any work the day before. He also wanted to prep himself for Steve to come into his office asking what had happened. He had been trying to put together the right words to say, but nothing besides the truth made sense.

Keelan was still on cloud nine from all the love he and Teeka had made the day before, and he was feeling pretty good about life. It was around ten o'clock that morning when he finally got a knock on his door. He sat up in his chair, cleared his throat, and straightened his tie before he said, "Come in."

"Good morning, Keelan," Steve said when he walked in and shut the door behind him.

That day, Steve was wearing a light blue suit jacket with a white silk shirt and brown slacks. The shoes he wore matched the jacket, and Keelan had to admit that Steve had always been a smooth-dressing motherfucker.

"Hey, boss," Keelan said and motioned to the chair on the other side of his desk. "Please, have a seat."

"Don't mind if I do," Steve said.

When he was seated, Keelan waited for him to speak. Their eyes were locked on each other, and it was hard for him to read the look in Steve's. Finally, Keelan sighed and opened his mouth to explain.

"Look, Steve, I know why you're here. And first I just want to say—"

"He signed. ETCO is now part owner of Clout Enterprises!"

Keelan's mouth froze in place as he tried to comprehend Steve's words. He wasn't sure if he'd heard correctly. He swore Steve just said that Edward signed the papers.

"Seriously?"

"Yes! All thanks to you!"

"To me?" Keelan was confused.

"Don't act modest now, son." Steve grinned. "You knew this was happening today. I don't know how you pulled it off after breaking things off with Miss Clout, but whatever it was, it worked!"

"Uh, yeah," Keelan said and let his voice trail off.

Obviously, Alecia had told her father what happened between them, but Keelan couldn't for the life of him understand why he still went through with the business deal. Although business was business, Alecia was his princess. Keelan couldn't see Edward putting anything over her. Still, he was happy that he had.

"Keep up the good work," Steve said and pulled something out of his pocket. "Oh, and before I go, I can't forget this." He handed Keelan a long, triangular-shaped object. It was a gold nametag with Keelan's name on it. Next to his name were the words *Vice President*, a welcome sight for his eyes. Keelan broke into a broad smile.

"Thank you, sir," he said and held his hand out for Steve. "I won't let the company down."

"I know you won't," Steve told him. "That's why I gave you a new office on the third floor to match that nametag. One word: windows."

"I don't have words. Thank you, boss."

"You're welcome," Steve said and stood up. "I need to go and make sure everything is in place for the banquet tomorrow. Edward said that he would stop in, but his flight leaves in the evening."

"Did he say whether Alecia would be there?"

"After you dumped her for Teeka? I doubt it."

"Sir, I did not dump—you know about me and Teeka?"

"I had my suspicions, especially since the two of you decided not to come into work yesterday." He cleared his throat. "I hope you know what you're doing with that one. She's not one for any nonsense."

"And I don't plan to bring any into her life—I mean *anymore*."

"As long as you make sure she comes in this office smiling every day, you have my blessing on the matter. If it weren't for her this place would be turned upside down."

"Oh, trust me I know. You think I don't know who types up all of the company's statements?"

"I don't know what you're talking about," Steve said as he opened the door to the office. "Have a good day, Keelan."

"You too, boss," Keelan replied.

His smile said it all. He was on top of the world. Rolling up the long sleeves of his off-white button-up, Keelan leaned back into his seat and thought about sending Teeka a message to tell her about his good news. He changed his mind, deciding he would tell her that night at dinner. Somehow, everything had worked out. This week was a magical one because so much had happened, and he truly felt like a new man.

He started to get back to work, but a vibration in his pocket stopped him. He pulled his phone out and raised his eyebrow because he did not recognize the number on the screen. It was a Milwaukee area code, though, so he figured someone from home was trying to get in contact with him.

He put the phone to his ear and answered. "Hello?"

"I finally decided to call you as a man and see what your reason for breaking my daughter's heart was."

"Mr. Clout, it's nice to hear from you too."

"Don't humor me, boy. When my daughter called me crying Wednesday evening, asking me to book her a flight back to Milwaukee, I wanted to wring your neck."

"I'm sorry. I never meant to hurt Alecia."

"I always told her that she was too good for you. You were never nothing more than just a thug from the hood. But no, she didn't listen to me, and now look at what you did. You left her for your secretary. What was it? You used her up until you couldn't anymore, is that it? You are lucky the board outvoted me on Wednesday, otherwise the merger would have never happened."

"I'm sorry, Mr. Clout. . . . Actually, no. No, I'm not sorry."

"Excuse me?"

"I'm done apologizing for deciding what is and isn't good for me in my life. You're right about one thing: Alecia should have never been with me. Not for the reasons you're saying, but because eventually I would grow enough balls to leave that controlling bitch alone."

"You motherfucker! Don't you ever call my daughter a—"

"I want to thank you so much for your business with ETCO, Mr. Clout. I look forward to our future endeavors. If you have any questions, feel free to shoot me an e-mail. See you at the welcome banquet tomorrow."

Edward was still bumbling out insults when Keelan disconnected the call. He tossed his phone on the desk and felt a tickle at the back of his throat. When he opened his mouth, a loud laugh escaped his lips. Well, at least now he knew the reason why the merger had happened. He couldn't believe he used to be intimidated by Edward. Keelan had been so worried about getting on his bad side, but now that it had actually happened, he could truly say that he didn't give a shit.

Ping!

The noise came from his computer. It was an e-mail from Teeka, and he was still smiling when he opened it.

Lunch?

He opened the reply box and began to type away.

I was starting to think that you forgot about me. And yes, lunch would be great.

After about thirty seconds, his computer sounded again with her reply.

How could I forget someone as amazing as you? And perfect. I was thinking we would try that new Mexican spot on the corner down the street.

Keelan had seen the spot that she was talking about and had also wanted to see what their tacos were about. It was supposed to be authentic Mexican food, nothing like the bubble guts on a shell that Taco Bell served.

Sounds good. I'll meet you at your desk in fifteen. I have something to tell you.

He sent his message and closed out of his e-mail so that she couldn't bombard him with questions about what he was talking about. He wanted to tell her face-to-face so he could see the smile on her lips. Alecia had gone back to Milwaukee, he was the vice president of a company he hadn't even been at a full year, and he had a good woman by his side.

"Ahhh," he said like he'd just taken a swig of soda. "Life is good."

And the story of love is a long, sad tale, ending in a grave.

Chapter 14

Teeka

The night of the banquet had finally arrived, and Teeka was giddy like it was the prom she didn't get to go to. She had come to the home she'd grown up in and was in her old room, getting ready. She sat in front of the vanity, messing with her hair. She'd gotten a fresh flat-iron, and it would be the first time that Keelan had ever seen her hair straightened. She hoped that he liked it, and her dress, for that matter. She'd opted for a blue velvet off-the-shoulder dress. It came all the way down to her feet, which she loved, since her feet would be hidden. It would seem as though she were gliding.

"So, I heard you done messed around and fallen in love."

The voice came from behind her, and when Teeka looked in the vanity mirror, she saw her mother standing in the doorway. She was dressed in a way that let Teeka know that she was in for the night. Her pink bonnet was neatly in place on her head, and the cream-colored satin nightgown underneath the matching robe looked all too comfortable. Rashanda's smile was contagious, and Teeka felt the corners of her lips fighting to slant upward.

"I don't know what you're talking about."

"Mm-hmm." Rashanda placed her hand on her hip and used the other to wave a finger. "I don't see any other reason for you to be dressed like a pageant queen. I've been watching you since you sat down in that vanity, fussing with your hair. You look gorgeous, my young queen. Absolutely darling."

"Thanks, Mama," Teeka said and grabbed the golden pin to put in her hair.

"Here. Let me," Rashanda said and took it from her hands. "My grandmama always wanted some diamonds to wear in her hair, so my granddaddy worked day and night. It took him two months to save, but finally he had enough money to buy this for my grandmama. She gave it to my mama when she turned eighteen, she did the same for me, and I—"

"You did the same for me," Teeka finished for her.

She couldn't remember how many times she'd heard the story in her life; definitely more than a hundred Sometimes she thought that Rashanda reminded her so often so that she wouldn't do something crazy like sell it—which she would never do. She cocked her head slightly so that her mom could put the pin in place. When she was done, she reached in her pocket and pulled out a diamond choker and the bracelet to match.

"Mama, those are your favorites." Teeka gasped as she let her mother place the choker on her neck.

"Exactly why they better come back in one piece! Your daddy got me those, but I know he would have loved to see you in them tonight."

"Oh, Mama!" Teeka kissed Rashanda's hand after the bracelet was buckled in place. "Thank you. Tonight means a lot to me."

"Because of that boy?"

"Yes." Teeka sighed and playfully rolled her eyes. Her mom was relentless. The subject wasn't going to be dropped until she got the information she wanted. "His name is Keelan."

"I know." Rashanda winked at her daughter through the mirror. "Sandy called and told me everything yesterday."

"Oh my God! Steve told her?"

"That's his wife and you're like a daughter to him. Of course he told her. And she told me," Rashanda gloated. "I heard he was a fine young man, too. Well, I guess I'll see for myself when he picks you up. He is picking you up from here, right?"

"Yes. He should be here any minute now. The banquet starts at eight."

"Perfect," she said and gave Teeka a suspicious look.

"What?"

"Oh, nothing," Rashanda said and smiled slyly. "I just *also* heard that he put an end to his engagement for you. Is that true?"

"No!" Teeka spat out a little too suspiciously. "I mean, no. We've been spending time together for the past seven months, and when she came back into his life, he thought the right thing to do was go through with the wedding. But he loves me, and not her. Soooo . . . here we are."

She thought she'd done quite a good job of summarizing the last month of her life, but seeing the bewildered look on her mother's face, she started to second guess that theory. She burst out laughing and put her hands up.

"Mama, relax. He's a good guy. What is it that you always tell me? Every man comes with some shit; you just have to decide which shit is worth it. Isn't that right?"

"I really hate when you use my own words against me." Rashanda sighed. "Well, Steve vouched for this man. I still have questions about the situation, but you're grown and can make your own decisions. At least he has a good job. Sheesh. I just want to see you happy, baby."

"And I am happy. More than that, actually." Teeka stood up and whirled around in her dress. "What do you think? Is the dress too tight? Does it look like too much?"

"You look like Cinderella," Rashanda said and put her hand on her chest. "Oh, my goodness. You are absolutely stunning, darling. Let me go grab my camera."

"Mama," Teeka complained.

"Oh, hush, girl. You didn't go to prom, remember? You owe me!"

Rashanda bustled out of the room and down the hall to grab her digital camera. She hadn't even been gone for a minute when the doorbell rang.

"I'll get it," Teeka called out and hurried to the front door of her mother's one-story ranch-style home. "Put some pants on, Mama!"

"Girl, this is my house!" Rashanda called back. "And don't leave until I find this damn camera!"

Teeka was shaking her head when she opened the door. Her knees threatened to give when she got the first glance of Keelan Metoyer. The brotha was already naturally fine, but that night he was looking godly. Her heels gave her an extra three and a half inches, but he was still taller than her. The shirt under his black suit was the same color blue as her dress. His hair was freshly cut, and in each ear was a square-cut diamond that glistened in the moonlight. She was almost blinded by his pearly whites before he licked his lips.

"You clean up nicely. Did you do something new with your hair?" he joked as he eyed her head.

"Very funny." She grinned, and her eyes fell on a single rose in his hand. "Is that for me?"

"Nah, it's for this other girl named Teeka," he joked again and handed it to her.

"Thank you, baby," she said, taking the rose and putting it to her nose. "And you don't look too bad yourself. Come in. My mom is trying to find her camera. I'm sorry. She's about to drag this out. I didn't go to my prom, so she's going to make up for lost time."

"Don't worry about it." Keelan laughed and stepped through the doorway so Teeka could shut the door. "If my mom was here, trust me when I say she would be doing the same thing. Why didn't you go to your prom, if you don't mind me asking?"

"No one wanted the fat girl as their date, I guess." Teeka pointed to one of the pictures her mother kept hung up.

It was of her during her junior year in high school. She was in a size sixteen back then, and she could see it all in her face. She was happy that puberty had finally caught up to her and rounded her out. She was truly an ugly duckling that had turned into a swan. Teeka shuddered slightly looking at the picture. She wished her mother would take it down.

"Well, we can make up for all of that tonight, can't we? And if they don't know yet, the entire office is going to know that we're the makings of a couple after tonight."

"Is that a bad thing?" Teeka asked and leaned into him.

"No," he said and pressed his nose against hers. "But you better stop. If I didn't know any better, I would say that it seems like you're trying to get into some trouble right here in your mother's doorway."

"What if I am?" Teeka asked and kissed him.

There was a sudden bright flash of light, and the two of them broke apart quickly to see where it had come from. Rashanda must have finally found her camera, because there she stood, at the end of the hallway, with it glued to her eye.

"Okay, I got that one. Now do something else," she instructed and waved her finger around.

"Mama, aren't you even going to introduce yourself?"

"I will after I get these pictures. Now, pose and do something cute. Keelan, put your arm around her waist." She told Keelan what to do as if she'd known him for years.

He must have known not to make Rashanda ask twice, because he did as he was told without protest. They took at least twenty pictures before Rashanda was satisfied.

When she finally put the camera down, Teeka stopped holding in her stomach and took a deep breath.

"Okay, Keelan, this is my mom, Rashanada. Mama, this is Keelan."

"Nice to meet you, ma'am," Keelan said and kissed Rashanda's hand.

"Mm-hmm," she said. "You are very handsome. I can see why my daughter likes you. I can only guess what the other reasons are. You better not break her heart, though. Her daddy might not be here, but I sure got me a forty-eight tucked nicely under my mattress."

"Mama!"

"I'm just playing with him." Rashanda chuckled but shot Keelan a look that told him she was serious. "I'm not going to hold the two of you up, though. You both look lovely and are going to give the other couples a run for their money tonight."

"Thank you, ma'am. It was nice meeting you, and I will be sure to steer clear of that forty-eight. I promise."

"Bye, Mama. I love you." Teeka kissed her mother on the cheek before she ran back into her room to grab her clutch and shut off the light. "Okay, I'm ready!"

And with that, she and Keelan were off. She couldn't get rid of the butterflies in her stomach. What would everybody say? Especially since he had just broken off his engagement. Would they judge her, or call her a homewrecker? She hoped not, because that would be the day she had to smack an ETCO employee.

She and Keelan rode in silence all the way to their job, but he reached over and grabbed her hand on the ride. If only he knew how the simple gesture of him rubbing her hand with his thumb had calmed her nerves. Who cared what anyone else thought? What was understood didn't need to be explained.

"We're here," Keelan said finally. "Aw, man. Valet? They pulled out all of the stops tonight."

Keelan pulled his car to the front of the building and waited patiently behind another car. From the looks of the visitor parking lot and from what she could see of the parking garage, the place was pretty packed already, and it was only twenty minutes past eight.

"Yeah, you should have seen the invitation list that Steve had me send out. Anybody who is anybody is here tonight, not even including the people from Clout Enterprises."

The valet got to their car and held Teeka's door open. Keelan came around the back of his car and helped her out. He handed the valet his car keys and gave him a fifty-dollar bill as a tip. Teeka linked arms with his and let him lead the way.

As soon as they stepped into the banquet hall, her breath was taken away. There were ice sculptures in the center of the huge space, and along the far wall were tables full of food and drinks. There were at least a hundred tables set up, and they all had blue or white tablecloths with snowflake-shaped plates in front of each seat. It was like a winter wonderland, and strobe lights bounced off the walls. Music played in the background, and Teeka recognized the song as "Promise" by Jagged Edge. She hummed the tune as they made their way through the crowded room until they reached their table.

Steve and Sandy were already there, and at the first sight of Teeka, Sandy jumped out of her seat. She was wearing a rose-colored dress with long sleeves and the back completely cut out. To be in her early fifties, she looked great. Her body was still pretty fit, and she loved to show it. That was probably why she and Rashanda got along so well. They were the true definition of "black don't crack." She rushed over to Teeka and grabbed her hands so she could get a better look.

"Oh, T. K., you are a sight to see!" she gushed and embraced her. "Steve, doesn't she look lovely?"

"Of course she does!" Steve's voice boomed from where he sat at the head of the table.

"You must be this Keelan that I've heard so much about." Sandy offered him a kind smile. "It is nice to finally meet you. Wow, I see what all the fuss is about over you." She nudged Teeka and whispered something that only they could hear. "You better hold onto him, T. K. Steve is giving him a fifty thousand–dollar raise and another one in six months."

"Sandy, leave that girl alone and let them sit down." Steve motioned to two seats beside him and Sandy.

Across from them was a man Teeka didn't recognize. He was a brown-skinned man, and although he had a head full of black hair, his age showed in his face. He looked like he was trying to keep a pleasant expression on his face, but in reality, he didn't want to be there at all.

"You missed the speech," Steve told Keelan when they were all seated.

"That's my fault," Teeka butted in. "My mama wanted to take a hundred pictures of us before we left."

"And why wouldn't she? I mean, look how good the two of you look together," Sandy said.

The man across from them coughed slightly, and when Teeka glanced at him, she saw him glare at Keelan briefly.

"I hope that this doesn't affect our business ventures, Mr. Clout." Steve addressed the man. "I know that Keelan was engaged to your daughter at one point in time."

"No problem. You see, Keelan has actually done me and my family a favor," Mr. Clout responded. "I don't let anyone who will never be in my tax bracket affect my business. My Alecia saw that she deserved better and acted on it. I do, however, wish the two of you the best."

"Thank you," Teeka said as Mr. Clout offered her the fakest smile she'd ever seen in her life.

"But I must get out of here," Mr. Clout said, standing to his feet. "My flight leaves tonight at eleven. Thank you for the lovely event. I hope you have a great time as I make my exit. If you have any other questions, please find my assistant, Elizabeth, before she finds the tequila table."

"Let me walk you to the door." Steve stood up as well.

When they were gone, Sandy grabbed the cocktail in front of her plate and threw it back. "Boy, if his daughter is anything like him, you sure dodged a bullet. I haven't met a man more into himself than that in so long. Oh my goodness, it's a wonder why he isn't just married to himself!"

They all shared a laugh, but Teeka saw the serious expression on Keelan's face. She placed a gentle hand on his cheek and kissed him softly on the lips. "Hey, fuck him," she said. "He's nobody."

"Yea, he's a prick," Keelan said and glanced at the liquor table. "He never thought I was good enough to date his daughter. Always found some kind of way to put me down and remind me that I'm from nothing."

"But look at you now. Don't ever let anyone else's thoughts of you affect the way *you* feel about yourself. You are amazing in all aspects, Keelan Metoyer. Don' ever forget that."

"What would I do without you?" Keelan smiled down into her pretty face. "Do you want something to drink from the liquor table?"

"A sex on the beach, if they have one. I'm about to go use the little girls' room while you do that. I'll be right back."

They both stood up from the table and left Sandy in deep conversation with a lady from the HR department. Teeka walked past many people who asked if she and Keelan were an item. She told them she would give them an answer once she emptied her bladder. Well, she didn't say it exactly like that, but it was similar. When she reached the hallway that led to the bathroom at the end of the hall, she felt relief. It was like swimming through a sea of nosey sharks, and she was happy that the hallway was pretty much empty.

When she got to the women's restroom, she rushed to get into the biggest stall and relieve herself. After she was done, she hurried to wipe and flush so that she could wash her hands. She didn't want Keelan to be waiting too long for her. As she opened the stall, someone else came into the bathroom. She didn't pay them any attention as she continued to wash her hands. The woman came and stood right next to Teeka so she could refresh her makeup.

"Nice dress. And I have always loved your hair."

The voice froze Teeka's heart, because it was one that she recognized. When she whipped her head, she saw Alecia standing next to her. She was dressed for the event in a long silver dress that shone in the lighting of the bathroom. Her makeup was flawless as usual, and her hair was pinned neatly back with a bang.

"I–I thought you were back in Milwaukee."

"Oh, I was." Alecia applied a little lip gloss before putting it back in her Chanel clutch. "But then I came back for the banquet. I mean, I was invited after all."

"Oh, okay," Teeka said, drying her hands with a paper towel. "Look, Alecia. My intentions were never to steal Keelan from you. I'm sorry for whatever pain this whole thing might have caused you."

"I'm glad you said that." Alecia gave Teeka a sinister smile through the mirror. "Because I plan to steal him back tonight."

Teeka would never have expected what happened next to be reality. Alecia pulled a small handgun from her clutch before she turned around and pointed it at Teeka. Teeka gasped and took a step back out of instinct. Her eyes went to the door of the bathroom as she wondered if she could make a run for it.

"Don't even try it," Alecia said, reading her mind. "If you move, I'll put one in that fat stomach of yours."

"Alecia, think about what you're doing for a second." Teeka spoke evenly and put her hands in the air.

"Did you think before you got into bed with an engaged man? Huh, Teeka? Did you think about me while you were sucking his dick?"

"I didn't know about you, Alecia. I swear. If I did, I would have never dealt with Keelan." She thought it to be a bad time to throw in that the two of them were split up when she met Keelan.

"But what about when you found out? You couldn't just leave him alone, could you? You had me looking like a complete fool in the office!"

"We tried, Alecia. We tried to cut it off. We really did, but it didn't work. Keelan loves me."

"No!" Alecia shook her head violently. "He can't love you, because he loves me, you see. I'm the one who's been here through it all. I'm the one who pushed him to finish school and make something of himself. Me! I'm the one who should be on his arm tonight and every night after. Don't you see? Can't you see how you're in the way?"

"Alecia, put the gun down and we can talk, okay?"

"No! You bitch! You may have Keelan wrapped around your finger, but not me! Soon he will see that it's me that he wants. Not you. Did you know that the hallway that leads to this bathroom is the only one in the entire building without a camera? I found that out on my many visits here to see *my* man.

"So, here's what's about to happen. I'm going to shoot you in your chest and leave. When they find your body, no one will know what happened to you. But don't worry. I'll be here to take care of Keelan."

"No!" Teeka screamed

She didn't know what had overcome her, but listening to Alecia explain to her how she was going to kill her and take Keelan pissed her off. She lunged at Alecia and grabbed at the hand that held the gun. The sudden jerk upward caused the gun to go off and shoot the ceiling.

"Get off of me, you big *bitch!*" Alecia huffed as the two women tussled over the gun.

"He will never be yours, Alecia!" Teeka shouted in her face. "Do you hear me? He doesn't want you anymore. You're being *crazy!*"

"You can call me whatever you want!" Alecia shouted back and scratched the side of Teeka's face with her sharp nails. "But after tonight, it won't matter. Teeka will be no more!"

Teeka's face stung, but she couldn't stop fighting. She pulled her head back and brought it forward with as much force as she possibly could. The blow broke Alecia's nose on impact, but that only enraged her more.

"My nose!" Alecia shouted and backhanded Teeka with the strength of a man. "Do you know how much this thing cost? You're going to pay for that!"

Alecia's hit was powerful, but not powerful enough for Teeka to let go of the gun. They were in a power struggle, trying to point the gun in each other's direction. Their grunts filled the bathroom until finally, Alecia backed Teeka against the tile wall and pressed the gun between them.

"He will never be yours," Teeka said, staring into the other woman's eyes. "Even if he and I aren't together, he would never choose you. He doesn't want you, Alecia."

"Well, he doesn't have a choice," Alecia whispered. "Good-bye, Teeka."

Boom!

Both women stared at each other in shock when the gun went off. When the initial shock went away, the pain set in. It was coming from Teeka's side, and it felt like she was on fire.

"Y—you shot me," Teeka said, and Alecia backed away from her.

Teeka's hands flew to the side of her dress and touched the spot where she felt the pain. When she brought her fingertips up, she saw the bright red blood on them. Gasping, she slid to the floor and tried to apply pressure to the wound. It was no use, however. Her blood just seeped through her fingers.

"See what you made me do?" Alecia said and put the side of the gun to her head in a distraught manner. "You made me shoot you. All you had to do was leave him alone, Teeka. All you had to do was let us be a family. I even pushed my wedding back to appease this man, but no! He didn't want to marry me anymore because of you!"

As she was rambling on, Teeka's entire life was flashing right before her. Her mind fell on Keelan's face, his handsome face, and a single tear fell from her eye.

Is this the price to pay for love? she thought as she felt herself growing weaker by the minute.

Knock! Knock!

"Is anybody in there? The door is locked, and I have to pee!"

"Yeah, me too! Open up!"

The voices outside of the bathroom must have brought Alecia back down to earth. She inhaled sharply and looked at the gun in her hands. She did a full three-sixty spin while hitting herself in the head.

"I hear somebody in there. Hey! Open the door! We really need to go."

"Screw this! I have had too much tequila! I'm about to go and find security. This is just ridiculous!"

"What have I done? I can't go to jail. Not after everything. Oh my God, my future!" Alecia stopped spinning when she was facing Teeka. "This is all your fault. Don't you see? If you weren't such a slut, I would have never done this."

Blinded by rage, she held the gun up, that time aiming for Teeka's head. If she was going to get caught, then she might as well finish the job. Just as she was about to pull the trigger, the door busted open with a loud bang.

Right before the world around her faded to black, Teeka could have sworn she saw a man who resembled Keelan tackle Alecia to the ground. Then everything went blank.

Epilogue

Keelan

One Year Later

If there was one thing that Keelan learned about life, it was that taking it for granted could cost a pretty penny. He stood in his third-floor office overlooking the city Chicago. It was summertime, so there was a lot of traffic in the downtown streets. He enjoyed watching them—the people, that is. It was like, for a split second, he had a glimpse of their lives.

He smirked and stepped away from the tall window and went back to his desk. Just as Steve had promised, he got a new office to go along with his fancy new nametag. The only thing was, nothing at the office was the same. Ever since Teeka had been gone, things were out of order. Reluctantly, Steve had ended up hiring a new secretary, but it was different. No one could keep the office running as smoothly as Teeka did, but that was something everyone would have to get used to.

Keelan sighed deeply and thought back to the night that had changed his life a year before. His heart tugged, because he knew that it was his fault that Teeka had been put in that position. He never once thought to question Alecia's mental state after the breakup, but he for sure never thought that she would do anything as crazy as attacking Teeka.

When Chauncey asked him which girl was his date, it had thrown him for a loop. Chauncey proceeded to tell him that he could have sworn he'd seen Alecia step into the banquet, but Keelan told him that he had to be tripping. Alecia was all the way back in Milwaukee. However, when Teeka was gone for almost ten minutes in the restroom, he began to grow alarmed. He went off looking for her, only to find a line outside of the women's room. He heard some women complaining about the door being locked and another swear that she'd heard tussling inside. He leaped into action without thinking and kicked open the wooden door just in time to stop Alecia from shooting Teeka.

But he was too late; Teeka had already been shot. He would never be able to rid his mind of the image of her leaned against the bathroom floor, surrounded by a pool of her own blood. It was like it was he who had been shot, because he felt an electric shock to his heart. He remembered watching the stretcher roll her body away, and how all the breath had left his body. Why hadn't he been there for her? She needed him, and he wasn't there. He'd promised her that he would never hurt her again, and he had broken that promise.

Knock! Knock!

The sudden sound of a knocking on his office door jerked him from his thoughts and back to reality. He sat down on top of his desk and cleared his throat.

"Come in!"

"Hello, Mr. Metoyer." Ava, the middle-aged secretary entered his office. "I'm sorry to barge in like this, but there is something wrong with my phone. I've been trying to tell Mr. O'Brian to fix it, but he has been so wrapped up in meetings all day that he hasn't been much help. Ava was a sweet woman, but once you got her going, it was hard to get her to stop. The lady was a chatterbox and could talk an ear off from there to China.

Keelan smiled and let her ramble on about her broken phone for a minute before he interrupted her. "It's okay, Ava. I don't mind you coming up here," he said. "What's going on?"

"Your twelve o'clock is here," she said with a smile.

She stepped out of the way so someone could enter the room, and her arms flew out like a protective mother to make sure they got in without an issue.

"Thank you, Ava." Teeka's voice was pleasant, and she smiled genuinely at the woman. "I appreciate all of your help, but you really didn't have to come with me up the elevator."

"The hell I didn't! Your mama isn't about to fuss at me if you fall and go into early labor."

Keelan grinned, thinking about how his future mother-in-law had definitely made an impression on the secretary. Whenever Ava saw Teeka in the office, she was making sure that Teeka didn't need any help, since she was in her third trimester.

"Thank you, Miss Ava," Teeka said before the woman excused herself from the office. "Hi, baby. Why are you all holed up in here on this beautiful day?"

"I was just thinking," Keelan said and opened his arms for Teeka to fall into.

"Oh, really," Teeka said and gave him a peck on the lips. "Thinking about what?"

"About you, and how lucky I am to have you in my life."

And that he was. Teeka had arrived just in time to the hospital to receive medical attention. They were able to remove the bullet, since it was just a flesh wound, but she had lost so much blood they kept her for a few days. In those few days, Keelan realized that he had almost lost her twice in one month. The second time was almost permanently. It was then that he could see a wedding in his future, except this one would be with the right woman.

Of course, his plans changed a few months after Teeka was all healed up. She told him that she was pregnant and that he was going to be a father. Although it didn't happen in the order that he would have liked, he was ecstatic. They were going to be a family, and with Alecia in prison for attempted murder, there wasn't anyone who could get in their way.

"Yes, you are," she said and placed her hand on his chest. "You ready to go? Your son is kicking my ass because he wants a burger."

"*He* wants a burger, or you do?"

"Same thing." She shrugged and stepped away from him. "Come on, honey. If we hurry up, we can get a quickie going in the car."

"In the car?" Keelan raised his eyebrow and grabbed his car keys. "Are you sure that's good for the kid?"

"I'm thirty-eight weeks today. The doctor said sex is good for labor, and I want him to come on his due date, so I need you to do your fiancé duties and give me some dick."

"Oh, really?" He laughed and took her by the hand. "If those are my duties, I can definitely get used to them."

He squeezed her hand before leading her out of his office. She was so beautiful, and he didn't understand how he had gotten so lucky. In his mind, he was still earning her love, but he planned to show her how worthy of it he was every day.

"I love you, Teeka Metoyer," he told her, calling her by his last name.

"And I love you too, Keelan Metoyer. More than you'll ever know."

The two of them shared one last kiss before Keelan flicked off the lights. Hand in hand, they walked out of the office to continue another day in their forever love story.